This was a man who trusted no one. A man alone, his spirit raw with unhealed wounds.

Had he known many women? Surely he had. Latigo's rugged features and dark, feral grace would be enough to draw the gaze of any female he passed. But love? Rose mentally shook her head. Loving a man like Latigo would be like loving the wind.

His knuckles brushed her leg as he reached for the wrappings again. The unexpected touch sparked a ripple of awareness through Rose's body. She turned to find him looking up at her, his eyes intent but guarded.

"Who are you?" she whispered again, quivering as his gaze pierced her defenses like a stone-tipped arrow.

"To you—no one and nothing," he murmured. "A passing ghost with the first light of sunrise."

"So when will you go?" Rose heard herself asking....

Dear Reader,

This month we've covered all the bases. You'll laugh, you'll cry, *you'll find romance.* We are thrilled to bring you *Apache Fire* by longtime historical and contemporary romance author Elizabeth Lane. As with all of her books, this Western sizzles with emotion and romantic tension. It's the story of a beautiful young widow with a newborn son, who finds love and hope in the arms of the Native American army scout she's hiding on her ranch.

In *Lost Acres Bride* by rising talent Lynna Banning, a rugged, by-the-book cattleman must contend with the female spitfire who inherits a piece of his land—and gets a piece of his heart! And Tori Phillips returns with another of her CAVENDISH CHRONICLES, *Three Dog Knight*, about a shy earl and an illegitimate noblewoman who forge a marriage of convenience based on trust, and later love, despite the machinations of an evil sister-in-law.

Rounding out this month is *Blackthorne*, Ruth Langan's first medieval novel in nearly four years! Packed with intrigue and emotion, this is the tale of a haunted widower, the lord of Blackthorne, whose child's governess teaches him how to love again.

Whatever your tastes in reading, you'll be sure to find a romantic journey back to the past between the covers of a Harlequin Historicals® novel.

Sincerely,
Tracy Farrell, Senior Editor

Please address questions and book requests to:
Harlequin Reader Service
U.S.: 3010 Walden Ave., P.O. Box 1325, Buffalo, NY 14269
Canadian: P.O. Box 609, Fort Erie, Ont. L2A 5X3

APACHE FIRE

ELIZABETH LANE

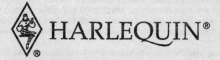

HARLEQUIN®

TORONTO • NEW YORK • LONDON
AMSTERDAM • PARIS • SYDNEY • HAMBURG
STOCKHOLM • ATHENS • TOKYO • MILAN • MADRID
PRAGUE • WARSAW • BUDAPEST • AUCKLAND

ISBN 0-373-29036-5

APACHE FIRE

Books by Elizabeth Lane

Harlequin Historicals

Wind River #28
Birds of Passage #92
Moonfire #150
MacKenna's Promise #216
Lydia #302
Apache Fire #436

ELIZABETH LANE

has traveled extensively in Latin America, Europe and China, and enjoys bringing these exotic locales to life on the printed page, but she also finds her home state of Utah and other areas of the American West to be fascinating sources for historical romance. Elizabeth loves such diverse activities as hiking and playing the piano, not to mention her latest hobby—belly dancing.

For Alec
September 23, 1997

Chapter One

Arizona Territory
April 7, 1876

Latigo's vision was a red blaze of pain. He sagged over the neck of his spent mustang, teeth clenched as he battled to stay conscious. He had been riding most of the night, every lurch of the horse like a lance thrust into his bleeding shoulder. The Colby Ranch couldn't be much farther unless, in this cursed stupor, he had somehow become lost.

The ghost face of the waning moon hung low in the western sky. Startled by hoofbeats, a miniature owl exploded out of its burrow and flapped screeching into the darkness.

Latigo cursed, fighting pain as he struggled to calm his spooked mount. He had lived all his life in the desert, and he was as much at home here as the sharp-nosed coyotes that ranged along the lonely arroyos. But tonight he was no coyote. He was wounded prey, and in the danger of darkness even the wind's familiar voice was an alien moan.

With excruciating effort, he focused his eyes on the

notched peak that was his beacon point. He could feel his
life oozing through the makeshift bandage that covered the
bullet wound in his shoulder. In the seven hours since the
ambush, he had lost a dizzying amount of blood. If John
Colby refused him shelter...

But how could Colby refuse, when his very honor was
at stake? Ten years ago, during the bloody Apache wars,
Latigo had saved Colby's life, and the rancher—more out
of pride, to be sure, than gratitude—had vowed to repay
him one day. Now it was time to call in the old debt.

Under any other circumstances, Latigo would just as
soon have let the matter go. He was a man who asked little
of others, especially where whites were concerned. But
now he had no choice. Not if he wanted to live.

As he clung to the horse, he fueled his strength with his
own anger at what had happened. Hours earlier, on the
San Carlos Reservation, he had been guiding two U.S.
government agents on an inspection tour. As their mounts
passed through a narrow ravine, a hail of rifle fire had
erupted from the rocks above and behind them. The two
federal men had died at once, but the bullet meant for
Latigo's heart had struck a handbreadth too high and to
the left. Reeling with shock, he had managed to spur his
horse and gain some distance before the four attackers had
time to mount up and come after him. He had barely
glimpsed their faces, but he had seen enough to know they
were not Apaches.

Twisting painfully in the saddle, he peered into the darkness behind him. He had not sighted his pursuers since
yesterday afternoon when he'd holed up in a rocky crevice
to wait for nightfall. Surely he had lost them. Whites
weren't worth spit as trackers, and they'd had no scout
along. Surely he could afford to roll into the brush and
rest for the space of a few precious breaths.

But he could not even think of stopping. The ebbing

strength in every part of his body told him that if he were to lie down he would never get up again.

A snort from the mustang jolted Latigo to sudden alertness. He felt the horse shudder beneath him and caught the eager prick of its ears. Instinctively his hand groped for the empty holster where his U.S. Army issue Colt would have been, had he not dropped it when the bullet slammed into his body. He was weaponless except for the braided rawhide whip that lay coiled like a rattlesnake along the flank skirt of his saddle. Latigo's prowess with the whip had earned him the Spanish name by which he'd been known for half of his thirty-three years. But little good that would do him now, when he could scarcely raise his arm without a stab of nauseating pain.

Latigo's thoughts scattered as his ears picked up a distant shrillness on the wind. *Horses.* A dozen perhaps, maybe more, about a mile ahead. They sounded close together, as they might be in a corral.

The Colby Ranch.

Had he found it, or was he riding into a trap?

The half-wild mustang bugled eagerly, trotting hard in its urgency to be with its own kind. Latigo was too weak to stop the animal. He clenched his teeth as the pain jolted through him. *Hold on,* he ordered his shock-numbed arms. *Just hold…on…*

Fire…smoke from the blazing wagon blinding her eyes, searing her throat…her mother's scream, and the cold twang of arrows striking flesh…her gentle father pitching facedown next to the mules, his fingers clawing lines in the powdery red dust…savage Apache faces streaked like bloodied hatchets with vermilion war paint, eyes glittering, as they moved in for the kill…no!…please, God, no!

Rose Colby awoke in a frenzy of silent screams.

Her fingers clutched the patchwork quilt as she battled

her way back to reality. Her heartbeats echoed like gunfire
against the wall of her ribs.

It's all right. Beneath the long muslin nightgown, her
body was drenched in sweat. *It's all right. You were only
dreaming.*

She lay rigid while the nightmare faded, quivering in
the warm darkness of the bed she had shared with John
Colby for more than a third of her twenty-six years. Yes,
it was all right, she reassured herself. The Apaches had
long since been beaten by the army and herded onto res-
ervations. The adobe walls of the big house were as thick
as a fortress, every window barred with wrought-iron grill-
work. John's Colt .45 Peacemaker lay loaded on the nightstand. The vaqueros had taught her how to use it, and she
could hit a playing card dead center at fifty paces.

You're safe, Rose. Perfectly safe.

But Rose knew she would never feel safe from the terrors that lurked in her own mind. No walls, however
strong, could shut out the nightmare visions that had
haunted her for nine long years.

Brushing back her tawny mane of hair, she sat up, slid
her bare feet to the floor and pattered across the cool Mexican tiles. The hand-carved mahogany cradle sat against
the near wall, sheltered by the inward slope of the roof.
Bathed by moonlight, her two-month-old son lay deep in
slumber, his eyelids closed, his upflung fists curled like
tiny pink chrysanthemum buds. His breath whispered
sweetly in the darkness.

Mason, she called him—John Mason Colby, after her
husband and her own father. She would raise her boy well,
Rose vowed, aching with love. He would grow up to be a
fine man, and he would carry on the names he bore with
pride, honor and courage.

Pride… Honor… Courage… Duty. Moonlight gleamed
softly on the words etched around the border of the silver

medal that hung on the wall above the crib. The medal had been John's, awarded to him by the territorial governor for valor during the Apache wars. John had treasured it. So would his son.

Rose's throat hardened with emotion as she bent low to feather a caress across the downy silk of her baby's hair— dark, as John's hair must have been in his youth, although she had never known it to be other than gray. What a tragedy John had not lived to see this baby, the heir he had wanted—demanded—for so long. He would surely have forgiven her, then, for the long, barren years and the heartbreaking miscarriages. The two of them might have even known some happiness, drawn together at last by their love for this beautiful child.

Closing her eyes, Rose inhaled the sweet, milky, baby aura that cloaked the tiny body. *Let him sleep,* her practical side argued. But her motherly instincts cried out for her son's warmth in her arms. She reached into the cradle only to freeze in midmotion, her heart convulsing in sudden alarm.

Outside, just below the window, the sound of a horse.

Rose darted to the nightstand and caught up the loaded Peacemaker. Maybe it was nothing—one of the vaqueros returning early from the mountains, where they'd moved the herds for spring grazing, or some visitor from Tucson, or—

But what was she thinking? The grandfather clock in the downstairs hallway chimed two in the morning. No one would be so foolhardy as to travel at this hour. No one, at least, with any good intent.

Gripping the heavy pistol, Rose crept along the wall and peered around the edge of the window. Except for the baby, she was alone in the house. The vaqueros were out with the herd. Esperanza, the cook, and her husband, Miguel, who tended to things around the place, had left that morning to visit their newborn grandchild in Fronteras. Rose herself had insisted they go—foolishly, she realized now. Whatever trouble lurked outside, she would have no choice but to deal with it alone.

An artery pulsed along the curve of her throat as she scanned the moonlit landscape, the barren front yard where John had never allowed so much as a paloverde or creosote bush to sprout because it might provide cover for marauding Apaches; the open-sided *ramadas* and the adobe bunkhouse; the corrals where those horses not taken on the cattle drive milled and stamped.

Yes, something was out there.

Rose pressed closer to the glass, the pistol leaden in her shaking hand. She had fired the big gun at tins and bottles, but never at any living target, let alone a human being. Her Quaker parents had raised her to detest violence. All the same she knew, with a ferocious maternal certainty, that if threatened, she would kill to protect her child.

At first she saw nothing. Then, directly below her, almost hidden by the overhanging shadow of the roof, the dark shape of a solitary horse emerged, its head drooping, its saddle empty.

A gasp of relief escaped Rose's taut lips as she sagged against the wall. A riderless horse was a matter for concern, but it posed no immediate danger, unless—

Nerves screaming, she pressed toward the window again. The horse could be a ruse, she reminded herself, a trick to lure her outside. She would be a fool to drop her guard now, when an army of intruders could be waiting in the shadows.

Rose's breath stopped as the horse shifted its stance to reveal, dragging from a stirrup by one entangled boot, the dark, limp form of a man.

She pressed close to the glass, forgetting to hide herself. Judging from what she could see, the rider appeared to be a stranger. He was tall. Rose could calculate that much from the length of his trapped leg and the lean sprawl of his body. His clothes were plain, dark and trail worn. But beyond that, she could not tell how badly he was hurt, or even whether he was still alive.

She gripped the gun in an agony of indecision. To go downstairs and open the door would jeopardize her own safety and, infinitely worse, that of her baby. But how could she leave a man—a good man, for all she knew, maybe with a wife and children waiting at home—to die on her very doorstep?

As Rose hesitated, torn to the point of anguish, she saw the man's arm move, saw his hand stir and lift. His fingers strained, quivering toward the stirrup, only to fall back, clenched in pain and frustration.

A moan of pity broke in Rose's throat. Whatever the peril, no decent soul could turn away from this human being.

Laying the gun on the bed, she flung on her flannel wrapper and knotted the sash tightly around her waist. Then she picked up the weapon again, paused to thumb back the hammer and, with a last glance at Mason's small, sleeping form, hurried down the dark hallway toward the stairs.

Her steps faltered as she neared the massive front door. For the space of a heartbeat she clung to the heavy crossbar, gathering her courage. The entryway was pitch-black, the house eerily silent. If only she'd thought to bring a lantern…

But the stranger was in pain and need, and there was no more time to be lost. The moon was shining outside, Rose noted as she shoved back the bar. She would be able to see well enough.

Her knuckles whitened on the pistol grip as the door creaked open. For a moment she held her breath, gulping back old terrors as she waited for a rush from the shadows. But this time, except for the solitary horse drooping next to the hitching rail, there was nothing.

"Steady, boy." Rose approached the animal cautiously, fearful that it might bolt and drag its injured rider back into the scrub. "That's it…easy…" She caught the reins that were dangling loose over its neck and looped them around the rail.

The rider had neither spoken nor moved. He lay as still as death in the moonlight, while Rose labored to free his worn boot from the stirrup.

The leathers, she swiftly discovered, had become twisted around his ankle as the horse dragged him along the ground. So stubbornly were they tangled around his high-topped boot that she could not tug it loose. Rose hesitated, then laid the pistol on the ground. The man was surely too far gone to pose any danger.

Panting with effort, she tugged and twisted, but the stranger's boot was caught fast. To free him, she would need to slide the boot off his foot, worsening any possible bone fractures in the process.

Praying she wouldn't hurt him too badly, Rose cradled his leg against the curve of her waist and began, slowly and carefully, to work away the boot, which was so old and worn that the leather had molded like a second skin to the lean, bony contours of his foot. She was so intent on her task that she forgot her peril until the stranger spoke.

"No tricks, lady."

The hoarse whisper struck Rose like a bullet. She turned to find herself staring down the barrel of her own discarded gun. The stranger's face lay in shadow, but there was no mistaking the raw desperation in his voice.

"You heard me, lady. I don't want to hurt you, but try anything cute, and you won't live to be sorry!"

Rose knew she should be frightened, and she was. But bubbling hotly over her fear was a tide of anger. Her trembling hands balled into fists as they dropped to her sides.

"You crazy fool!" she snapped. "Can't you see I'm trying to help you? I could've left you out here to die, and maybe I should have!"

Her words echoed on the silent wind. For the space of a long breath the stranger did not respond. Then Rose heard the sound of sharp-edged laughter in the darkness. Laughter that ended in a grunt of pain.

"You're hurt," she said.

"Hell, yes, I'm hurt," he snarled. "Get me loose from this horse, and then you can do something about it."

"That's exactly what I was trying to do when you interrupted me," Rose said coldly. "May I go ahead now?"

"Go on." His hand held the pistol steady as she turned back to working the boot off his foot.

"You could have broken bones," she said. "Tell me if I hurt you."

"Won't make much difference if you do." His breath sucked in, then rasped painfully out of his lungs. "I'm looking for John Colby. Is this his place?"

"It is. But he's…not here." It would not be wise to tell the stranger John was dead, she reasoned, at least not until she knew who he was and what he wanted.

"Are you Colby's daughter?" The man winced as she repositioned his leg to support it against her hip.

"No, I'm John Colby's…wife." Rose felt his heel loosen from inside the boot. Holding her breath, she began easing the leather from around the threadbare stocking. When she glanced around, she saw that his gun hand had fallen to the ground. He was watching her cautiously, his jaw clenched against the pain.

"So, when will your husband be back—uh—Mrs. Colby?"

"What is it you want with him?"

"I—*blast it, woman*—" He muttered a string of curses as his foot slipped free of the boot, allowing the leg to drop. His hand, however, kept its grip on the pistol.

"You can let go of my gun," Rose said coldly. "I don't intend to harm you."

"I'll think about that after I've seen John Colby." His voice grated with determination. "When did you say your husband would be back?"

"I didn't." Swallowing her fear, she forced herself to crouch beside him. He had propped himself on one elbow, the pistol clutched in his free hand. A chill knifed through Rose, stabbing to the marrow of her bones.

"What are you doing here?" she whispered, her throat dry and tight. "What do you want with John?"

A muscle twitched below his sharp cheekbone. "Let's just say I've shown up to collect on an old debt," he muttered.

"You mean to kill him, don't you?" The words burst out of Rose with an audacity she might not have possessed if her husband had been alive.

"No, I only need his help…his word." The stranger coughed, doubling over in sudden agony. "Get me in the house," he said. "Now!"

Rose's eyes swiftly measured his length and bulk. He was at least six feet tall, with broad, heavy shoulders and a deep chest. Too big a man for her to drag up the steps, let alone lift. "Can you walk?" she asked cautiously.

"My legs are fine. Just damned sore." He struggled to rise, then sank back in obvious pain. As his arm shifted, the moonlight revealed an ugly, dark blotch still oozing crimson down the left side of his shirt.

Drops of sweat glistened on his skin as he strained to get up. "Give me your hand."

Rose knew she had to take control now, while she could. "Give me the gun first," she said quietly.

His black eyes flashed with sudden wariness. "Who's in the house?"

"Nobody who could do you any harm. Give me the gun."

He hesitated, then shook his head groggily. "Can't trust you," he mumbled. "Can't trust anybody till your husband gives his word. Let's go inside, Mrs. Colby."

Rose thought of her son, asleep in his cradle upstairs. Anxiety made her bold. "No," she said.

"No?" He glared at her, as if questioning her sanity.

"Not until you give me the gun."

"From here, lady, I'd say you were in no position to argue."

"That's where you're wrong," Rose retorted, masking her fear with ice. "You're badly wounded, and I'm the only one who can help you. Shoot me, and you won't last till morning."

He blinked, as if trying to clear some unseen darkness from his vision. His gun hand quivered. "Your husband—"

"John died four months ago." Rose thrust the truth hard into him like the point of a lance. She saw him slump, saw the resistance ebbing out of him. "Give me the pistol," she said more gently. "Believe me, I'm all you've got."

His eyelids drooped, then, with effort, jerked upward again. The stranger had lost a great deal of blood, Rose surmised. It was all he could do to stay conscious. He did not even resist as she reached out, grasped the Peacemaker by its long barrel, lifted it from his hand and carefully released the hammer.

"Come on," she said, shoving the weapon into the knotted sash of her robe. "Let's get you up those steps before you pass out."

Crouching close, she managed to work her shoulder under his right arm. His body was rank with sweat and blood, his clothes saturated with wood smoke. The blending odors ignited memories of death and terror in Rose's mind, but she forced them aside. This man was too weak to fear, she reassured herself, even though every instinct whispered that she was wrong.

"Help me," she ordered, gathering her strength. "Now!"

A grunt of agony exploded through his teeth as they lurched upward together. Rose staggered under his weight, fighting for balance as he struggled to get his footing. His body was as hard as ironwood, all bone and sinew through his clothes.

"Can you make it up the steps?" She strained against him, her flesh hurting where his hand gripped her shoulder.

"I'll make it." He gained the first step, then the second, biting back curses. She could feel his trembling heat along her side; she could feel the labored pounding of his heart.

Something flashed through Rose's memory—the image of a wounded coyote whelp she had once found in the brush, half-dead, its eyes still glinting with a desperate defiance. Hungering for something to nurture, Rose had begged John to let her take the wretched creature home and care for it, but he had drawn his pistol and shot it before her horrified eyes. "You've got no sense at all, woman," he'd said. "A coyote's a wild animal. First chance a varmint like that gets, it'll turn on you for sure."

A wild animal.

The man at her side had that same hunted air about him, and no matter how he might be suffering or what he might tell her, Rose knew she could not afford to trust him.

They had gained the porch. The stranger was reeling like a drunkard. It was all Rose could do to keep him upright. All the same, she forced herself to stop short of the door.

"I'm not taking you under my roof until I know," she declared, bracing her weight against his ribs. "Who are you? What did you want with my husband?"

"Latigo." He spoke with excruciating effort. "I knew your husband from the Apache wars. He said if I ever needed help…"

The words trailed off as his knees buckled, then his body collapsed in Rose's arms. She tried to hold him, but his weight was too much for her. His blood left a streak of crimson down the skirt of her dark blue wrapper as he slid to the porch, shuddered and lay still.

Panic shrilled alarms in Rose's head as she groped for his pulse. Reason argued that she and the baby would be safer if he died, but when her fingertips, searching along his jugular, found a weak but steady flutter, she broke into a sweat of relief. He was alive, but his life was trickling away with every heartbeat. There was no time to lose.

Urgency, now, drove her to fling open the door and seize the stranger's feet, one booted, one covered only in a half-disintegrated dark woolen sock. As she dragged him along the tiles toward the kitchen, Rose prayed silently that she would know what to do. She had nursed the cuts and sprains of the vaqueros and cared for John during those last terrible months when he lay barely aware of her, but she was no doctor.

He groaned as she turned his body to slide it across the threshold into the kitchen where she kept water and medical supplies. "I know it hurts," she muttered, "but I have to get you in here where I can work on you." Rose shoved back the table to clear more space, then maneuvered him into position. She would have to dress his wound on the floor. Unless he could get up by himself, there was no way for her to lift him onto anything higher.

Water. Yes, he would need all the fluids she could force down him. Rose darted to the counter and filled a pottery cup from the tall pewter pitcher. Moonlight etched ghostly windowpane squares across the tile as she crossed the kitchen and dropped to her knees beside him.

The stranger—Latigo—moaned as she lifted his head and cradled it in her lap. His face was in shadow, so obscuring his features that she had to grope for his mouth. His skin was as smooth as new leather beneath her fingertips. An unexpected tenderness surged through her as she tipped the cup and pressed it to his cracked lips. "Drink," she murmured. "Please—you've lost so much blood."

At first he did not respond. The water filled his mouth until Rose feared she would drown him. It trickled out of one corner to run down her sleeve as she tilted his head to keep him from choking. *Please,* she begged silently. *Please.*

He sputtered weakly. Then she felt the ripple of his throat as he began to swallow. "Yes," she whispered, tipping the cup higher to give him the last drops. "Yes, that's it, drink it all."

She withdrew the cup, then hesitated, wondering whether she should get him more water. No, she swiftly concluded, too much at one time might make him sick, and she could wait no longer to stop the bleeding.

"Latigo, can you hear me?"

He made no sound.

"Latigo!" Sick with dread, she seized his shoulder and shook it. Relief swept through her as he moaned incoherently.

"I've got to clean out your wound. It's going to hurt. Do you want some whiskey?"

Again he did not answer, and Rose realized she was wasting precious time. Leaving him where he lay, she scrambled to her feet and strode to the cupboard, where she rummaged for matches to light the lamp that Esperanza kept on the counter. By its flaring yellow light she filled a basin with water, then retrieved her medical kit, some clean rags and a bottle of John's rye whiskey from the pantry. These she placed on the shadowed floor next to Latigo's unconscious body. Then she rushed back to fetch the lamp from the counter.

Light danced eerily off the open-beamed ceiling as she picked up the lamp. It glistened on hanging copper pots and flickered on strings of garlic and dark red chilies as she hurried across the kitchen. The tiles were smooth and cold beneath her bare feet.

Latigo had not moved. He lay where she had left him, the agonized hiss of his breathing his only sign of life. Light pooled around his lanky frame as Rose bent down to set the lamp on the floor. It flooded his face, casting his features into stark relief—the tawny skin, the straight nose and sharp, high cheekbones, the long, square jaw, the broad forehead, crowned by hair as black as the wing of a raven.

Rose's flesh had gone cold. Panic surged through her body, propelled by memories so vivid and terrible that she could not fight them back. The smoke. The blood. The savage, painted faces.

She closed her eyes, battling instincts that threatened to send her bolting out of the kitchen. The man was helpless, she reminded herself. He would die without her aid. Maybe he would die anyway, but she had no moral choice except to try to help him.

Rose willed her eyes to open, willed herself to look down at him as she reached for the basin and a clean cloth. She would perform her Christian duty, she resolved. But no charity on her part could wipe out the horror of the past.

And nothing could alter the fact that this dark stranger, this man who called himself Latigo, wore the face of an Apache.

Chapter Two

He was running free, his boyish legs bounding along the rocky crest of a sage-swept ridge. The dawn wind whispered in his long, black hair. The soles of his moccasins skimmed the path as he mounted higher and higher, pursuing some precious golden thing that glimmered just beyond sight and reach. "Seek, boy," the aging di-yin had told him. "Climb high. Only then will you find the path to who you are and where you must stand."

Latigo awoke to thin gray light as the dream faded. His body jerked to sudden awareness. His eyelids fluttered open. Then, with a caution born of dangerous years, they swiftly closed to narrow slits, allowing him to size up his situation before moving.

His shoulder burned like hellfire, but the tightness of new wrappings told him his wound had been dressed. However badly or well remained to be seen. Someone had put a clean shirt on him that scratched his neck and smelled of laundry soap. That was something a woman would do, he reasoned foggily.

A woman.

Yes, his memory was beginning to clear. Latigo's ears recalled the husky timbre of a white woman's voice, telling him to lie still, but her face was nothing but a disembodied cloud. Someone had dragged or carried him indoors because he was lying on a hard floor, covered by a fleecy wool blanket that smelled of cedar, as did the pillow that supported his head. But where was he? What had happened last night? *Think, man.*

Latigo's tongue was a dry pebble, his throat so brittle with thirst that he could not bring himself to swallow. His hands stirred, then froze as he realized his wrists and ankles were bound with some sort of coarse, soft twine.

The discovery sent a shock jolting through his system. Latigo's pulse jumped, snapping his senses to sudden clarity. He remembered the ambush, the long, punishing ride through the desert and the sight of the ranch gate. He remembered slipping into blackness, then waking up on the ground, scraped and battered, with one boot twisted in the stirrup. He remembered a woman with a pale, frightened face and moonswept hair. He remembered her eyes, violet blurs, their color startling even by moonlight.

And he remembered that John Colby was dead.

Latigo fought the urge to struggle against the ties that wrapped his wrists and ankles. Whoever had taken him prisoner was likely close by, maybe watching him right now. To preserve the element of surprise, which was his only weapon, he would have to remain perfectly still.

His pupils shifted warily beneath half-closed eyelids as he strained to see in the wan morning light. Off to his right, he could make out the legs and underside of a massive wooden table, and beyond that the tiled base of a cast-iron stove. The kitchen appeared large enough to contain an entire Apache *rancheria*, but then, that should come as no surprise, Latigo reminded himself. The size of white men's dwellings tended to far outstrip their needs, and John Colby owned, or had owned, the biggest spread of land south of the Gila.

Latigo's furtive gaze scanned the room, lingering on the solid, lime-washed walls, the padlocked plank door and the high, iron-grilled windows. The place was built like a stockade, he groused, feeling more and more like a caged animal. Even if he could get untied, escaping from such a fortress would not be easy.

By now his body had fully awakened to its discomfort. His skull throbbed like the dull beat of a tom-tom. Every breath lanced agony through his wounded shoulder. His back and legs ached from lying on the cold floor, and hunger clawed at his stomach—good signs, he reminded himself. Pain and hunger meant his body was alive and fighting.

Shoving his useless physical complaints aside, Latigo continued his furtive exploration of the kitchen. He glimpsed an open door, leading, he surmised, to another room in the house. To the right of the doorway—

Latigo's breath stopped.

On a bench beside the door, bathed in a shaft of morning sunlight, a young white woman sat nursing a baby.

Thunderstruck, he studied her through the screen of his lashes. Propriety, drilled into him by years in the white man's world, warned Latigo that he had no business casting eyes on such a woman. But his gaze was drawn to her.

The top of her robe had fallen to one side, baring the slope of her shoulder and the ripe, satiny curve of her breast, concealed only where the baby's round head lay dark against her creamy skin. Tiny sucking sounds drifted to Latigo's ears, triggering an unexpected tightness around his heart, an unspoken hunger for the warmth and tenderness he had lost as a child and never known as a man.

Not that the sight was new to him. Chiricahua mothers nursed their children openly in the *rancherias*. But something about this woman, her tenderness, her vulnerability, struck a quivering chord of response. She reminded Latigo of a painting he had seen once in an old Spanish church, a careworn Madonna cradling her heavenly infant, her expression so poignant and knowing that it haunted him to this day.

In happier times John Colby's widow would have been a radiant beauty, he mused, his eyes tracing one sunlit curl where it tumbled like a swirl of honey over her bare shoulder. But the desert was not kind to pretty, young white women. Hot sun and parched air burned the life out of them in a few short years. Hard work and childbearing usually finished the job by the time they were thirty. This one had already begun to fade. Still, there was something about her, a soft resilience like the luster of tumbled river stone.

But he had more urgent things to do than gape at a woman, Latigo told himself harshly. Right now, his most pressing concern was getting untied and finding a way out of this place.

He forced his gaze lower. That was when he noticed the heavy pistol lying on the bench beside her, its barrel glinting in a finger of sunlight. He went cold inside as the truth sank home.

This woman was both his rescuer and his jailer. She had cleaned and dressed his wound, then bound him hand and foot and kept guard with a pistol to make sure he didn't escape.

Latigo cursed his own rotten judgment. He had made his first mistake in seeking refuge here, gambling his safety on the word and reputation of a white man he had not seen in years. And he had made his second mistake in trusting Colby's fragile-looking young widow.

She had saved his life. But what good would that do him if she'd sent for the law—or worse, if she were associated with the bastards who had murdered the two government agents? Either way, he would be a dead man.

Latigo's gaze lingered for an instant on the woman's wistful Madonna face. Maybe she hadn't betrayed him after all, his instincts whispered. Who knows what he might have said or done in the midst of his pain and exhaustion. Maybe he had frightened her, and she had tied him up to protect herself.

Maybe, but that was a chance he could not afford to take. Somehow he would have to win her confidence and persuade her to untie him—that, or untie himself. Once he got loose, it would be easy enough to get his hands on the gun and make a fast getaway.

Knowing there was little time to lose, he closed his eyes, moved his head slightly, and feigned a semiconscious moan.

Rose had been drowsing, lulled by her own weariness and the soothing tug of the tiny mouth on her nipple. At the low sound from the man on the floor, her eyes shot open. She jerked bolt upright, her frayed nerves screaming.

The Apache, Latigo, was stirring beneath the blanket. His long legs strained at the thick wool yarn her shaking hands had wrapped around his ankles. His eyelids opened, then swiftly closed.

Only then did Rose realize her breast was exposed. Hot faced, she flung a corner of the baby's blanket over her bare shoulder.

The stranger's eyes opened again. This time his feral gaze swept her defiantly from head to foot. Feeling as vulnerable as a nesting dove, Rose gulped back her fear and forced herself to speak calmly.

"I've sent a man into Tucson for the sheriff," she lied. "Until he gets here, I suggest you keep still unless, of course, you want to open up that bullet hole and risk bleeding to death. I won't bind it for you a second time."

His obsidian eyes glinted like a captive hawk's. "Did

anybody see to my horse?'' he asked, as if his own condition were of no importance.

"Your horse is in the corral with the others. There's plenty of hay and water there.'' That much, at least, was true. She had unsaddled the poor, spent animal herself and turned it in with her spare cow ponies. She remembered fingering the long, coiled whip as she carried the saddle to a dark corner of the barn. She remembered the worn boot, still tangled in the stirrup leathers.

"You were lucky.'' Rose spoke boldly, even though the mere act of touching an Apache had all but drained her of courage. His bleeding body, so close, so real, had rekindled her nightmare in all its horror. Even now, it was the most she could do to meet his fierce black eyes without cringing. "From the looks of your shoulder, the bullet passed through without hitting anything vital,'' she said. "But you've lost a dangerous amount of blood. That's why you must keep absolutely still.''

"Is that why you've trussed me up like a bald-faced calf at branding time?'' His sharp-edged words challenged her in English that was as fluent as her own. This Latigo, whoever he might be, was clearly no ordinary reservation Apache.

"I don't intend to hurt you,'' he said, his gaze flickering toward the pistol on the bench. "Just cut me loose, give me some food and water and a fresh horse, and I'll be on my way. That's the least you owe me.''

"*Owe you?*'' Rose clutched her son beneath the blanket, remembering, now, what he had said about collecting on an old debt. "Your business was with my husband, not with me,'' she declared coldly. "I'd never set eyes on you before last night. What could I possibly owe you?''

His black eyes narrowed. "The last ten years of your husband's life.''

His words struck her with the impact of a slap. Rose

stared at the man, rifling her memories for some spark of recognition and finding none.

"John never mentioned his life being saved by anyone, let alone an Apache," she retorted, flinging the words with a bravado she did not feel.

He flashed her a contemptuous look. "For whatever it's worth to you, Mrs. Colby, only half of me has the honor of being Apache. My mother was a Chiricahua, my father a Spanish Basque. But I'm telling the truth about your husband. I saved his life ten years ago when I led his company out of an ambush in the Dragoon Mountains."

"The Dragoons?" Rose's sleep-fogged mind searched what she knew of the past. When Cochise's bloody uprising had flared in the mid 1860s, John Colby had helped organize a volunteer militia out of Tucson. As its captain, he had bravely led more than a score of forays against the Apaches. On one excursion along the Gila, he'd come across a seventeen-year-old girl wandering the desert in a state of shock, her family murdered and their wagon burned. A widower nearing fifty, he had taken the dazed young Rose Thomas home to his ranch and, a few weeks later, made her his bride. Within days of their marriage, he was riding patrol again.

All this Rose remembered. But she had no recollection of John's discussing the Dragoon Mountains. Apart from ranch matters, he had communicated little with her when he was home. He had never told her where he'd been or described the things he'd done. And he had surely never mentioned a man named Latigo.

The stranger waited, his eyes flinty with distrust. It would be dangerous to lie to such a man, Rose calculated, but then, hadn't she lied to him already?

"Did you ride with John's militia?" She asked, knowing a yes would trap him in his own deception. John Colby and his fellow volunteers had hated Indians and would never have tolerated Apache blood in their ranks.

Latigo's thin mouth tightened in response to her question. "I was scouting for the army," he said, gritting his teeth against the pain in his shoulder. "We didn't much care for the local militia boys. The trigger-happy fools tended to stir up more trouble than they prevented—"

"Why, that's not so!" Rose interrupted, flaring with sudden outrage. "My husband's militia protected settlers all over this part of the territory! They were heroes!"

The look he gave her was so scathing that it shocked her into silence. "More than once we had to rescue them from disasters of their own making," he continued in the same flat tone, as if she had not spoken. "That's how I met your husband."

He shifted sideways on the floor, straining upward as if he were struggling to sit.

"Lie still," Rose spoke in a sharp whisper. "I told you, you'll start the bleeding again."

His eyes burned their desperation into hers, silently urging her to cut him loose and let him go. But her own fears shrilled the warning that she could not trust this man. Last night he had pointed John's gun at her and threatened to shoot her with it. She had no choice except to keep him bound and helpless.

Beneath the blanket, the baby's warm little body stirred, then settled into slumber. Rose felt the stranger's wild, dark presence like an aura in the room. The skin at the back of her neck tingled as his gaze flickered over her, lingering on her face, probing the depths of her courage.

"What have you done?" she demanded in a low, tight voice. "Who are you running from?"

Hesitation flickered across his face. Then his expression hardened, and Rose realized that his distrust was as strong as her own. "You wouldn't believe me if I told you," he said, wincing as he spoke. "But I give you my word, I'm not a criminal."

"How can I be sure of that?"

"I'm not a liar, either." His eyes locked Rose's in a proud gaze that defied her to doubt him. Against her will, her thoughts flew back to last night. She remembered cradling his head between her knees to keep him still as she cleaned his wound. She remembered the smoky fragrance of his hair and the feel of his flesh beneath her fingers, cool and hard, like living bronze. On touching him for the first time, a freshet of disturbing heat had surged through her body. Rose felt it again now as his gaze gripped hers.

Every instinct told her the man was dangerous. But she had to be sure. If he had saved her husband's life, she had no right to turn her back on him, not until she had some idea of what was in his heart.

"Tell me what happened," she said. "I can't promise to believe you, but I think I'm entitled to hear your story."

Morning sunlight warmed the quiet air, melting the shadows in the corners of the kitchen. Latigo hesitated, then his eyes narrowed with the effort of collecting his thoughts. He was weak from pain and blood loss, she knew, but Rose resolved not to spare him until she had heard everything.

"Untie me," he said. "I won't harm you."

"No." She shook her head. "Not yet."

His eyes flashed, as if he had sensed a weakening in her resolve. Rose's arms tightened around her son. "Go on," she said, lifting her chin. "You said you were a scout. Did your trouble have something to do with the army?"

"The army?" His bitter chuckle ended in a grunt of pain. "Believe me, there were no soldiers in sight. Just two government inspectors, all the way from Washington. I'd been assigned to guide them on a tour of the San Carlos." His eyes narrowed to slits, as if he were trying to shut out something he didn't want to see again. "They're dead—shot from ambush, both of them. The bullet that went through my shoulder was supposed to have killed me, too."

"Apaches?" The word sprang without thought to Rose's lips.

His glare cut her off like the flash of a blade. "Not Apaches. Not unless Apaches are sporting store-bought Stetsons, Springfield rifles and fifty-dollar saddles these days. They were as white as you are, Mrs. Colby, and I saw them murder two federal agents. That's why they can't afford to let me live."

Rose stared at his sharp Apache features, struggling against the nightmare that lurked in the shadows of her mind. She smelled the smoke, heard the screams....

"That sounds like a wild tale if I ever heard one!" she heard her own voice saying. "What if I choose not to believe you?"

Latigo's eyes hardened. "That's your choice."

"But it doesn't make sense! One might expect it of Apaches, but why would white men do such a thing?"

The question caught in her throat as the clatter of galloping hoofbeats and the snort of a horse echoed across the front yard. Rose's head swung toward the window as the long night's strain crashed in on her. She was so tired, so scared, and now, at last, somebody was here.

"Turn around, Mrs. Colby—slow and easy, now. I don't want to hurt you."

Rose's heart plummeted as she realized what had happened. All the while Latigo was talking, his hands had been busy beneath the blanket, stretching and loosening the yarn that held his wrists. She had glanced away for the barest instant, but he had struck with a rattler's quickness to seize the pistol from beside her on the bench. Now the weapon was in his right hand, its muzzle thrusting up at her. Instinctively she shifted her body to shield her son.

"Who's that outside?" he demanded in a low voice. "You said you sent for the sheriff."

"No." Rose blurted out the truth. "I had no one to send. I lied to you because I was afraid."

"Then who's outside?" He was struggling to sit up, his jaw clenched against the pain.

"I don't know. But if you're telling the truth about the murders, why are you holding a gun on me now? Why didn't you go to the sheriff and report those men?"

Latigo's free hand yanked the yarn from around his ankles. He gripped the edge of the table and hauled his way to his knees, then to his feet. The heavy Colt quivered unsteadily in his hand.

"What makes you think the sheriff would believe me?" His black eyes glittered with irony. "After all, you didn't."

Rose could only stare at him as a sharp rap sounded on the front door. The hour was far too early for a social call. Maybe it was one of the vaqueros. Maybe something had gone wrong in the mountains.

The rap on the door became an insistent pounding. Latigo's eyes met Rose's in terse confirmation that the visitor was not about to give up and go away.

"Go on," he ordered. "Put your baby down. Then, whoever's out there, get rid of him."

Heart pounding, Rose fumbled swiftly beneath the blanket to tug her robe over her breast. With the gun following her every move, she crossed the kitchen to the flannel-lined basket that served as her son's downstairs cradle. Half-asleep, Mason whimpered as Rose eased him away from her body and, with trembling hands, lowered him to the soft padding and tucked the blanket around him. He sucked one tiny rosebud fist, his helplessness tearing at her heart.

With imploring eyes, she turned on the tall stranger.
"Don't make me leave him here."

Latigo's expression hardened. Then he paused, torn by
a conflict that Rose could read in his bloodless face. He
was wounded and desperate. Keeping the baby in the
kitchen would insure her cooperation and his own safety.
Surely he realized that. Still, he hesitated, a muscle in his
cheek twitching subtly as the pounding on the door grew
louder and more urgent.

"Please," Rose whispered, "let me take him. He's all
I have."

Latigo's sinewy body tensed, then his shoulders slackened as he exhaled. "I don't hide behind children," he
growled. "Take him. But no tricks, Mrs. Colby. I've got
the gun, and I'll be watching every move you—"

His words ended in a groan as his knees buckled and
he crashed unconscious to the floor.

Rose crouched beside him and pried his long, brown
fingers from around the pistol grip. His eyes were closed,
his breathing shallow but regular. Even in repose, there
was a hawklike ferocity about the man, but surprisingly,
she was no longer afraid of him.

"I don't hide behind children."

The words echoed in Rose's mind as she gazed down
at the dark face, with its straight, black brows and clean-
chiseled features. An Apache's face, to be sure, but what
thoughts and motives lay behind it?

If Latigo had truly saved her husband, she owed the man
a great debt—

"Rose! Blast it, Rose, are you in there?" The shout
from outside was muffled by the walls of the house, but
Rose had no trouble recognizing the voice. Scrambling to
her feet, she seized the baby's basket under one arm and
fled from the kitchen, closing the door behind her.

She hurried across the dining room, and moved toward

the small anteroom that had served as her husband's office. There she placed the basket in the hollow beneath John's massive walnut desk. If more trouble broke out, she wanted her son safely out of harm's way.

"Rose!" The pounding from outside would have cracked a less substantial door. Rose hesitated again, then slipped the pistol into a desk drawer and hurried out of the room.

In the front hallway she paused to wrap her robe tightly about her body and knot the sash. Taking a deep breath, she slid back the heavy bolt, lifted the latch and opened the door.

"Rose! Thank heaven!"

The man on the threshold was tall and barrel-chested, with ruddy, handsome features and ginger hair that curled over the collar of his starched, white shirt. A longtime friend of John Colby's, though twenty years his junior, Bayard Hudson had been a regular visitor to the ranch— even more regular, Rose had come to realize, since John's death.

"Bayard?" She feigned a sleepy yawn, her gaze darting to his gun belt. "What on earth are you doing here? You must have ridden most of the night to arrive at this hour."

"Are you all right?" His windburned eyes were laced with red. "I saw blood outside, a trail of it across the porch. And your robe, Rose, there's blood on that, too!"

"Blood?" A picture flashed into Rose's mind—Latigo, helpless on the kitchen floor. Bayard had no more love for Apaches than John had. He would likely shoot first and ask questions later.

"Oh—" She laughed nervously. "One of the vaqueros, he—uh—slipped and cut himself on his own knife last night. A silly accident. I patched him up and sent him back to the herd." She was chattering, talking too fast. "It was nothing serious, but I couldn't go back to sleep. I—I'm afraid I'm not very presentable this morning.''

"Nonsense, you always look beautiful.'' His gaze wandered up and down her body, lingering where the neck of her robe had loosened to reveal a hint of shadow between her breasts. "But can't you get someone else to doctor those Mexicans of yours? I can't say I fancy the idea of you touching those swarthy little heathens.'' His thick hand settled onto her shoulder, its weight too warm, too heavy. "You ought to send them packing and hire yourself a bunch of real American cowboys. That's what I'd do if I was running this spread.''

"My vaqueros are good workers.'' Rose squirmed away from his clasp and edged out of reach. "They know horses and cattle, and they send their pay home to their families instead of throwing it away on liquor and women in town.'' She swung back to face him, arms folded across her chest. "And now, Bayard, suppose you tell me what you're doing here. You didn't ride thirty miles just to tell me how to manage the ranch.''

"I could use some breakfast,'' he said. "We can talk while I eat.''

"Esperanza isn't up yet,'' she lied, praying her inhospitality would annoy him to the point of leaving. But Bayard Hudson only snorted his disgust.

"Well, go and wake the lazy old hen! You're too easy on the hired help, Rose. You need a man around the place to see that things are properly run.''

"I'm raising a man for that very purpose. But until John's son is old enough to take over, I'm the one in charge.'' Rose arranged her features into a smiling mask. "Go and sit down in the dining room, Bayard. I'll heat up some beans and fresh coffee and bring them in to you.''

"Bacon and eggs would be nice, too, while you're at it. But you needn't go so fancy for me, Rose. I'll eat in the kitchen, and we can visit while you cook. I like watching a woman work.''

"No!" Rose scrambled for a way out. "The baby—he's asleep, and you might wake him. Go on, sit down, this won't take a minute.''

"Fine. I like my eggs sunny-side up.''

"Yes. I know.'' Her knees went liquid as Bayard ambled into the dining room and slid one of the high-backed leather chairs away from the table. Only after he'd settled his broad frame onto its seat could she force herself to turn and walk back toward the kitchen. Heart pounding, she opened the door wide enough to slip through, then closed it carefully behind her.

Latigo had awakened. He was sitting up on the floor, his back propped against the whitewashed wall next to the door frame. His face was haggard with pain.

"What's going on out there?'' His mouth moved with effort.

"It's an old friend of John's, and he's expecting breakfast.'' Rose gathered some kindling sticks from the wood box and thrust them into the stove. As she blew her breath on last night's embers they began to glow.

"He doesn't know I'm here?''

Rose shook her head.

"Where's the gun?''

"You actually think I'd tell you?''

A ghost of a smile flickered across his lips as he settled back against the wall, watching her cat-fashion through the half-closed slits between his eyelids as she filled the enameled coffeepot and set it over the fire. The beans Esperanza had cooked two days ago were in the pantry, cool in their thick earthenware jar, but the bacon, if she wanted it, would have to be brought from the smoke cellar, the eggs gathered from the backyard henhouse. She cared precious little about pleasing Bayard Hudson, but if she could turn such errands to her advantage...

No, Rose concluded swiftly, the peril was too great. If Bayard were to get restless and wander into the kitchen at the wrong moment, anything could happen. She had to be here to keep him out.

Rose ladled some beans into a shallow iron skillet and hurried back to place it on the stove. Latigo's gaze followed her every move: His feverish black eyes seemed to burn through her flesh.

"Maybe you'd better hide in there." She jerked her head toward the open pantry door.

He shook his head, and Rose realized that even now he didn't trust her. The pantry, with its thick, windowless walls and heavy door, could too easily become a prison.

"You could unlock that kitchen door and let me out," he said.

"You're too weak to run. You'd pass out in the yard." Rose scooped the half-warmed beans onto a plate, added two slices of brown bread and poured some coffee into a porcelain cup. Her shaking hand splattered the hot liquid onto the counter. Reflexively she reached for a dishcloth, then, realizing she was only wasting time, flung it down, piled the breakfast things onto a tray and, with a last frantic glance at Latigo, rushed out of the kitchen.

Bayard was teetering backward on the rear legs of his chair, his fingers drumming impatiently on the tabletop. Rose bit back a surge of nervous irritation. Bayard Hudson was a good man, she reminded herself. Any sensible female would throw herself into his arms and beg him to protect her from the brooding stranger in the kitchen.

Sensible?

A grim smile tugged at Rose's lips. No one, least of all John, had ever given her credit for having much sense. Before his accident, she had been a trophy, with little more expected of her than to adorn his home and produce the heirs he'd so stridently demanded. All that had changed, however, in the past six months. She ran the ranch now, and she would deal with the man named Latigo on her own terms.

Bayard scowled as she arranged the simple breakfast on the cloth before him, but he did not complain. His warm gaze followed her as she pulled out a chair on the opposite side of the table and settled uneasily into it.

"You're not going to join me?"

"I'm more tired than hungry. Forgive me, Bayard." Rose brushed a lock of hair out of her face, her heart sinking as she noticed the spark her gesture ignited in his hazel eyes. "Your visit can't be a social call at this hour," she said, feigning an air of cheerfulness. "What are you up to?"

"Posse business." He scooped a hunk of bread into the beans, took a hungry mouthful and washed it down with a swig of coffee. "We rode out of Tucson last night and made it as far as the hot springs. While the rest of the boys bedded down for a few hours, I decided to ride over this way and make sure you were all right."

"As you see, I'm fine. You could've saved yourself the trouble." Rose laughed uneasily, her hands clenched into fists below the tabletop. "Posse business, you say?"

"Uh-huh. Half-breed army scout named Latigo murdered two government agents on the San Carlos Reservation. The wire from Fort Grant said the bastard was headed south, maybe this way. When I got here this morning and saw that trail of blood across your porch, the idea that it could be yours—"

Rose watched him gulp his coffee. She felt light-headed, as if a noose had been jerked around her throat, shutting off the blood supply to her brain.

Was the wire from Fort Grant a mistake, or had Latigo

lied to her? Was she protecting an innocent man or harboring a killer?

"I don't like the idea of your being alone out here," Bayard was saying. "Those Mexicans of yours, hell, they've got no more loyalty than jackrabbits. They'll turn tail and leave you at the first sign of trouble. You need someone strong, someone who cares about you. You need a man."

"What?" Rose had been staring down at the weave of the linen tablecloth. Preoccupied with her own thoughts, she had only half heard him. She glanced up to discover that he had stopped eating and was gazing at her with an intensity that raised goose prickles beneath her robe.

"Bayard—"

"It's time," he insisted. "John was my friend. He would want me to take care of you and the baby." He paused long enough to take in her stunned expression. "Don't look so surprised," he said. "I've been in love with you for years, Rose. Now that you're free, and you've had a few months' time for mourning, I'm asking you to be my wife."

Chapter Three

Rose stared at the man across the table, hoping she had misunderstood him but knowing she had not. His boldly stated words left her no room for evasion.

"Well, Rose?" He was beaming at her as if she had already said yes. After all, what woman wouldn't jump at the chance to marry Bayard Hudson? He was handsome, well-to-do, and one of the most respected men in Arizona.

So why had her skin suddenly gone clammy beneath her robe?

She sensed his impatience, sensed the tension in him as his body poised to spring out of the chair and sweep her into his embrace. Rose thought of the dark stranger in the kitchen. Lives could depend on her getting Bayard Hudson out of the house as swiftly as possible.

"You've been very kind to me, Bayard," she murmured, staring down at the tablecloth. "But it's far too soon. John has barely been gone four months. Out of respect for him, if nothing else, I should wait."

"The man who was your husband and my best friend died last summer when that horse bucked him out of the saddle onto his head." Bayard spoke sharply, making no effort to hide his impatience. "It was his body you tended for those last months, but it wasn't the man we knew and loved, Rose. It wasn't John.''

"Your breakfast is getting cold," she said.

"Forget breakfast!" The chair legs grated across the tiles as he slid away from the table and strode around it to stand behind her. Rose stiffened as his warm hands settled onto her shoulders. "Dash it, but you're tense," he murmured, his strong, blunt fingers working her knotted muscles. "What's the matter? You aren't afraid of me, are you?"

Rose shook her head in denial.

"Then what—?"

She forced a tired smile. "Forgive me, Bayard. You just didn't pick a good time to propose, that's all. I've had a long night, and I'm not thinking very well."

His hands continued to knead her shoulders, their motion slowing to a sensual caress. "You're a beautiful woman, Rose," he murmured, "too beautiful to be alone, without a man. Just say yes." He bent close to her ear, his lips skimming her tousled hair. "You'll never be sorry, I promise."

Rose shivered, imagining Latigo behind the kitchen door, his sharp Apache ears hearing every intimate word.

"Rose, darling…" Bayard's voice had deepened to a breathy rasp. His mouth nibbled a damp trail down the side of her neck as his fingers nudged aside the collar of her robe to expose the naked slope of her shoulder. "Do you know how long I envied your husband? How long I've wanted to—"

"No!" Rose spun away from him, toppling her chair in a spurt of nervous panic. The crash resounded like a gunshot through the empty house, freezing her in midmotion.

Bayard righted the chair, his expression as bewildered as a slapped child's. Silence lay leaden between them, broken only by the ponderous tick of the grandfather clock in the entry. Little by little Rose began to breathe again.

"You *are* afraid of me," Bayard said. "Rose, I swear I would never hurt you."

"No, of course you wouldn't." Wanting only to have him gone, she molded her features into a conciliatory smile. "You've caught me off guard, that's all. I'm honored by your proposal, Bayard, but I truly need some time to think about it."

"I've waited a lot of years for you, Rose, and I'm not a patient man. All the nights I've lain awake, imagining you in my bed, in my arms..." He made a move toward her, then hesitated, realizing, perhaps, that he had said too much. "So when do I get my answer?" he demanded. "In a day? A week?"

Rose's gaze flashed toward the kitchen door. It was open a crack, and she realized Latigo was not only listening but watching. She groped for a reply, anything that would placate Bayard and send him on his way.

"I was thinking of longer," she hedged, already knowing what her answer would be but desperate for him to leave.

"A month, then. But don't expect me to take it in good grace. I'm anxious, girl. Anxious to make you mine."

"Shouldn't you be getting back to your posse?" She edged toward the front hallway, praying he would follow her.

Still, maddeningly, he lingered. "I don't like leaving you here with that half-breed Apache murderer on the loose," he said.

"Oh, for heaven's sake, I'll be fine!" Rose punctuated the words with a toss of her head. "A lone desperado would never take on a ranch this size."

"Maybe not." He exhaled like an agitated bull. "But

keep John's big pistol handy—I know you can use it. If you see a stranger, don't take any chances. Shoot to kill.''

"I hardly think that will be necessary." Her eyes flickered toward the kitchen door.

"Is something wrong, Rose?"

Her heart convulsed for an instant. "No—no," she answered much too quickly. "You caught me unprepared, that's all. I prefer to look my best when people come calling, and I haven't even combed my hair." The laugh she attempted came out sounding like a nervous hiccup. "Off with you, now, I need to get dressed and start my day!"

Bayard stood his ground, his thumb absently rubbing the butt of his pistol. "Not until you kiss me goodbye," he declared.

Rose struggled to ignore the sinking sensation in the pit of her stomach. Right now, she reminded herself, the only thing that mattered was getting the man out of here before he discovered Latigo and someone wound up dead.

"I'm waiting, Rose."

"You'll go if I kiss you?"

"I'm a man of my word, sweetheart."

Rose forced herself to stop thinking as she strode back across the room. She had meant to give Bayard a light peck, but his arms closed around her like the jaws of a trap. His full, wet lips captured hers with a force that pressed her spine into an arch, jamming his belt buckle hard against her belly.

"Rose..." He was panting like a stallion. Frightened now, she began to struggle, but he was a large, powerful man, and her twisting movements only served to heighten his ardor. "Rose...dash it, girl, if you only knew how long I've wanted you." He kissed her again, his hands groping downward toward her buttocks. Rose could sense Latigo's mocking black eyes watching everything from the kitchen doorway. She knew he could not help her.

For an instant she went rigid in Bayard's arms. Then, as his hot palms slid lower, she gathered all her strength into one desperate, wrenching shove.

"No!" she gasped, twisting away from him and spinning free. "I'm not ready for this."

"You were married to an old man, Rose." He reached for her again, his face flushed, his lips damp and red. "It's time you found out what having a younger fellow is like."

"No!" Dizzy with rage and fear, she clutched the back of a chair, keeping it between them. "You have no right to touch me! You've insulted me, dishonored my husband's memory. I want you gone!"

He took a step backward, startled by her vehemence. "Now, Rose, honey, I didn't mean to upset you."

"Get out, Bayard." Her voice was flat and cold, her body drained of its emotional energy. "I'm sorry if I misled you, but I have no desire to marry you or anyone else. This ranch was John's, and it belongs to John's son. I intend to raise the boy here—by myself."

His eyes bulged with the outrage of a man accustomed to getting his own way. "You'll change your mind. I can make you change your mind. You'll see."

Rose tightened her lips, her silent glare saying more than any words she might have uttered. His voice faded, then rallied once more.

"You'll find I don't give up that easily," he declared, retreating toward the entry hall. "Mark my words, Rose. One day you'll come to me on your knees. You'll kiss my boots, and you'll *beg* me to marry you!"

When she did not answer, he turned and strode out the front door, closing it behind him with a bang.

Rose stood poker-spined, listening to the snort of his horse as he mounted and rode away. Only when the galloping hoofbeats had faded into silence did she slump, trembling, onto the chair.

"That was quite a performance, Mrs. Colby."

Latigo had opened the kitchen door. He was on his feet, leaning unsteadily against the frame. His face was as gray as river mud. His right hand clutched the long, sharp kitchen knife she had used to slice the bread.

Rose glared at him, too unstrung to be frightened. "You can put that thing down," she snapped. "Bayard is gone, and you've certainly nothing to fear from me!"

"I'll be the judge of that." He remained stubbornly where he was, his eyes glazed and feverish.

"Bayard told me you killed those two government men," she said.

"So I heard." His lips thinned as a shudder of pain passed through his body. "Now you've heard two versions of the same story. Which one have you decided to believe?"

"I don't know."

"Then why didn't you turn me over to your hot-handed friend? He was packing a gun. It would've been easy enough to let him take me." His pupils glittered like shards of black flint. Rose quivered as she forced herself to meet his gaze.

"I had to be sure," she said. "If Bayard had taken you back to that posse, you would never have lived to reach Tucson, and I would never know if I'd done the right thing."

"You...did right." His speech had begun to slur. His hand dropped to his side, as if the blade had taken on the weight of a sledgehammer. "But under the circumstances, I'd say that you're either very brave or very... very...foolish."

The knife slid down his leg and clattered to the tiles. For the second time that morning, his body went limp, his knees buckled and, as Rose sprang from her chair, he slumped to the floor.

Sinking to her knees beside him, she eased him onto his back. A glance at his shoulder revealed blood seeping through the fabric of the old cotton shirt she'd found to put on him. The fall had most likely opened the wound, and he was already so weak from loss of blood that she feared for his life.

Feared?

Rose fumbled for his pulse, her eyes fixed on his proud Apache features—the sharp, high cheekbones, the bitter, oddly sensual mouth. This man was still her enemy, she reminded herself. If he died, she would be rid of him. She and the baby would be safe.

Her trembling fingers found the pulse point along the side of his neck. He was alive, but his flesh was clammy, his heart racing like the wheels of a runaway train.

Who was this man? What, if anything, did she owe him? Rose struggled to slow her pinwheeling thoughts and examine what she had heard.

It *was* possible that he had saved her husband's company from an Apache massacre, she conceded. But what about the two government agents? The story about the white assassins was so preposterous it might as well have been a joke. Even his bullet wound could be explained in any number of ways. For all she knew, the dark-eyed devil was the world's most convincing liar, and the price of trusting him could be her life and her child's.

Was she harboring an innocent victim or a cold-blooded murderer?

Whatever Latigo was, Rose knew she could not turn her back and let him die.

He moaned incoherently as she jerked his shirt open to get at his bandaged wound. Stop the bleeding, that was her most urgent task. Then she would need to get him to bed and get him warm. Leaving him on the floor had been a mistake. The cold tiles, she realized, had chilled away his strength. But then, she had not been thinking clearly. She had been so afraid of the man, so unnerved by his fierce Apache features that even her thoughts had frozen.

Strange, she mused, how her fear had diminished now that she knew him.

Knew him?

The man had menaced her with a gun, Rose reminded herself as she ripped off the ruffled hem of her nightgown and wadded it against the seeping wound. He had arrogantly claimed that she was in his debt and told her stories that defied belief. No, she did not know this mysterious stranger at all, and she would be a fool to trust him.

But he would live, she vowed. He would live to tell her his whole story.

Off the kitchen was a small, unoccupied servant's room with a bed. Rose stopped the bleeding as best she could. Then she picked up Latigo's stockinged feet and slid his body carefully across the tiles. The isolated room had only one tiny window, high and securely barred. Its heavy door could be locked from the outside. When she was not tending to his needs, she could shut him in and feel safe.

But she would get the pistol and keep it close at hand whenever the door was open, she resolved. She could not afford to let Latigo get the best of her again.

She raced back to John's office. There she took a moment to check on her sleeping son and retrieve the Peacemaker, which she thrust into the sash of her robe as she hurried back to the kitchen.

Panting with effort, she dragged Latigo's body into the tiny room and turned down the bed. A beam of morning sunlight trickled through the window to fall across his inert legs. It was only then that Rose noticed his dust-caked cavalry trousers. Something fluttered in her stomach as she assessed his condition. Yes, she swiftly concluded, for the sake of hygiene and comfort, his dirty clothes would have to come off.

First she gingerly peeled away his remaining boot, then his threadbare stockings, resolving to burn them at first opportunity. Then, gritting her teeth, she bent over him to undo his belt buckle and the fastenings of his trousers. The uncivilized wretch had been bare skinned beneath his shirt. The lower part of him would likely be the same, Rose reasoned, steeling herself as she worked the stubborn buttons through their holes. But what could it possibly matter? After all, she was no longer a blushing schoolgirl. She had been a wife, a mother, a helpless man's nurse.

"Do you do this to all your prisoners?"

His rough whisper jolted her like a swig of white lightning. Rose gasped as her startled glance met his eyes. Her hand flashed for the pistol. In an instant she had jerked the weapon out of her sash and was aiming it at his chest.

He grinned groggily. "You...won't need the gun, Mrs. Colby," he mumbled. "I'm not a man to object if a pretty woman wants to take down my britches."

"I'm just trying to get you to bed!" Rose snapped, her cheeks flaming as his grin broadened. "But now that you're awake, you might as well do the job yourself." She edged backward, brandishing the pistol. "Go on. Get those filthy trousers off. Then climb between the sheets and stay there. If nothing else, I'll see that you live to hang!"

"I'm touched by your concern." His expression had hardened again. His right hand fumbled awkwardly—too awkwardly—with the first of four remaining buttons. A spasm of pain rippled across his face as he tried to reach downward with the arm on his wounded side. "Unfortunately," he muttered through clenched teeth, "I happen to be left-handed."

"Take all the time you need." Rose thumbed back the hammer of the gun, ignoring his thinly veiled plea for help.

Oh, she knew what he was thinking. Get her to come closer, then overpower her and grab the pistol. But this time she wasn't falling for his tricks. This time she was the one in charge.

Cursing under his breath, Latigo managed to undo the first button, then the second. On the third, he hesitated. His eyelids drooped, then blinked open as if he were battling waves of unconsciousness. Was it a performance, designed to lure her into lowering her guard?

"I know what you're thinking," she said. "But it wouldn't make any difference if you did get the gun. You're too weak to go anywhere. You've proved that by passing out twice. You need me, Latigo."

"Need you?" His eyes glinted sardonically. "A minute ago you were threatening to see me hang."

"Did you kill those two government agents?"

"No."

"If that's true, you have nothing to fear from me." Rose's grip tightened on the pistol. Her hand was trembling, and she knew that Latigo had noticed.

"Nothing to fear?" His tongue moistened his dry lips. "How do I know there isn't already a price on my head, and you're just waiting to collect it? A widow woman, even on a big ranch like this one, could find herself in need of money—"

"Go on," she interrupted icily. "Get those pants off."

"Anything to oblige a lady." A mocking smile flickered across his face. "But I'm warning you, don't expect to see—*oof!*" His words ended in a grunt as he tried to brace himself on one elbow and inch his trousers down over his hips with his free hand. He was truly in pain, Rose realized, noticing the ashen ring around his lips as he sank back onto the floor. But she could not let herself feel pity for him. This man was a wild, wounded animal who could be every bit as dangerous as he looked.

"I'm waiting." She willed herself to keep her gaze impassive, to keep the pistol pointed squarely at his chest.

He lifted his head, his slitted eyes chilling in their contempt. "It seems you have a choice, Mrs. Colby." He spat out each word as if it were snake venom. "Either you can allow me to stand up and let gravity take its course, or you can trust me enough to get down here and give me a hand."

Rose hesitated, every instinct screaming flight as the intimacy of the small room closed around her. "Get up, then," she said. "But no tricks, not if you want to live."

"You wouldn't shoot me," he said. "Hell, you couldn't shoot anybody—a woman like you, soft, pampered—"

"Don't bet your life on it!" Rose snapped in sudden fury. "You don't know me! You don't know anything about me!"

"And you don't know much about me, either, lady." He grimaced, clenching his teeth with the effort of hefting himself to his feet. "If you did, you'd put that big horse pistol away and—*damn!*" He staggered to his feet, one hand clutching the bedpost for support, the other holding up his unbuttoned pants.

"The trousers," she said. "Get them off and get into bed before you end up on the floor again."

"I'd advise you to turn your back. I may not dress as decorously as most men you know, and I wouldn't want to offend your womanly—"

"Turn my back?" Rose's sweat-slicked grip tightened on the pistol. She swallowed the dryness in her throat. "I'd just as soon turn my back on a snake!" she said. "Go ahead, I've seen a man before—and a better man than you, I'll wager!"

The whites of his eyes flashed dangerously. Then without another word, he turned his back on her and let his trousers drop to the floor.

Rose stood thunderstruck, unable to avert her eyes from the full sight of him. She had tolerated her husband's aging physique and grown used to it over the years. She had even come to accept his appearance as an example of the way any man would look without his clothes.

Until now.

Latigo's naked body was as sleek as a cougar's, tapering from powerful shoulders to a lean, sinewy waist. His long legs were crowned by high, taut buttocks, and his muscles flowed in feline curves, coiled strength beneath skin that captured the light like molten copper.

Rose's hand slackened around the pistol. He was magnificent. Even with the ugly, bloodstained bandage marring his shoulder, Latigo, mixed-blood Apache and possible murderer, was the most beautiful man she had ever seen.

"If you're waiting for me to turn around—"

The edge in his voice shocked Rose back to reality. Her breath jerked. Her fingers seized on the pistol just in time to save it from clattering to the floor.

"Get into that bed." The words emerged as a shaky whisper. "Go on, you arrogant, disrespectful, presumptuous—"

A small but piercing wail from beyond the kitchen ended her tirade. Her baby was awake and crying, and his needs pulled at her instincts with a power no mother could resist.

Latigo's broad shoulders had tensed at the cry, but he did not turn his head. Rose kept her eyes on him as she backed warily toward the door. "Get into bed and rest," she ordered. "I'll be back later with something for you to eat, unless I decide you deserve to starve."

A rough chuckle—or was it a growl?—rumbled in his throat but that was all. He was still standing next to the bed, his splendid back held rigid in an unspoken statement of disdain as Rose closed the door, slipped the bolt and fled on trembling legs to the sanctuary of her little son.

Latigo heard the bolt click into place. Then, giving in to waves of dizziness, he crumpled into the bed.

Crisp and fragrant, the clean sheets enfolded him like a shroud, their fineness one more reminder that he didn't belong in such a place. He'd have been better off taking his chances in the desert. At least he might have died in peace there, leaving his bones to be bleached by the sun and nosed by passing coyotes. Instead, here he was, caged and cosseted like a house cat, lying behind a bolted door, in a pretty white woman's house.

Rose. That was the name that panting bull had called her. Rose Colby. She looked like a rose, all right, even smelled like one as she leaned over him, fragrance spilling from between her lovely, milk-swollen breasts. For all his weakened condition, it had been as much as he could do to keep from pulling her down on top of him and burying his face in that warm, satiny cleft.

Damn the woman!

Latigo's vision swam as he lay on his back and gazed up at the small, barred window. He hated being closed in, where he couldn't see the sky or feel the wind! He had to get out of here. And once he did, he vowed, he would die rather than let the whites lock him up in their jail.

Half in panic now, he raised his head and struggled to move his legs. They lay like inert slabs, defying all his efforts to rouse them. John Colby's widow was right, he realized, sinking back onto the pillow in black resignation. He was too weak to go anywhere.

For now, he would bide his time, Latigo resolved. He would submit meekly to Rose Colby's ministrations. He would allow her to feed him, to nurse his wound and to ravish his senses with her unsettling womanly presence.

But he would not lower his guard for so much as a heartbeat. Any slip—an open door, an unguarded moment—could be his key to freedom, and he would be ready to seize it. Get the gun, steal a horse and head straight for the Mexican border—that's what he would do at first opportunity.

And heaven help Mrs. John Colby if she tried to stop him.

Chapter Four

Latigo woke to a spill of amber light through the barred window of the tiny room. Sunset. He muttered a bewildered curse. Had he slept for a day? A week? His blurred mind had lost all sense of time which, for him, could make the difference between life and death.

A mélange of mouth-watering smells drifted through the crack beneath the door. Chicken soup, richly laced with garlic and onions. Freshly baked bread. Hot coffee. Latigo's empty belly growled in ravenous response to the delicious aromas. If the violet-eyed Widow Colby had chosen to torture her prisoner, she could not have devised a more exquisite punishment, unless she were to—

His thoughts scattered as the bolt clicked open on the other side of the door. In a flash he was fully awake, every muscle tense and quivering.

As he struggled to raise his body, the door swung open. Latigo's breath stopped as he saw Rose Colby standing on the threshold, the light making a halo of the sun-colored hair that she wore in a loose bun.

She hesitated, then stepped into the room. Only then did he notice that she was carrying a tray with a bowl, a spoon and thick, buttered slices of bread on a china plate. Latigo's vacant stomach emitted another loud rumble, causing her left eyebrow to twitch in wary amusement.

"I, uh, see you're hungry." She was wearing a calico apron over a faded chambray gown that narrowed enticingly at her slender waist. She looked young and tender and vulnerable.

"How long have I been asleep?" Latigo eased his pain-racked body upward as she put the tray down on the nightstand and bent close to adjust the pillow behind him, washing his senses with the subtle aroma of lavender soap. He imagined reaching up and tugging the pins from her hair, letting it fall around his face in a cascade of fragrant, golden silk. He imagined fondling it, smelling it, tasting it.

But those kinds of thoughts were crazy, he reminded himself harshly. Rose Colby was a white woman, pretty, pampered and spoiled. She wouldn't condescend to spit on a man like him, let alone allow him to touch her. His time would be better spent figuring out what she'd done with the pistol and how he could get his hands on it.

"You've been asleep for nearly twelve hours, and I can see it's done you a world of good," she said briskly, pulling a chair up to the bed and sitting down. "Are you able to feed yourself?"

"Won't know till I try." He inched higher in the bed, the friction of fabric against bare skin reminding him that he was naked beneath the bedclothes. "Give me the tray," he said. "I'll manage."

"In a minute." She unfolded a linen napkin from the tray and spread it over his lap to protect the bedding from spills.

"You're being awfully good to me, Mrs. Colby," he ventured. "Why?"

She glanced up sharply. "Maybe I'm curious. Or maybe I just like a good story, and I do intend to get one, you know." Her answer was flippant, almost careless, but her trembling hands jiggled the spoon in its bowl as she lifted the tray and set it across his legs. She was still afraid of him, Latigo calculated, even though she was trying her damnedest not to show it. Colby's widow had courage, he conceded, for a white woman.

Dizzy with hunger, Latigo took the spoon awkwardly in his right hand and dipped it into the soup broth.

"It's all right," he muttered, determined that she would not see him spill. "Go about your business. I'll manage fine."

She waited in stubborn silence. When she did not leave, he focused his attention on raising the spoon to his mouth. But it was no use: he was as weak as a newborn colt. The soup dribbled from the shaking spoon and splattered back into the bowl.

"Here." Her warm fingertips brushed his knuckles as she slipped the spoon from his hand. Latigo watched uneasily as she picked up the bowl and raised it close to his face.

"Don't worry," she said with an air of crisp bravado. "I'm an old hand at this. I had to feed John this way for four months before he...passed away."

She dipped into the soup and thrust the first spoonful between Latigo's parted lips. The delicious warmth trickled down his throat, jolting his deprived system to ravenous hunger. He gulped eagerly, noisily, shamelessly, as fast as she could spoon the precious liquid into his mouth.

She fed him with a practiced efficiency, but he could not help noticing that her hand trembled as she raised the spoon to his lips. Her gaze flickered away at every meeting of their eyes. Was she truly afraid of him or only repelled by his dark Apache features? Latigo could not be sure. He only knew that winning her trust would be like gentling a high-strung mustang mare. He would have to approach her gently and cautiously, and he could make no false or sudden moves that would startle her away.

Meanwhile, there was food and warmth and beauty here, and he could not resist savoring it all. Latigo filled his belly with nourishment and his eyes with the sight of Rose Colby, and little by little, he began to feel like a man again.

Rose put the bowl and spoon down on the tray, shaken by Latigo's darkly intense gaze. "You can manage the rest," she said, breaking off a hunk of bread and sopping it in the dregs of the broth. "Here—you're going to be fine. I can tell you're already feeling better."

He accepted the bread in his elegantly long fingers, eating slowly now that the worst of his hunger had been slaked. "I'm obliged to you, Rose Colby," he said. "And now, if you have any common sense, you'll fetch my boots and clothes and give me leave to ride out of here."

"You're not strong enough yet," she said. "You wouldn't last an hour in the saddle."

"Why should you care? I've invaded your home, held you at gunpoint, been as surly as a three-legged coyote with the mange—"

"I care because you saved John—at least that's what you claim." Rose caught the dark flash of his eyes. "If you're telling the truth, I owe you for my son's life as well as my husband's." She exhaled nervously. "I want you to tell me how it happened."

Latigo had finished his meal. A twinge of pain flickered across his face as he sank back against the pillows. Rose stood up, lifted the tray from his lap and placed it on the nightstand, her breast brushing his shoulder when she leaned over him. Her face felt prickly hot as she lowered herself onto the edge of the chair. "Go on," she said. "I'm waiting."

"Do you want the pretty version of the story, or do you

want the truth?'' His hard eyes glittered with irony. A dark knot of premonition tightened in the pit of Rose's stomach.

"Tell me the truth," she said.

"You may not like it."

"Go on. Tell me how you met John, and how you saved him."

A cactus wren piped its evening song through the open window. Latigo hesitated, swallowed, then spoke slowly into the silence that followed.

"Your husband's company had a reputation for fighting Apaches who couldn't fight back," he began, his voice as expressionless as book print. "Old ones, young ones, women—it didn't matter as long as they were Apaches. This time they'd been chasing a bunch of Diablo's squaws they'd spotted out foraging in the brush. They'd followed the women up a box canyon, bent on Lord knows what—"

"No!" Rose burst out in spite of her resolve to listen. "That can't be true! John's militia fought armed Apaches on the warpath! He was a hero. He was even awarded a medal by the territorial governor. I have it upstairs."

"You wanted the truth." His eyes had narrowed to piercing slits. "Do you have the courage to hear it?"

Rose stared down at her clenched hands, passionately wishing she had never asked him to tell her this story, wishing she had sent him on his way to take his chances in the desert.

"Go on," she said, willing her voice to be as emotionless as his.

Latigo exhaled sharply. "One of the men in the company told me what happened. They'd managed to kill one woman and wound her baby when Diablo and his braves started shooting from the rocks above. The women scattered, and the Apaches blocked off the mouth of the canyon with a rockslide they'd rigged. By the time we came along, they had your husband's company pinned down with rifle fire and were closing in to finish them off.''

Rose listened numbly, her hands clenched in her lap. The story was preposterous, of course, she told herself. John Colby had been a brave and chivalrous man, while this Latigo had shown her no sign of being anything but a lying desperado.

"I was leading a scouting party two hours ahead of the main column," he continued in the same dispassionate tone. "We heard shots and guessed what had happened. There were only four of us, and we knew there was no time to get help. But one thing was in our favor—I knew the country, and I'd been in that canyon before. There was a way out, a side branch, hidden by rocks. The other scouts set fires to create a diversion while I went in after the trapped men. I had to save them. It was my job."

"And you led them out, I suppose. You saved John and the whole company all by yourself." Rose's pulse hammered as she challenged him. "You're lying!" she snapped.

"Lying?"

"John would never have pursued a band of helpless women and babies! And your story—it's too neat, like something out of a dime novel! You didn't save my husband's life or anyone else's! You're making it all up so I'll feel obligated to—"

The blaze of cold fire in his eyes shocked her into silence. "Your husband was wounded when a bullet grazed his left thigh," he said. "I bandaged it myself. The wound wasn't deep, but it would have left a scar."

"No, you couldn't possibly..." Rose remembered the raw, pink groove, newly healed, along John's upper left leg. She had seen it whiten with time. She had touched it every day as she tended his all-but-lifeless body.

"Listen to me, Rose Colby." The last rays of the dying

sun blazed their reflected fire in his eyes. "I don't know where you were during the Apache wars, but nothing about that time was noble or heroic. It was dirty and bloody and just plain, damned awful, and each side was as bad as the other."

"My parents were massacred by Apaches," Rose whispered, gazing out the window at the bloodred sky. "We were on the way to Prescott, and I'd left our camp to gather some *nopales*. I came back just in time to see them die. John's company found me the next day, wandering through the brush, half out of my mind."

He stared at her as if seeing her for the first time. "I'm sorry," he said. "I didn't know."

"You were part of it, too," she lashed out at him. "You were with the army, fighting against your own people. If things were as bad as you claim, why didn't you leave?"

Something hard slipped into place behind his eyes. "Let's just say that I had nowhere else to go."

Chilled by the cold finality in his voice, Rose stood up and reached for the tray. "You can rest the night here. I'll give you breakfast in the morning and enough food and water to get you to the mountains."

"And a gun. I'll find some way to pay you for it."

"You can have some of John's old clothes," she continued, ignoring his demand. "They should fit well enough. I had to burn yours, except for the boots—"

"You're not listening to me, Rose."

Her breath caught at his use of her given name. "No," she said. "No gun. Supplies are one thing, but what if I'm wrong about you? What if you really murdered those two men? How can I, with any good conscience, give you the means to kill others?

"Anyway, your story doesn't make sense to me." Rose paused in the doorway, the tray balanced on her hip. "Why should white men ride onto the Apache reservation and shoot down agents from their own government?''

''Does it make any more sense to you that *I* would shoot them?'' he asked. ''I was responsible for their safety! I would have been the first one blamed.''

''Unless you'd somehow managed to be shot along with them.''

''From behind?''

Rose had no answer for that. She set the tray on the kitchen table and turned back toward the door, still hesitant. Lock him in and walk away, her common sense argued. She had already heard enough of this stranger's talk to shake her world.

''Was there something else you wanted?'' he asked.

The edge in his voice unnerved her. ''No,'' she said. ''I only meant to tell you there's water in that clay pitcher on the dresser, and there's a necessity under the bed if you need it. Be careful getting up.''

He gazed at her in mocking, slit-eyed silence. Flustered, Rose spun away, swung the door shut and jammed the bolt into its slot. Then she wilted against the wall, eyes closed, heart slamming her ribs.

How could she let the man unsettle her so? Everything he said, everything he did, threw her off balance, causing her to question things she'd always been sure about, leaving her vulnerable, exposed and shaken.

Even now, his image flashed through her mind as she had last seen him—Latigo, half Apache, half devil, sitting up in bed, his beautiful, tawny chest and shoulders naked except for the dressing on his wound, the bedclothes scrunched around his hips—his jet-black eyes seeing her secret thoughts, thoughts no decent woman should be having.

It was as if, suddenly, she no longer knew what she believed, or even who she was.

Her thoughts flew to the baby. She had left him upstairs, fast asleep, less than an hour ago. He could be awake and crying, needing her.

Rose crossed the kitchen to the hallway and raced upstairs, urgently needing the comfort of her child in her arms. Mason was her anchor. He was her link to reality, to John and to her own duty.

Rose stole inside the bedroom to find her son still fast asleep beneath the soft lambs-wool blanket she had crocheted before he was born. Tenderly she bent over the cradle, her gaze caressing every delicate curve of his tiny face. She ached to gather him up, to hold him close and lose herself in the bliss of cradling his precious little body. But Mason needed his sleep, she reminded herself. He would be cross if she woke him too soon.

As she glanced up, her eyes caught the last glimmer of sunset on John's medal where it hung on its blue ribbon above her son's cradle.

Pride...Honor...Courage...Duty.

The words mocked her as the image of John and his cohorts, riding down on a band of helpless squaws and papooses, flashed through her mind. She slumped over the cradle, her whole body quivering. If Latigo was to be believed—and the evidence of the scar was too strong to deny—John's militia had gunned down Apache women and children with no more mercy than the Apaches had shown her own family.

She had always believed John to be brave and honorable, and she had vowed to raise Mason by his father's code. Now that code had crumbled away to reveal something she could not even pretend to understand.

Rose struggled to rationalize what she had heard. How could she judge what John had done? Terrible things had happened on both sides of the conflict. Even Latigo had said so. John and his fellow volunteers had done no more than repay the Apaches in kind, following the old biblical law of an eye for an eye. Was that so wrong, in view of what Apaches had done to her own family?

Torn, Rose gazed down at her sleeping son—John's son, too, she reminded herself. In a few years Mason would be old enough to ask questions about his father. How could she tell Mason the truth about his father when she knew so little of it herself? The quest for answers would be long and painful, Rose knew. And her search would have to begin now, before the trail grew too cold to follow.

She had not known many members of John's militia. Of those she had met, most of the older ones had died, and the younger ones had moved on. There was Bayard, but— no, she could not go to Bayard! Not now!

Rose sighed raggedly as she realized her one sure source of knowledge lay downstairs, locked in the little room off the kitchen. For all his rough manners, Latigo was the one man she could count on to give her honest answers. He might hurt her. He might outrage and offend her, but he would not lie.

Tomorrow he would be gone. She needed to talk with him now, tonight, while she still had the chance.

Crossing the room, she raised the lid of the chest that stood against the far wall. Inside, John's clothes lay clean and neatly folded. John was gone. Why had she kept them?

Maybe this was why.

Piling everything on the bed, she selected a cotton union suit, a soft gray flannel shirt, some woolen socks, and a pair of new Levi's to give to Latigo.

The thought of opening the door and seeing him there in the narrow bed, his black Apache eyes as fierce and alert as a hawk's, sent a strange hot chill through her body. The man was everything she hated and feared. All the same, she burned to know the secrets that lay behind that bitter face, behind the anger, behind the sadness that seemed to steal over him at unguarded moments.

Hurrying across the room, she discovered Mason awake and cooing. He smiled up at her as she lifted him.

Then, she kissed one rosebud ear, clutching the fresh clothes under one arm and cradling her baby with the other, Rose made her way down the darkening stairs. This time, she vowed, she would ask all the difficult questions, and this time she would not turn away from the answers.

Latigo's pulse leaped at the sound of Rose's footsteps. Strange, he mused, how he had already come to recognize the light, graceful cadence of her walk, the agitated rush of her breathing, the husky little catch in her voice when she spoke. Even blindfolded, he would know this woman from all others.

Sitting up in the bed, he waited tensely for the sliding of the bolt. He had not expected Rose Colby to return so soon, but he was far from dismayed at the thought of seeing her again.

Time seemed to stop as the door swung open.

"I brought you some clothes," she said, stepping into the room. "You can have your boots in the morning."

"Are you that determined to keep me prisoner?" he asked, half-amused.

"It's for your own good. You're still very weak."

"For my own good, I should be leaving right now. I don't fancy the idea of playing tag with that posse in broad daylight."

"Then stay until nightfall tomorrow." She tossed the bundle of clothes onto the foot of the bed. A wry smile tugged at Latigo's lips as he noticed the union suit—one trapping of white civilization he had stubbornly rejected.

"Your husband's?" he asked.

"Yes." Taut and expectant, she lowered herself to the

edge of the chair. Nested in the crook of her arm, the baby gazed at him with innocent, violet-blue eyes. Her eyes.

"You never told me how your husband died," he said.

"You didn't ask. It was an accident."

"An accident?" He stared at her.

"Why should that be so surprising?" she asked.

"You'd mentioned hand-feeding him. From that, I assumed it was an illness, maybe a stroke."

She shook her head. "It happened last summer. John had ridden out alone to check on the herd—something he often did. When his horse came back with an empty saddle, I sent the vaqueros out to look for him. They brought him back in the wagon just before nightfall, unconscious. Evidently he'd fallen, or been thrown, and struck the back of his head on a rock."

"I'm sorry," Latigo said, reminding himself to be gentle with her. "If it's too painful—"

"No, it helps me to talk about it. Most people don't seem to understand that." Rose sat in near darkness now, her beautiful, sad face obscured by shadows. "At first we didn't expect him to last through the night. But John was a strong man. He lived for four months, if you could call it life. He was bedridden. He couldn't stand or speak, and he didn't seem to know anyone, not even me."

"And you took care of him?"

"I was his wife."

Latigo gazed at Rose Colby's delicate face through the soft veil of twilight. Pampered, he had called her. Spoiled. Lord, how could a man be so wrong?

"Of course, I couldn't have cared for John all alone," she added swiftly. "I had Esperanza to help with the housework and cooking, and Miguel to keep the ranch running. And there was Bayard, of course."

"Bayard?" The name triggered a taste as bitter as creosote in Latigo's mouth.

"Bayard rode out from Tucson as soon as he got word of John's accident." She paused, head tilted, lost in thought. "You know, I truly can't imagine what got into him this morning. Bayard was wonderful the whole time John was dying—sitting with him by the hour, bringing us things from town...."

"If he was so wonderful, maybe you shouldn't have been so quick to run him off!" Latigo growled.

He regretted the remark instantly, but it was too late to call it back. He saw her body stiffen and, even in the darkened room, caught the fire, like flecks of Mexican opal, in her splendid eyes.

"My relationship with Bayard Hudson is none of your concern!" she retorted sharply. "You asked me how my husband died, and I was telling you. That's all you need to know!"

Silence hung between them. Then, deliberately, Latigo allowed himself to laugh. "You have a fine way of slapping a man's face without touching him, Rose Colby," he said.

"If that's true, maybe I should do it more often!"

"It is true, Rose. Everything I've told you is true."

"How can I be sure of that?" The anguish in her voice was real. She wanted to trust him, Latigo sensed, but she was still fearful.

"Would it be easier if I were a white man?" he dared to ask.

"That's not a fair question," she answered. "There are different kinds of white men and, I suppose, different kinds of Apaches."

"That's very generous of you," Latigo said dryly. "So, what kind of Apache am I? Have you decided?"

"I don't know. I don't know *you*."

She made a move to rise, then settled uneasily back onto

the chair as if she'd changed her mind. Once more the darkness lay heavy and still between them.

Latigo battled the urge to reach out and demand to know what she was doing here. Her husband's clothes had only provided her with an excuse to come to him—she could just as easily have delivered them in the morning. If she were a different sort of woman, he might have construed it as an invitation. But Rose Colby was not bent on seduction. Her modest, distant manner and the presence of her child were enough to tell him that.

"Light the lamp," he said. "I want to see your face. And I want you to see mine."

She hesitated in the darkness, then rose from the chair with her son in her arms. "The lamp's in the kitchen. Wait here. I'll go and light it."

"You'll need both hands," Latigo heard himself saying. "Give me the baby. I'll hold him for you."

Her lips parted as her arms tightened around the blanketed bundle. Only then did Latigo realize what he had done. In his readiness to be helpful, he had demanded the ultimate token of her trust, a trust he had yet to earn.

"It's all right, Rose. I would never harm your son."

"I know."

Despite her words, she did not move, and Latigo knew better than to push her. "Never mind about the lamp, then," he said. "Darkness makes it harder for each of us to know what the other is thinking. Maybe that's not so bad after all."

For a long moment, the only sound in the tiny room was the soft rush of her breathing. Then she took a step toward him and very carefully held out her baby.

Latigo's heart jumped as she thrust the small, squirming bundle toward him. His outstretched hands received the precious weight like a blessing.

"I'll get the lamp," she said, and walked swiftly into the kitchen.

The baby whimpered, then relaxed, gurgling contentedly as Latigo settled the tiny body awkwardly against his chest. In all of his adult life, he could not remember having held an infant.

An alien sweetness, frighteningly close to tears, stole through him as he cradled Rose Colby's son in his arms. Most men his age had sons of their own. Daughters, too, and wives and homes. But a family had no place in the life of a man caught between two worlds. He was alone and destined to remain so, a fugitive spirit, tied to no place, bound to no other human soul.

Light flickered in the kitchen as Rose struck a match and touched it to the lamp wick. The glow moved with her as she crossed the tiles to stand in the doorway.

"Mason seems to have taken to you," she said as she placed the lamp on the dresser. "He's settled right down. You should be flattered, he doesn't do that with everyone."

"Well, let's hope the boy acquires better sense as he gets older," Latigo remarked dryly.

A wan smile flickered across her face. "I can hold him now."

"He's fine where he is."

She settled back onto the chair, making no move to take the baby from him. Latigo watched her, savoring her gentle beauty and the fragile warmth of her child against his heart.

This was foolhardy, his instincts shrieked in the stillness. John Colby's widow had lost her family to the Apaches and he could not afford to trust her. True, she had not given away his presence this morning. But under different conditions, she could easily betray him. Lovely, brave and gentle she might be, but he could not allow himself to fall under her spell.

"What are you doing in here, Rose?" he asked, his voice unexpectedly rough. "You could be taking an awful chance, you know. I could overpower you, force you to get me the gun, take you and your baby hostage to use against that posse."

"You don't hide behind children, or women, either, I take it. At least that's what you said."

"But what if you're wrong about me?" he persisted. "What do you want so much that you'd take this kind of chance?"

"The truth." Her eyes, reflecting the lamplight, held tiny gold flames. "I want to know exactly how you came to be on this ranch, and I want to hear everything you know about my husband."

"Even if you don't like my answers?"

Her pale throat moved as she swallowed, then nodded. "I need to know for my own sake, and for Mason's one day, when he's old enough to understand."

Latigo shifted his body higher on the pillows. The baby stirred in his arms, turning to gaze up at him with wide indigo eyes, and he knew that whatever he said, it would be for both of them. And whatever he said, it would be true.

But would it be the whole truth? Could he trust her with everything he knew?

Gazing at her through the amber haze of lamplight, he cleared his throat and began with a question.

"Rose, how much do you know about the so-called Indian Ring?"

Chapter Five

*T*he Indian Ring?

Rose stared at the man in the shadows. She had never heard of the Indian Ring, but something about the name, or perhaps the way Latigo had said it, sounded so sinister that it triggered cold prickles along the flesh of her forearms.

"Your husband never mentioned the Ring to you?" he pressed her. "You never overheard him talking about it with his friends?"

"My husband believed women should keep still and tend to their knitting. His friends did come to the ranch sometimes, but I was never invited to join them." Rose twisted the hem of her apron, her eyes on her son lying contentedly in the cradle of Latigo's bare brown arms. In the dancing lamplight, Latigo's lean Apache face had softened to tenderness, which tore at her defenses. She forced herself to meet his calm gaze. "If you want to talk about the Indian Ring, you'll have to start by explaining what it is," she said.

Latigo's eyes narrowed. Cool evening air drifted in through the barred window, smelling of dust and rain. Thunder rumbled faintly from beyond the horizon.

"Most people would say the Ring never existed," he said. "But I know better."

"Maybe so, but I'm not following you!" Rose broke in impatiently. "Are you implying the Indian Ring had something to do with John?"

"I was hoping you might be able to tell me that."

"You're speaking in riddles."

"I know." Pain rippled across Latigo's face as he shifted his weight against the pillow. Seeing his discomfort, Rose leaned forward and lifted Mason out of his arms. His eyes watched her guardedly, their black depths whispering unspoken secrets, and suddenly she was afraid.

"Can I get you something?" she asked, taking an emotional step backward.

He shook his head.

"This is taxing your strength," she persisted.

"I'm all right."

Rose held her son close, seeking comfort in his small, warm nearness. "Tell me about the Indian Ring," she said softly.

"The Ring is secret, and powerful." Latigo bit back pain as he spoke. "It's made up of white men who've profited from the Apache wars, legally by selling beef and supplies to the army, illegally by smuggling guns and whiskey to the Apaches."

"And you think John was involved?"

"I didn't say that."

"But it's certainly no secret that this ranch has furnished beef to the army for years."

"Let me finish." His eyes warned her to listen. "The men in the Ring got rich off the Apache wars during the sixties. It suits them to keep things stirred up, especially with all the talk of the railroad coming in. That's the last thing the Ring wants to see because most of them would e ruined. They're banking on the hope that nobody will want to lay track through hostile Indian territory.''

Rose stared at him in disbelief. "You're saying that the Ring deliberately causes trouble with the Apaches? That sounds awfully farfetched to me."

"Not as farfetched as you might think. You remember he Camp Grant massacre in '71?"

"Yes, of course I do." Rose's flesh went cold as she spoke. No one in the territory could have missed hearing about the slaughter of 125 peaceful Arivaipa Apaches by an armed mob of Tucson citizens.

"But John wasn't there!" she protested, springing once more to her husband's defense. "He was out on the range with the herd! And you know as well as I do there were only five white men involved in the massacre—the rest were Mexicans and Papago Indians."

"All true." Latigo's eyes glittered like sharp black flints. "But I worked as translator for the army commission hat investigated the massacre. The five whites all had connections to the Ring—as hirelings, most likely. The Ring's leaders are prominent men. They call the shots and pay the money, but they don't get their hands dirty."

Thunder rolled dimly, echoing along the fringe of Rose's awareness as she stared at him, horrified. "You're saying John could have been involved in the Ring and in the massacre?"

"Rose, there's no proof either way."

"And Bayard?"

"Again, there's no proof. When you get right down to , there's no proof the Ring even exists. Any such proof ould be a very dangerous thing to possess."

Rose sank back into the chair, feeling strangely light, as the marrow had been drained from her bones. "Your wound," she said, forcing the words out of her tight throat.

"The murder of the two government agents—you're saying that was the work of the Ring, too?"

"Again, there's no proof. But I know what I saw. And I know that the two federal men were looking into smuggling activities on the San Carlos, which could also have been the work of the Ring. If I hadn't escaped the ambush, it would have been natural for the authorities to blame the murders on the Apaches and call in more troops. As it was—"

"They had to blame you." Rose closed her eyes for a moment as she struggled to make sense of the things she had just heard. She had asked Latigo for the truth and resolved to accept it, but he had shown her a glimpse of something so large and dark that it defied belief.

"What I've told you is true," he said in a low, flat voice. "Every word of it."

"But you've told me nothing! You've only raised more questions, more suspicions."

"I've told you what I know. If I've failed to answer your concerns about your husband, it's because I have no answers myself."

"Then answer me this, at least!" Rose's arms tightened around her baby. "If you suspected John was involved in the Ring, why did you come here last night demanding his help?"

Rose saw Latigo hesitate, as if his mind were scrambling for an answer that would placate her. "There was nowhere else to go," he said with the icy pride of a man who detested being a supplicant. "I had to gamble that Colby would honor his promise. It was that, or die in the desert."

"Then you did believe John was an honorable man?"

"I barely knew your husband. It was a chance I had to take."

"Then you've been no help at all!" Bursting with frustration, Rose stood up with a suddenness that startled the baby.

"All you've done is confuse me!" she snapped, worn beyond patience. "My son and I don't need your kind of trouble. Tomorrow I want you gone. Then I'm going to do my best to forget I ever saw you!" She turned away from him and strode toward the door.

"You believe me." The sound of his voice followed her, compelling in its power. "You can't run away from that. I know you believe me, Rose."

"What difference does it make?" She wheeled to face him, framed by the doorway. "I can't help you! I can't prove your innocence! I've got a ranch to run and a boy to raise!"

"I'll be gone by sunup," he said quietly. "But there is one thing you can do."

"What?"

"Get me a gun," he said. "That's all I'm asking."

"No!" Rose shook her head adamantly. "Right or wrong, I won't be a party to more killing on either side! John owed you a debt, so did I. When you leave tomorrow, consider it paid!"

Before he could argue or call her back, she had spun into the kitchen, flung the door shut behind her and slipped the bolt. Startled, Mason began to fuss, then to wail.

"It's all right, little love." She gathered him to her shoulder, soothing him with one agitated hand. She had half expected to hear Latigo shouting at her through the door, but the silence from the small room was grim and final. The tall Apache was a proud man, too proud to demand her return.

Legs wilting, Rose sank onto a chair and fumbled with the bodice of her gown. The baby rooted hungrily at her breast, found the nipple and began his noisy, eager sucking.

You believe me. You can't run away from that. I know you believe me, Rose.

She squeezed her eyelids tightly shut, willing the words to fly from her mind. If Latigo was truly innocent she could not, in good conscience, turn away and leave him to his fate. It was her moral duty to aid the cause of justice. That's what her father would have said, and that's what he would have done.

Oh, why did it have to be so difficult? Right or wrong, she wanted no part of what this man represented—the danger, the deceit, the violence. She wanted only to be left alone, to raise her son in peace on this ranch that was his legacy.

No, she could not allow herself to become involved. The danger was too great.

By this time tomorrow everything would be all right, Rose reassured herself. Her dangerous guest would be gone, and Esperanza and Miguel would be back from Fronteras. The quiet pace of life would go on as if the events of the past twenty-four hours had never happened. And she would not allow herself to think about the black-eyed stranger who brooded in silence now behind the locked door. She would not think about the way he had stopped her breath, standing naked as Adam beside the bed, the morning sun rippling copper light over his muscular back and taut buttocks. She would not remember the sight of him lying against the white pillows, his powerful arms cradling her son with a father's gentleness. She would not allow herself to feel the piercing power of his hard, black eyes or hear the flinty, sensual whisper of his voice.

You believe me...I know you believe me, Rose.

The baby had stopped nursing and lay in the crook of her arm, gazing up at her in the twilight. The first drops of rain lashed the window, leaving trails of wet dust down the outside of the glass. The bolted door remained ominously silent.

No, she would be a fool to open it. He could be waiting on the other side, ready to overpower her and demand the pistol; and even in his weakened condition, those muscular arms would be more than a match for her own strength.

You believe me...

Rose tugged her bodice together and lifted the Peacemaker from its hiding place behind the bread box. Then, clutching her son, she fled upstairs to the sanctuary of her bedroom.

The storm moved slowly but with monstrous power. For what seemed like hours, Rose huddled at the upstairs window, cradling the baby as she watched the savage play of nature over the flats and mesas.

Below her in the locked room off the kitchen, the stranger waited for dawn. Rose pictured him lying alone in the narrow bed, still weak from his wound. She imagined him listening to the storm, his Apache eyes blacker than the night around him, his lean body stirring beneath the blankets, too restless for sleep.

As her eyelids began to droop, she imagined herself moving downstairs, floating through the doorway to lean over him in the darkness. She felt his hands reaching up, his long, masculine fingers unpinning her hair, his arms drawing her down to him, holding her as gently as he had held her son until, at aching last, his beautiful, sensual mouth claimed hers in a kiss as wild and passionate as the storm that raged outside....

A sudden quiver shot through Rose's body, jarring her fully awake. She had been dozing, she realized. Her mind had drifted into a forbidden dream, a dream so scandalous that the memory of it triggered a flush of heat across her face. She was exhausted, she realized as she wrenched her-

self back to reality. What she needed was a few hours of
sleep.

Mason slumbered in her arms, his lashes a feathered
shadow against his pale baby cheeks. Turning away from
the window, she carried him to the cradle, eased him tenderly onto the pad and tucked the soft blankets around him.

Weary beyond coherent thought, she stumbled back
across the room, unfastened her gown and the busk of her
corset and peeled off the entire costume. Her dress and
petticoats crumpled around her in an untidy heap. Rose
was too tired to pick them up. Clad only in her chemise
and drawers, she turned down the covers and crawled between the sheets. Her head had scarcely touched the pillow
before she sank into sleep, oblivious except to the savage
thunder that crashed in her dreams.

Fully clothed, Latigo lay on top of the quilt, watching
the reflected lightning play across the ceiling of his prison.
He had dressed as soon as Rose left the room, determined
to be ready for whatever might happen next. Since her
departure, however, the hours had crawled at the pace of
slow death.

He had already tested the door, his desperate fingers
probing every inch of the frame, the hinges, the surrounding mortar, in search of some weak spot he could exploit.
He had done the same with the bars on the window, but
had discovered nothing that promised an easy escape.

Now, seething with frustration, he could only lie here
and torture himself with the golden image of Rose Colby
sitting beside the bed, her opal eyes intent on the path of
the spoon from the bowl to his lips; Rose bending over
him in the twilight, her lovely, swollen breast brushing his
ear as she lifted the tray from his lap; Rose moving, smiling, speaking in the husky little whisper that stirred his
senses like the stroke of a fingertip…

This was no good, he lashed himself. He had to get out of this place, now, before he slipped any deeper into danger.

The center of the storm was passing over the ranch. Rain poured like a waterfall off the eave outside the window. Lightning crackled across the sky, striking so close that light and sound crashed together in an earsplitting boom that shook the house to its foundation.

Latigo could not see the corral, but he could hear the horses milling in wild circles, squealing in terror and slamming their heavy bodies against the rails. Soon no fence would be able to hold them. Unless they were driven into the barn, they would break out and stampede into the night.

Then what?

Latigo swung his legs to the floor and stumbled to the bolted door. "Rose!" He pounded the door with all his strength, praying she would hear him above the storm. "Rose, damn it, you need—"

The room flashed blue-white as a bolt of lightning split the heavens. The thunderclap was instantaneous, so close and so loud that Latigo felt as if he had been knocked across the room.

The scream of a horse mingled with the roar of the storm. A horse in agony, injured, down.

"Rose!" His fists bruised as he battered them against the wood. "Rose—"

He heard the slam of the back door, heard her quick footsteps, and suddenly she was there, throwing back the bolt, flinging the door open. She was soaked with rain, her hair streaming water, her wet flannel wrapper clinging to her body. In the blue darkness, her eyes were huge and frightened.

"The horses—they're getting out—I can't manage them alone." She was panting—no, sobbing. "One of them is hurt! Oh, please, hurry!" She thrust something toward him—his boots. Latigo bent over and began jerking them onto his feet. He felt sore and light-headed, but he knew he had to help her.

"You were out there alone?" he rasped, anger battling relief. "In this storm? You could've come for me sooner!"

"I was asleep. Come on!" She flew across the kitchen, pulled open the back door and vanished into the storm outside. With a muttered curse, Latigo plunged after her.

He rounded the back corner of the house to be greeted by a scene from a nightmare. The downpour had turned the yard to a muddy sea. A lightning flash revealed the shattered fence and the gleaming wet shapes of horses, milling, rearing, galloping off like phantoms into the rainy darkness.

Latigo forced his pain-dulled mind to think as he raced across the yard. The barn door was closed. If he could get it open and get even one horse inside...

But what was the use? Latigo's body sagged with despair as he realized he was already too late. The spooked ponies had scattered to the four winds and were already thundering into the rainy night. On foot, there was no hope of catching even one of the miserable beasts.

A flicker of lightning illuminated Rose crouching beside the fallen horse. With a sigh, Latigo sloshed back across the yard toward her. She lifted her anguished face as he came close.

"It's my fault," she whispered. "I could have put at least some of them inside before I went to bed. But I was so tired. I didn't even think of it."

"You couldn't have known the kind of freak storm we were in for." Latigo had meant to vent his frustrations on her, but his voice came out raspy with tenderness. "In an ordinary rain, the horses would've been fine. It's not your fault, Rose. It's not anybody's damned fault."

The injured horse snorted and raised its head. Its mud-coated legs thrashed helplessly. Latigo had wrangled horses in his early army days, and his instincts told him this one was badly hurt.

"Can't you do something?" Rose whispered.

"I can put the poor thing out of its misery—that is, unless you'd rather pull the trigger yourself."

"Please," her tearful voice pleaded with him. "This one's my horse, my pet. His name is Sundown. He was a wedding gift from John. I've ridden him around the ranch ever since."

"All right, I'll take a look." Latigo masked his emotions with gruffness. How had this woman survived so many long, harsh years on the desert, the loss of her family, the slow death of her husband? She was too tender-hearted for such a life. A woman like Rose Colby was meant to be cherished and protected, to be surrounded with love.

Willing his thoughts to fade, he crouched in the mud and examined the horse's legs. He was conscious of Rose's voice, crooning to the animal in the darkness, of her eyes watching him anxiously through the black curtain of rain.

In the left hind leg, midway between pastern and hock, his probing fingers discovered an ugly swelling. A bad sprain, or even a break, he reckoned. Worse, the animal had evidently cut its leg on the broken fence and was bleeding badly, its rich, dark blood mingling with the muddy rain.

"Can't we do something?" Rose's voice was laced with tears. "Can't we at least get him into the barn?"

"Maybe. But if the leg's broken I wouldn't bet on the horse ever being worth riding again. It might be kinder to get the pistol and let me shoot him for you."

"No."

He glanced up, startled by her vehemence. She was cra-

dling the horse's head in her lap, rain streaming down her
pale face.

"He's in pain, Rose."

"But you can't be sure the leg's broken," she whispered. "Otherwise you'd have said so. Please."

Latigo's shoulders sagged in resignation. "We should
stop the bleeding before we try to move him. I'll need
some wrappings, and some clean bacon drippings if you
have them."

"In the house. Wait here." She scrambled to her feet
and raced toward the house, the black rain sweeping behind her.

Latigo sank back onto his heels as she vanished from
sight. His shoulder and head throbbed. By now, he should
have been headed for the Mexican border. Instead, here he
was, playing horse doctor for a woman who, by turns,
touched, intrigued, aroused and maddened him.

The horse, a sleek bay gelding, its white blaze splattered
with mud, snorted and raised its head. Latigo stroked the
tense, wet neck, murmuring soothing phrases in Apache.
He had not relished the idea of shooting the poor animal,
but he was no miracle worker. If the leg was truly broken,
the horse would be better off dead.

He could see Rose now, struggling toward him, her arms
laden with wrappings. Her stubborn courage tugged at his
emotions. The woman was a sentimental fool, getting soft
and weepy over a horse, he reminded himself. Even so, at
that moment, Latigo knew he would do anything to keep
her heart from breaking.

"Sorry to take so long," she gasped. "I had to check
on the baby."

"It's all right. Keep him still, if you can." Latigo took
the wrappings and motioned her toward the horse's head.
He would support the leg well enough to block the bleeding, then try to get the animal onto its feet.

Rose cradled the massive head in her lap, crooning tender little phrases Latigo could only half hear. Her wide, soft eyes watched him as he wrapped the leg, following each circling movement of the cloth.

"Finished," he muttered, glancing up at her. "Now we have to get him up. Take his halter and coax him. I'll add some encouragement from the other end." He picked up a stick from the ground and, as Rose scrambled out of the way, brought it down none too gently on the gelding's hindquarters.

The startled animal lurched to its feet, nickering with pain as its weight came down on the injured leg.

"That's it." Latigo encouraged the horse, nudging it gently forward as Rose caught the halter. "That's it, old boy. Favor that leg. Keep it off the ground."

"Come on, Sundown." Rose's voice broke as the horse stumbled. The rain continued to stream down, plastering Rose's nightclothes to her slender frame.

She caught the door, and they staggered inside, into the dry darkness. "Hold him. I'll light the lamp," she said.

Latigo heard her fumbling in the dark, heard the scrape of a match. An instant later, warm, golden light from a hanging lantern pooled around them.

Rose was drenched and shivering, her lips edged faintly with blue. She looked so cold and exhausted that Latigo battled the urge to pull her close and warm her chilled body against his own.

"We've got to get you dried off," he said gruffly, guiding the injured horse into an open stall.

"The horse first." She reached for a clean towel that hung nearby.

"No, *you* first." His fingers circled her wrist. Gently but firmly, he lifted the towel from her hand and began to sponge the moisture from her dripping hair. She closed her eyes in weary acquiescence. Her breath eased out in a long, quivering sigh.

Rose's water-soaked flannel wrapper clung to every curve of her body. Latigo willed his responses to freeze as he worked the towel down the small of her back, taking exquisite care against any accidental brush of his fingers. Nothing touched her except the wadded towel. Even so, he could feel that she was trembling. And he could feel the hot current rising in his own blood, its ardor mounting with the slightest press of the cloth.

She was uncorseted beneath the wet wrapper, her body as lithe and firm as a deer's, and yet, he sensed, indescribably soft. Her buttocks swelled gracefully below the point where he dared touch, even with the towel, lush beneath the clinging fabric. Her damp skin smelled faintly of lavender, blending in his nostrils with the subtle womanly aroma of her body.

Latigo's hand had stopped moving. He could hear the low rush of her breathing, the warm silence of the barn. He could feel the drumming fever of his own pulse as he battled the compelling urge to touch her, to turn her in his arms, strip away her wet clothes and sear her naked flesh with his heat.

Rose stood as still as glass. Her eyes were closed, her lips faintly tinged with blue—in dire need of kissing, or so it seemed. Time stopped as the towel dropped from Latigo's hand.

"The horse." Her voice was a raw whisper.

"Yes. The horse." Latigo recovered his senses. Chastened, he reached for a spare saddle blanket and wrapped it around her shoulders, bundling her tenderly, like a child brought in from the cold. She clutched at its folds, pulling it more tightly around her as he turned away, picked up the towel, and began rubbing down the injured animal.

What had possessed him? he lashed himself. Rose Colby

was a white woman, and a wealthy one at that. Here in the darkness, in a brief weak moment, she might have allowed him to touch her. But in the world outside, he would not be counted worthy to sweep the path where she walked. He knew it, and she knew it, too.

"Who are you, Latigo?"

The question startled him. He glanced back over his shoulder to see her huddled on a salt block, bundled to her chin in the faded, red Navajo blanket.

"I don't know anything about you. Where you came from, your people, how you came to be a scout."

"Maybe it's just as well you don't know," he said. "I'll be gone as soon as I can find a way out of here."

"That's not enough," she persisted. "I saved your life. You owe me some kind of explanation—who you are, what you are."

"I thought you said we were even."

"I changed my mind."

"You're a stubborn woman, Rose Colby."

"So they say." She sat very still, wrapped in the warmth of the blanket.

"You seem to know a lot about horses," she said.

"Most Apaches do. Even the women."

"You were raised as an Apache, then?"

"After a fashion." Latigo forced himself to keep working. His past was his own business. He had never revealed it to anyone. No person he knew would have cared or understood.

But Rose was waiting, her soft lips parted, her eyes bright and expectant in the lamplight, and for the first time in his life, Latigo felt the urge to share something of himself.

Outside, the storm was passing. The rain on the barn

roof had softened to a patter, the thunder to a distant rumble. In the peace of the barn, Latigo felt memories forming themselves into words. He took his time, waiting for them to come. Then, slowly, he began to speak.

Chapter Six

"I was born when the territory was still part of Mexico," Latigo began, his long brown hands working the towel over the gelding's wet coat. "The place, the date—those things I couldn't tell you if you asked me."

Rose watched him in silence, hesitant to speak and risk closing the tentative door that had opened between them. She had burned to know more about this bitter, mysterious man, and now she wanted to keep him talking.

"I barely remember my father," he said. "He was a Spanish Basque, and he came West looking for gold. As far as I know, he never found it. If I had to guess, I'd say he was long dead."

"And your mother?" Rose asked softly.

Latigo's hands paused for an instant. "She was a gentle person," he said. "Too gentle for what life dealt her. My father bought her from a gang of Mexicans. For almost five years he kept her with him. Then, early one morning, after he'd broken her nose and passed out drunk, my mother decided she'd had enough. She packed up some food and water, took me by the hand, and we walked for twelve days, all the way back to her people. I never saw my father again."

"I'm sorry," Rose said.

Latigo glanced around the barn, ignoring her sympathy. "Did you bring the bacon grease I asked for?"

"It's there, on that box by the door. Stay with Sundown, I'll get it." Rose sprang to her feet before he could argue, leaving the blanket draped over the nail keg. "What do you plan to do with it?"

"Make a salve to heal the wound. But I'll need some yarrow—"

"There's a patch of it on the south side of the barn."

"I'll go. You're wet enough already." He strode toward the door.

Latigo was back seconds later with a fistful of the scraggly green plant. Stuffing the leaves and stems into his mouth, he chewed them to a pulp, then began to knead them with a dollop of thick, cold grease in the palm of his hand.

Rose waited for him to go on with his story. When he did not speak, she broke the silence herself.

"You said your mother took you back to her people. She was Chiricahua?"

His face fell into shadow. "Yes. My mother was Cochise's half sister, so we were welcomed. Suddenly I had aunts, uncles, cousins. Taza, Cochise's son, was my playmate. It's the best time I ever remember."

"What happened?" Rose asked softly, aware that she was touching a painful and precious memory.

"The whites came. The *pindah likoyee,* with their guns, their god and their government. Everything began to change. My mother had taken a new husband and had two daughters. We'd broken off into a smaller band for the summer season. Some whites came by to trade. One of them was sick with measles."

His hands had stopped moving. Rose stared at him as the horror sank home.

"They died, all of them." His words echoed her thoughts. "All except me. Maybe my father's blood made me more resistant than the others. I don't know. But I lived to sing the death song over them all."

He knelt and began to unwrap the horse's bandaged foreleg. "I was still a boy—eleven or twelve, maybe. I wanted to go back to Cochise's *rancheria,* but I was afraid of somehow taking the sickness with me, so I tried surviving on my own. I almost starved before a band of soldiers found me. When they discovered I was part white, they turned me over to a missionary couple near Camp Grant." Latigo's shoulders had gone rigid. "And that," he said, "was the beginning of my so-called education."

He glanced up at her, his expression so bitter that Rose stifled a gasp. "Hold the horse still while I rub on the salve," he said. "It may hurt a little."

Rose gripped the halter, crooning to calm the nervous creature while Latigo rubbed the salve gently onto its wound. He worked in brooding silence, and Rose sensed that he regretted opening himself to her. This was a man who trusted no one. A man alone, his spirit raw with unhealed wounds.

Had he known many women? Surely he had. Latigo's rugged features and dark, feral grace would be enough to draw the gaze of any female he passed. But love? Rose mentally shook her head. Loving a man like Latigo would be like loving the wind.

His knuckles brushed her leg as he reached for the wrappings again. The unexpected touch sparked a ripple of sensual awareness through Rose's body. She turned to find him looking up at her, his eyes intent but guarded.

"Who are you, Latigo?" she whispered again, quivering as his gaze pierced her defenses like a stone-tipped arrow.

"To you—no one and nothing," he murmured. "A passing ghost, gone with the first light of sunrise."

"So when will you go?" Rose asked.

"Early. I'll only bring on trouble for you if I delay. You know that."

"Yes." Rose's eyes shifted to the straw that littered the floor of the barn. "And I know something else. You didn't kill those two government men."

He flashed her a bitter glance. "Congratulations. At this point, you're the only person in the territory who believes me." Without another word, he finished the wrappings, tied a knot and tucked in the ends.

"I'll stay out here with your horse tonight. Then I'll unwrap him in the morning and see how the leg's doing." Latigo loomed above Rose, cloaking her in his long black shadow. "If the leg doesn't heal—"

"I'll deal with that when the time comes," Rose said sharply. "Until then, there'll be no talk of shooting him."

"Will you have someone around the place who knows horses?"

"Miguel. He and his wife will be back from Fronteras any day now."

"Maybe...if the storm hasn't washed out every bridge from here to the border."

She glanced up at him in sudden alarm, then forced a shrug. "If that happens, I can take care of things here myself."

"Well, then, you'll have to, because I don't plan to stay around long enough for that posse to come by and pick me off. It's a long walk to Mexico. The sooner I get started the better."

"You're going to walk?" Rose stared at him as thunder boomed across the flats, its echo rumbling into silence. Her emotions pinwheeled, making no sense, even to her.

"Unless one of your cows is saddle broken, I can't see that I have a choice."

"No one can cross that desert alone on foot!"

Latigo's eyes had narrowed to slits. "Don't tell me you're concerned, Mrs. Colby. Have you forgotten I'm half Apache?"

His icy retort struck her like a lash. Stung, Rose turned away from him and stalked toward the barn door, her thoughts churning. *Let him go,* her common sense argued. *He's not worth your anger, not worth your grief. Let it be.*

But something in her heart would not listen. A few brief hours ago, she had declared that she wanted him gone. But Rose's inborn sense of justice had been seething all night. Now, as she reached the door and turned back to look at him, it exploded in a burst of indignant fury.

"How can you just leave like this? You'll have no life at all! You'll never be able to scout for the army again!"

"No great loss on either side." A muscle twitched in Latigo's cheek.

"You'll have a price on your head till the end of your days!"

"Would a rope around my neck be a better choice?"

"Don't you see?" she stormed. "You've been falsely accused. If you don't stay and fight to clear yourself, you'll carry that charge to your grave while the real killers go free!"

"That's all very brave and noble, Rose Colby." His voice was flinty with impatience. "But I have no evidence. I have no witnesses—none, at least, who could be expected to tell the truth. I have nothing but my own word, the word of a half-breed Apache."

Rose sighed, holding her exasperation in check. "But what if you could prove who was really behind the murders? Isn't there anyone who would listen and judge you fairly?"

Latigo's hands froze in midmotion, and for a moment, Rose thought, he looked almost hopeful.

"One man, maybe," he murmured, half to himself.

"John Clum, the Indian agent on the San Carlos. He hates the Ring as much as I do. If—"

He shook his head. "No, it wouldn't work. Clum's a fair man. Even the Apaches respect him. But even if he believed me, even if he was willing to take a stand, Clum has no power outside the reservation."

"But—"

"Forget it, Rose." His voice was flat and hard. "You've saved my life and canceled your husband's debt of honor. What happens to me now is none of your concern."

"But if John had connections to the Ring…"

"What if he did?" Latigo's obsidian eyes glittered. "Think about it, Rose. Would you sully your husband's fine reputation to help a man you barely know?"

Rose stared at him as his words sank home, brutal words that tore at the fabric of everything she had ever stood for.

She groped for a sharp retort that would put him in his place. But there seemed to be nothing left inside her but tears of frustration, rage and helplessness. They flooded her eyes, blurring her vision until she could barely see.

"I have to get back to my baby," she murmured, struggling to conceal her emotions. "The house will be locked till sunup, but if you want breakfast in the morning, just knock on the kitchen window. I'll be up early."

Latigo had not spoken or moved, and Rose could feel herself crumbling as the day's events caved in on her. Turning toward the door, she snatched up the skirt of her soggy wrapper and flung herself outside into the tail of the storm. Her ruined slippers spattered fountains of mud as she fled across the yard to the safety of the house.

Mason was still fast asleep. He lay sprawled on his back, his sweet baby breath filling the shadows around him. Rose paused to brush a fingertip along his downy petal cheek.

Then she turned back toward the bed and began stripping away her rain-soaked clothes.

Her teeth chattered in the darkness as she pulled a clean flannel nightgown from the depths of the cedar chest. Its dry warmth was bliss against her chilled skin.

Huddling on the edge of the bed, Rose used a towel to blot the rain from her hair. The motion reawakened the memory of Latigo's touch, the pressure of his fingers through the thickness of the fabric, the tingling ache that had crept through her body like the slow melting of spring ice in a mountain stream.

He had been so careful not to touch her skin, she recalled, so careful not to frighten her or give her any notion that he might...

Might what?

Might brush a questioning knuckle along the sensitive crest of her ear? Might slide his cool, tough palm along the curve of her jaw or trace the small of her back with a fingertip?

How would it have felt?

Annoyed with herself, Rose flung the towel into a shadowed corner of the room. What was the matter with her? The man was a blood brother to the savages who had murdered her family. Worse, he was a fugitive from the law, a man with no roots, no friends and no future. Even if he escaped hanging, Latigo would spend the rest of his life looking over his shoulder. She'd best forget she had ever met him.

Would you sully your husband's fine reputation to help a man you barely know?

Rose pressed her hands to her temples to shut out the echo of his words. No, she could not help Latigo expose the Indian Ring, not even if doing so might prove his innocence. She knew nothing, she had no evidence.

Seeking oblivion, Rose flung herself back into bed and

pulled the thick quilts up to her ears. Sleep was what she wanted, just a few precious hours until Mason woke up and needed her.

She closed her eyes and willed her quivering nerves to relax. But it was no use. Images flashed again and again through her mind—lightning splitting the black night; Sundown sprawled in the mud, nickering in pain; Latigo's soul-searing gaze; his fingers, long and brown and sensitive, their quiet skill, their gentleness...

As she struggled to sleep the images swirled from more distant depths—her father, his eyes as blue as heaven, his hand reaching out to stroke her hair; the burning wagon, the Apaches screaming their hatred to the sky...

No!

Rose sat bolt upright, trembling in the darkness as she fought to sweep the nightmare away. There were reasons for everything, even tragedy, her father had once told her. But in this bleak hour of the night, nothing in her life, aside from Mason, seemed to have any direction or purpose.

Now a dark stranger had flung down a challenge to all she held dear: to John's memory, to Mason's legacy of pride, honor and courage, and to her own thirst for justice. Could she live the rest of her life without knowing the truth about what he had told her?

With a restless sigh, Rose swung her feet to the floor and touched a match to the wick of her bedside lamp. The papers in John's office had lain untouched since his accident. Rose had never felt comfortable in the room's confined, masculine space. She had meant to go through John's papers, but the task had loomed before her like a dreary mountain, and she had willingly allowed other matters to interfere.

Now Rose knew she could not put it off another day. If the truth about the Indian Ring and John's involvement in it lay downstairs in that small room, she had to know before Latigo vanished from her life.

Shoving her icy feet into woolen slippers, Rose left the room and hurried downstairs in her long flannel nightdress. The grandfather clock struck two as she crossed the dining room and opened the door to John's office.

Lamplight flickered on the mahogany-paneled walls and on the framed photographs that hung there. John with the governor, John with the members of his militia. On top of the file cabinet sat a silver-framed tintype of John's first wife, Emily, holding their young son. Both had died of influenza in the early days of the ranch. John slumbered alongside them now in the little family graveyard on the crest of a nearby hill. Rose had planted poppy seeds on the three graves. Maybe with the rains they would sprout and blossom.

Setting the lamp next to the tintype, Rose lowered herself to the seat of the big, worn leather chair. Something of John's aura seemed to linger in the air—the pungent scent of his cigars, the horse-and-leather aroma of his clothes. She could almost imagine him materializing behind her, his expression stern as he scolded her like an errant child for this invasion of his private domain.

John Colby had been a meticulous man. Rose knew she would find his papers in orderly stacks, his files neatly alphabetized, his ledger books filled with precise columns. Still she hesitated, her hand quivering on the latch of the massive rolltop desk. Her flesh prickled as if she were opening a grave.

The pigeonholes were nearly empty but for a few unfilled receipts for the purchase of hay, grain and lumber. Rose ruffled impatiently through the papers and put them back where she'd found them. She should have known there would be no quick and easy answers, she lectured herself. Especially when she wasn't even certain what she was looking for.

Bracing for a long search, Rose opened the top drawer, which contained sheets of lined paper, spare pens, ink, sealing wax and a new, blank ledger book. She closed the drawer swiftly and, before she could lose heart, pulled open the next one.

This drawer was crammed with a jumble of what appeared to be bank records—account statements, canceled drafts, deposit and withdrawal receipts, loan documents. Maybe here, if she looked long enough…

Rose's mouth went dry as she realized what she was seeing.

John would never have left the drawer in such a disordered mess. Someone else had been here, someone conducting a hurried, frantic search of John's papers.

Heart thudding in the silence, she jerked open the remaining drawers in the desk, then sprang to her feet and dragged open the heavy file compartments.

Every drawer was the same. All of John's papers appeared to have been stuffed haphazardly into place by someone who had no time to be careful.

Rose sank back into the chair, her legs suddenly too weak to support her. Who could have done this, and when?

In the weeks following John's accident, scores of visitors had come to the ranch—John's friends and fellow ranchers, his old militia cronies, business contacts and townspeople. Even the governor had ridden out from Tucson to extend his sympathy and support.

Anyone could have slipped into John's office and rifled through his drawers. *Anyone.*

But what were they looking for? And had they found it?

A leaden inertia gripped Rose as she surveyed the chaos. All of the drawers had been searched, she realized. Whatever the intruder was seeking, either it had been found in the last drawer, or it had not been found at all.

What could John have had in his possession? What could he have known that would force someone to this?

Outside, the storm had passed. In its wake, the night was so silent that the tick of the great clock echoed through the house like a giant heartbeat.

Rose willed herself to move. Dragging out the drawer with the bank records in it, she dumped its contents onto the desk. She would pore over every scrap of paper, she vowed. She would not rest until she knew everything there was to know about her husband's affairs.

As she paused to move the lamp closer, her thoughts flickered to Latigo. His help could cut the task in half, Rose told herself. And surely he would be willing.

But no, this was her own quest. Whatever secrets she discovered here would be hers to guard or to share. Knowledge was power, and she would not be so foolish as to make a near-stranger privy to all the financial and personal details of John's life.

Resolutely she placed the empty drawer across her knees and picked up the first piece of paper. Holding it to the light, she glanced at it, judged it to be of no use, placed it back in the drawer and reached for a second paper.

By the time the next-to-last drawer had been dumped onto the desk, Rose's concentration had long since begun to blur. Her eyelids fluttered. Her head nodded, then jerked upward again. She couldn't stop now, she lashed herself. The very next paper she touched could hold the answer she was looking for.

She stared at a long column of balance sheet figures, looking for any discrepancy, any entry for which she could not readily account. The numbers crawled, zigzagging in and out of the column like little black ants. Rose felt her head falling forward. Her eyelids were like lead, and she could not keep them open.

The room floated into blackness as she fell asleep, her face resting on a scattered pile of John's old bank receipts.

Mason's hungry morning cry drifted down the stairwell to seek out Rose where she slept. Her eyelids jerked open, blinking in the gauzy gray light. Her neck throbbed as she sat up.

Then, forgetting her own discomfort, she hurried upstairs to the bedroom.

Mason's bare feet kicked the air, pink legs pumping as he wailed and gurgled. When Rose leaned over the cradle, his tiny face broke into a heart-melting smile.

"Come here, you little scamp!" She gathered him close, welcoming the warm surge in her breasts. The downstairs clock struck six as she settled into the rocker and opened her nightgown. Outside, veiled by thin lace curtains, a bone-white moon hung in the western sky. Dawn was stealing over the flats and mesas, a violet prelude to the harsh light of day.

Still drowsy, she dozed as Mason nursed. Only when the clock struck the half hour did Rose come fully awake. She remembered Latigo outside in the barn. She remembered the storm, the fleeing horses, the injured gelding. She remembered John's office, still strewn with papers from her frustrating search. Today she would finish, she promised herself. She would go through everything, no matter how long it took her.

Rousing herself, Rose boosted Mason to her shoulder and he elicited a lusty little belch. Then, moving swiftly, she gave him a light sponge bath on the bed and dressed him in a fresh diaper, shirt and gown. The laundry could not wait past tomorrow. If Miguel and Esperanza did not return by midmorning, she would drag out the heavy wash boiler by herself and—

"Rose!"

Startled, she dropped her hairbrush as the deep voice sang out from the yard below. For an instant she thought it might be Latigo. But Latigo would not have shouted.

"Rose! You awake in there?"

Heart plummeting, she raced to the front window. The sun was just rising over the mesas, streaking the rain-washed landscape with gold. She could see the ruined corral, the bunkhouse, the sheds and barns. The front yard was a sea of trampled mud dotted with puddles reflecting the morning sky.

"Rose, honey! Rise and shine! You've got a crew of mighty hungry men out here!"

Sick with dread, Rose pressed closer to the glass. She could see them now, clustered in front of the house, some of them already tying their horses to the rail. Even with the windows closed, it was hard to believe she hadn't heard them come in.

It was Bayard Hudson, with a seven-man posse, including the sheriff.

Rose snatched up the baby and raced down the stairs. Latigo could be anywhere—in the barn, in the yard, or even in the hills. If they spotted him...

But she could not afford to dwell on what might happen then. She had to get Bayard and his men into the house. If she could keep them occupied long enough, Latigo might be able to steal one of their mounts and get away.

She was aiding a fugitive, she reminded herself as she shoved back the heavy bolt. That in itself was a crime. But it was better than seeing an innocent man hang.

Tall, broad and handsome, Bayard stood on the front porch. A confident grin spread across his face as Rose opened the door. "See, what did I tell you?" he declared.

"You couldn't stay mad at me if you wanted to, could you now, Rose honey?"

"I'm not your honey, Bayard!" she whispered in a taut voice. "You can come in—the others, too. But unless you want me to embarrass you in front of your friends, I'd suggest you keep your hands to yourself!"

"Gettin' right feisty on me, aren't you, girl!" He laughed as he pushed past her into the front hallway. "That's all right. I like spirit in a woman!"

He paused long enough to beckon his cohorts inside. They had been hanging at the foot of the steps, and they followed Bayard's lead and trooped into the house, leaving a trail of muddy bootprints on the tiles.

Rose fixed a smile on her face and motioned them toward the dining room. Ordinarily she would have invited them to wash up at the outside pump, but there was too much danger of someone accidentally seeing Latigo.

She glanced toward the barn as she closed the front door. Where was Latigo?

Dear heaven, where *was* he?

Nerves screaming, she flitted into the kitchen and settled Mason into his downstairs basket. He lay sucking on one small, pink fist, smacking contentedly.

"I'm afraid you'll have to settle for my cooking," she called through the open doorway. "Esperanza's feeling poorly this morning."

"It's time you sent that old biddy back to Mexico and hired yourself a younger cook," Bayard said. "And what the devil happened to your horses? I told you, you need a man around here to take care of things, Rose. A real man."

"And I told you, I'm raising one for that very purpose." Rose shoved sticks of kindling onto last night's coals, then turned and began measuring coffee and water into the big enameled pot. "The horses broke out in the storm last night. I'm hoping they'll come back when they get hungry."

"We'll round 'em up for you after breakfast, won't we, boys?" It was Sheriff Oliver Haskell who'd spoken. He was a good friend of Bayard's, but then, everybody seemed to be a good friend of Bayard's.

"That's all right. Some of the vaqueros will be along later. Miguel's gone off to fetch them," Rose lied. She set cups and white china plates around the table, struggling to appear calm and cheerful. "Besides, I thought you had a fugitive to track down. What happened?"

"Lost the bastard in the storm." Roscoe Gallivan, the livery stable owner, paused to clear his throat. "Hell, you couldn't track a herd of elephants in that rain. We spent the night in that run-down cabin at the old Barton homestead. Damn, that coffee smells good!"

"It should be ready in a few minutes." Rose laid down knives, forks and spoons beside each plate, hoping no one would notice her trembling hands. "So you've given up? You're going back to Tucson?"

"For now." Bayard's gaze peeled away her clothes as he watched her move around the table. "But we're posting a thousand-dollar reward for that murdering half-breed, dead or alive, and the federal government will likely double that amount. Don't worry, Rose. For that kind of money, half the territory will be on his tail. Somebody's bound to bring him in soon."

"I'll check the coffee." Rose hurried into the kitchen, her legs all but collapsing beneath her skirt. Her hands shook as she sawed the bread into lopsided hunks and slid them onto a plate with a slab of butter from the pantry.

The coffee was boiling. She flashed into the dining room to leave the bread on the table, then wheeled back to the kitchen for the steaming pot and an iron trivet to set it on.

"Rose, honey?"

Bayard was leaning back in his chair, staring across the room in the direction of John's office. Rose's throat caught as she realized she had left the door open when the baby awakened her. Bayard had a clear view of the paper-strewn desk.

One ginger-colored eyebrow slid upward as his gaze swung back toward her. "Has somebody been going through your late husband's things?" he asked, subtly emphasizing the word *late*.

"Yes. I have." Rose filled his cup, battling the temptation to spill the scalding brew in his lap. "I've been getting by from one day to the next with the management of the ranch. I thought it was high time I learned more, especially about the finances."

Bayard looked pained. "Now, Rose, why trouble your pretty head about such dull things? A woman like you'd be better off thinking about cherry cobblers and lace curtains and blue silk ribbons in your pretty golden—"

Rose cut him off with an angry glare as she made her way around the table, splashing coffee into each cup. Bayard's hungry companions were already wolfing down the bread and butter. If they had noticed the exchange, they gave no sign of it.

"Let me help you with those papers," he persisted. "I can go through everything, sort it down to what's really important. Then we can look at it together, and I'll explain—"

"No."

"Rose." Was there a note of angry desperation in his voice, or had she only imagined it?

"You heard me, Bayard." She deliberately closed the office door, then swung back toward the kitchen and disappeared before he could argue further. She fetched the bacon from the pantry, carved off thin slices and laid them to fry in the big iron skillet on the stove.

A frantic glance out the window confirmed that no one was in the yard. But Latigo was a man accustomed to danger, Rose thought. Surely he would have heard the riders coming and hidden himself in a safe place.

Unless his wound had festered in the night and he was lying in the barn, out of his head with fever.

Or unless he had gone with the storm, for good.

Chapter Seven

Mason had begun to fuss, whimpering and sucking noisily at his fists. Rose moved the sizzling bacon off the heat long enough to lean over his basket where it sat on the kitchen table. At the sight of her face, he began to cry in earnest.

"What's the matter, little love?" She teased his velvety cheek with her fingertip. "You can't be hungry. I just fed you an hour ago. Here," she said, and checked his diaper with a cautious fingertip. "Dry and clean, and no bad old pins poking you! What's all the fuss about?"

She reached down, intending to pick him up, but the sudden appearance of Bayard in the kitchen doorway froze her in midmotion. She resisted the impulse to back away as he closed the door behind him and walked toward her, smiling.

"I just thought I'd see if you needed some company," he said.

"As you see, I'm much too busy for company," Rose answered icily. "The bacon's almost done, and I was just about to scramble some eggs, so if you'd be kind enough to go back and sit—"

Her words ended in a gasp as his big, fleshy hand captured her fingers. "Let me go," she muttered furiously. "I'll scream and embarrass you to death, Bayard. I swear I will!"

"Just hear me out, Rose." His voice was a breathy whisper. His damp thumb worked its way into her palm, stroking it suggestively as he spoke. "What's wrong, girl? You're as jumpy as a doe! I won't hurt you. All I want to do is apologize. I pushed you too hard yesterday, and I'm sorry."

"Let go of my hand," she said.

"Not until I've spoken my piece." His sweaty clasp tightened around her fingers. "I love you, Rose. And if patience is what it requires, then I'm willing to take this thing as slow as you like, as long as we both know where it's going."

Mason's whimpers had grown to a plaintive wail. Bayard gripped harder, ignoring Rose's struggle to reach her son.

"Let me go," she said. "Please."

"Dash it, woman, if I'm elected governor, you could be First Lady of the whole territory one day!" he rasped. "No other man could offer you such a future! Doesn't that mean anything to you?"

With a sudden twist, Rose wrenched herself loose and plunged toward Mason. Gathering him up in her arms, she swung back to face Bayard.

"I'm warning you," she began, only to freeze in sudden dread as a flicker of movement outside caught her eye.

Latigo?

Too startled to think fast, Rose jerked her head reflexively toward the window. Only then did she realize that if it was truly Latigo she'd seen, her movement could have betrayed him.

For an instant her heart stopped.

But Bayard only sighed. "Now, there's no call to be so

skittish, Rose. I wanted to speak my piece, that's all. Now that it's done, I'll go back in and sit down. We can talk later. Alone.''

He paused to straighten his collar, then strolled back toward the door and opened it wide to the dining room. "Oh, by the way," he said, pausing on the threshold. "I just sent Roscoe out to the barn to get some fodder for the horses. I knew you wouldn't mind."

"It's fine." Rose's legs had turned to jelly beneath her skirt. Her free hand gripped the edge of the counter as she struggled to focus her spinning mind. If it had been Roscoe Gallivan she'd just seen in the yard, Latigo could still be in the barn, sleeping or out of his head with fever.

But showing her alarm would only put him in more danger, she reminded herself quickly. She was powerless to help him. Powerless, even, to warn him.

Mason's cries had faded to forlorn little sobs. He sucked at the collar of her dress, wanting comfort. Rose moved the skillet back over the fire, working with one hand. *Don't think!* she admonished herself. *Don't even feel!*

But it was no use. Every second that ticked by was slow agony as she waited for a shout, a gunshot. She worked doggedly over the stove as her nerves screamed his name. *Latigo!*

Latigo crouched in the loft, hidden by a pile of feed sacks as the intruder rummaged noisily below. His mouth was dry, his stomach was rumbling, and his cursed shoulder had kept him awake most of the night. He should have headed for open country while he had the chance.

He had been rewrapping the horse's leg—badly sprained but healing cleanly—when he'd heard the sound of riders coming into the yard. A glance outside had confirmed his first guess. It was Bayard Hudson with the posse, and it would only be a matter of time before one or more of them came into the barn.

He had scrambled into the loft, a poor hiding place with no way out, but there'd been little choice. Now he could only pray that no one would have a reason to climb the built-in ladder and discover him.

Through a crack in the loft floor, he could see the man who had come into the barn. He was a husky fellow, graying and bearded, with the kind of belly that came of too much liquor and too little action. He wore his pistol belt awkwardly, with the holster positioned too far back for an easy draw—not the mark of an experienced gunman.

Even with his wounded shoulder, Latigo reckoned, he might be able to take such a man. Surprise him, knock him out, get the gun, then steal one of the horses. It wouldn't be all that difficult.

But what then? Even if he got clear of the ranch, a fugitive would be easy tracking on the muddy ground. And against an armed posse...

Dismissing the idea, Latigo focused his full attention on the man below. The stranger had paused to inspect the horse.

Watching, Latigo wondered how Rose Colby would explain the horse. The lady would need a good story, because those men would never believe she had doctored the big, nervous animal by herself. Unless she had her wits about her—

But why should Rose lie to save an Apache? She was among friends now, men she had known and trusted for years. All she had to do was tell them about the fugitive in the barn, and he would never trouble her again.

Despair tightened a knot in Latigo's stomach as he realized Rose had every reason to betray him.

The man downstairs had found a wheelbarrow and was piling it with hay. He paused to work a battered tin flask out of his hip pocket and take a long, throat-rippling swallow. Replacing the flask, he lifted the handles of the wheelbarrow and lumbered toward the open barn door.

Latigo had almost begun to breathe again when the man stopped, set the wheelbarrow down and turned back toward the interior of the barn as if he had forgotten something. He glanced up at the loft, sighed noisily, then walked straight toward the ladder and began to climb.

Latigo inched down into the straw behind the pile of feed sacks. He could hear the cows shifting restlessly in their stalls below. He could hear the man's labored panting, closer and closer as he mounted each rung of the ladder.

He glanced furtively around him for something he could use as a weapon—an abandoned iron tool, a stick of wood. But there was nothing but the heavy sacks and his own hands, which might be just as well, since the last thing he wanted was to kill the poor devil and be guilty of a real murder.

Latigo's pulse throbbed as the seconds crawled past. Maybe he could surprise the man, get the gun before he could react, then knock him out or tie him up. But that would be a gamble, too. The fool might have time to get a shot off. Even if he missed, the sound of the pistol would bring the rest of the posse running into the barn.

He pressed into the shadows as the man's heavy boots stomped across the floor of the loft. He willed his body to be perfectly still.

"Roscoe!" The shout came from below, from the direction of the barn door. "Hey, what's keepin' you, man? Your breakfast's gettin' cold in there!"

"Just gettin' some oats!" Roscoe picked up a sack and slung it over his shoulder, his muddy boot a handbreadth from Latigo's face. "I'll be right there. Wouldn't want to miss the show. That widow Colby's quite an eyeful, ain't she? An' all alone! How'd you like layin' yourself between them pretty legs of hers, huh?''

The lewd question was answered by a snort of laughter. ''Hell, you ought to ask Bayard Hudson. You see him followin' her around in there like a bull elk in rut? He'll have her afore he's through, I'd lay odds on it. Ain't nothin' gets between Bayard and what he wants. Leastwise not for long!''

''Hey, make yourself useful!'' Roscoe grunted as he carried the forty-pound sack to the top of the ladder. ''Catch this and toss it on the wheelbarrow. That way I can climb down without breakin' my neck.''

''Catch it? Hell, just toss it down. I'll pick it up off the floor! Say, d'you see this horse, all bandaged up like a doc had done it?''

''I did. And I noticed the green stuff drippin' out from underneath. Had a funny smell, like somethin' an Injun would use. Makes you wonder, doesn't it? But then, maybe them Mexican vaqueros of hers know a trick or two.'' Roscoe eased his panting body down the rungs. ''Oof, I'm gettin' too damned old for this posse business. When we get back to Tucson tonight, I'm gettin' me a hot tub and a pretty woman to scrub my back. Next time I'll stay home and leave the chasin' to the young bucks.''

''Think anybody else'll catch that murderin' breed?''

Roscoe had reached the bottom of the ladder. ''Good question. From what I hear tell, the bastard's pretty smart. Best damned scout in the territory, and as quiet as a ghost. Knows the country and all the Injun ways. Man like that's not gonna get caught easy.''

''But the reward, somebody's bound to turn him in.''

''They got to see him first,'' Roscoe grunted. ''Come on, let's go get our bellies full, and our eyes, too!''

Latigo's lungs emptied slowly as the wheelbarrow creaked out of the barn, followed by the two men. For a long moment he lay still, heart pounding as he willed himself not to move too soon.

The posse was going back to Tucson. He had heard it with his own ears. They were giving up the chase, leaving him free to make his way to Mexico. By the time they regrouped, he could be safely out of reach.

All he had to do was keep still until they rode away. It would be easy.

Too easy.

Latigo's spirits blackened as he realized he could be walking into a trap baited, set and sprung by the beautiful Widow Colby.

Who else would know he could be hiding in the barn? And who else would have devised such a devilish trick to lure him into the open?

Even as the realization struck him, his emotions raged against it. Rose had believed him last night. She had even urged him, however foolishly, to stay and prove his innocence. It seemed unthinkable that she would turn on him now.

But he would be a fool to deny it could happen. Last night Rose had been grateful for his help. She had been so warm, trusting and vulnerable that it had been all he could do to keep from taking her in his arms.

But in the cold light of dawn, she could easily have come to her senses. She could have remembered that in harboring a wanted man, she herself was breaking the law. Most likely Rose had let herself get good and scared. Then when the posse showed up...

Latigo cursed under his breath, feeling even more angry at himself than at her. If Rose Colby had betrayed him, it was his own fault. He, of all people, should have known better than to trust a white woman.

His mouth tightened in a bitter smile. One thing, at least

was certain. If he lived through the next few hours, he would be very slow to trust one again.

By the time the breakfast table was cleared away, Mason had fallen asleep in his basket. Rose piled the dirty plates, cups and silver into the big tin dishpan and set herself to washing.

She had desperately hoped her guests would mount up and leave after breakfast, but no one seemed to be in a hurry. The men lounged on the front porch or sprawled in the big leather chairs in the parlor, smoking, talking and laughing, just as they might have done when John was alive.

John had been strictly a man's man, she reflected as she plunged a greasy plate into the suds. Women had had no place in his life except to serve him—to cook his meals, mend his clothes, warm his bed and bear the sons that would carry on his name and preserve his land. He had married her with all the tender emotions of a man buying a broodmare, and when she had failed to meet his expectations—

"Here you are." Bayard's hand snaked around her waist from behind, lingering subtly on the curve of her hip.

"Don't, Bayard," she murmured.

The hand paused, then withdrew. "Can't you leave this work for Esperanza? I'd like to spend some time with you."

"I don't mind washing a few dishes."

Bayard gave a derisive snort. "If I know Esperanza, she's malingering. You're too easy on the old woman, Rose. If she can't handle the work, I'll send out one of my girls to help."

"Don't trouble yourself. Esperanza's bringing up her niece from Fronteras one of these—" Rose's body stiffened as his fingertip brushed the bare curve of her neck. "Bayard!"

"Sorry," he murmured. "I just can't seem to keep my hands off you. John was an old fool who didn't appreciate what he had. Let me—"

"Bayard, I'm warning you."

"All right." Once more the offending hand withdrew. "But I'm not really the monster you take me for, Rose. I want the best for you. I want to see you treated like the queen you are."

Rose reached for another plate and began scrubbing away at the bacon grease. At least Bayard seemed to care for her, she reminded herself. Maybe she should swallow her distaste and try harder to like the man.

But that wasn't possible this morning. Not with Latigo missing and the posse wandering all over the house and yard. Right now, all she could think of was seeing Bayard and his cohorts gone.

"At least, let me sort out those papers for you," Bayard said. "You've no experience dealing with shipping lists and ledgers and invoices, Rose. Without my help, how will you know what's really important?"

As he spoke, a sliver of ice seemed to pass through Rose's body, stilling the motion of her hands in the soapy water. When she'd first discovered the ransacked drawers in John's office, she had swiftly dismissed Bayard as a possible suspect. After all, he had been John's most trusted friend. What would he have to gain by such a furtive act?

Now, however, the very eagerness in his voice and manner sent a flesh-puckering chill down her back, and she knew she had been too trusting.

"Bayard," she said, resolving to test him, "I noticed something strange last night when I opened up John's desk for the first time. It looked as if someone had been going through his papers. Someone in a hurry."

"You're sure?" Bayard's voice had gone flat.

"Quite sure. The drawers and files were a mess. John would never have left things in such a state. You know how orderly he always was."

"And this is the first time you've opened the drawers since John's accident?"

"Yes." Rose's fingers toyed with a spoon in the water. "I'd meant all along to go through his papers, but the thought of all those memories..." Her words ended in a shrug. "Who would do such a thing, Bayard? Who would walk into John's private office and go through his desk without telling me?"

"No one who counted as a friend, and John had no enemies, Rose. I think you've been alone out here too long. Your imagination's starting to run away with you." His palm settled on her shoulder, triggering an involuntary shudder. "Show me what you found," he said. "Maybe you and I can solve this mystery together."

"You're too late." Rose scrubbed at a plate with grim efficiency. "I've already rearranged most of the drawers myself."

Bayard's hand tensed. "And you found—?"

"As you said, receipts, invoices, shipping bills, ledgers. But you're wrong about one thing. I had no trouble understanding what I saw." She forced a nervous laugh. "Aren't your friends in a hurry to get back to Tucson?"

"They can wait." His warm palm kneaded her taut shoulder muscle. "Roscoe mentioned you had an injured horse in the barn."

Rose's rib cage jerked as she took a too-sudden breath. "Sundown slipped and fell in the storm last night. But I think he's going to be all right. Miguel's good with horses."

"So am I. In fact, I'd like to take a look at him if you don't mind."

Rose had gone cold in the heat of the kitchen. "That's kind of you, Bayard. But it really isn't—"

"Nonsense. I wouldn't trust a Mexican cowboy with doctoring a pack mule, let alone an expensive animal like Sundown. I won't be a minute." He strode toward the kitchen door.

"I'll go with you." Her hands jerked, splattering dishwater on the floor. Something flickered in Bayard's eyes, and she knew even then she had made a reckless decision. But there was no going back now. She could not just let him walk into the barn and find Latigo there.

Rose paused to glance at her sleeping son. Then, with her heart in her throat, she accepted Bayard's proffered arm and allowed him to lead her outside.

Roscoe Gallivan and his friend had returned from the barn without incident. All the same, her instincts whispered that Latigo was nearby and still in danger. She had to find a way to warn him.

Moving in deliberate silence, Latigo eased the last heavy feed sack into place, adding it to the makeshift fortress he had built in the back corner of the loft. If any shooting started, the thick barrier would give him some protection, not that it would make much difference in the long run. What he really needed was a weapon of his own, or better yet, a way out of this rat trap.

He was rearranging the straw, taking care to cover his tracks and make everything look undisturbed, when a sound from the yard outside riveted him like a blow.

It was the sharp-edged peal of a woman's laughter.

"Why, Bayard Hudson, what a rascal you are! I declare, I had no idea you could be so outrageous."

Latigo vaulted into the shadows. Only as he was flattening his body against the base of the grain sacks did he realize the speaker was Rose.

Even then he was hard-pressed to believe it. His ears had come to anticipate her velvety near-whisper. But the voice he had heard was oddly strained, artificially shrill, almost as if she were shouting.

Was she shouting to warn him?

Or was this a side of Rose Colby he'd never seen before?

Latigo had no more time to ponder as the barn door creaked open. He heard the sound of footsteps and, once more, the brittle cadence of Rose's laughter.

"Watch your step, now, Bayard," she sang out in a voice that carried to the rafters. "We wouldn't want to soil those fancy new boots of yours, would we?"

"I don't know what you're talking about," Bayard muttered. "My boots are already so muddy from the storm that a little manure isn't going to make much difference. What's gotten into you, Rose? I've never seen you like this."

"Like what?" Her voice was moving away from him. Latigo could not see either Rose or Bayard, but what he heard was enough to paint vivid pictures in his mind. His jaw tightened as he told himself to keep absolutely still.

"Like I told you this morning," Bayard said, "You're as skittery as a wren! Come back here!"

"You said you wanted to see Sundown."

"The blasted horse can wait. I've been wanting to get you alone all morning." Bayard's thick boots crushed straw as he strode after her. "Stop playing games and come here, girl. If you didn't feel the same way, why did you offer to come out here with me?"

"The horse." Rose's voice had lost its bravado. She sounded nervous, even scared. Something hot and angry and desperate stirred in Latigo's chest.

"That's it, yes." He had evidently cornered her. Rose

had fallen silent. Latigo's hands clenched into fists as Bayard's husky breathing filled the dim silence of the barn.

"I could never hurt you," Bayard murmured. "Don't you know that by now? Dash it, girl, I'm in love with you. I want to give you the whole world!"

"I don't want your world." Rose's voice was low and tense. Latigo could sense her struggle in every syllable. "My world is this ranch and my son—John's son."

"Listen, girl, I know it's short notice, but the president of the Southern Pacific Railroad will be passing through Tucson in ten days. The governor is giving a reception and ball. Come with me. Walk into that glittering hall on my arm, and you'll see what you could have as my wife."

"I'm still in mourning for my husband. Or had you forgotten?" No one could have missed the cold edge in Rose's voice.

"Does it have to matter so much?" Bayard asked almost petulantly.

"It should, since the scandal could ruin you."

"That's a gamble I'd be willing to take. Kiss me, Rose. I want to taste you, taste your sweetness."

"Let me go!" She was struggling against him now. Latigo could hear the scuffle of feet in the straw. He could hear her desperate gasps and Hudson's lusty panting. He battled for self-control, knowing that to charge to her rescue would be suicide.

"No, Bayard, please!"

He heard her gasp, heard the unmistakable pop of a button, and suddenly Latigo was on his feet behind the low barricade, his caution blotted out by a reasonless, molten rage. Like a madman, he felt himself driving toward the ladder.

"Oof!"

Bayard Hudson's agonized grunt could only have been triggered by a sharp blow from a well-aimed knee. Latigo heard the sound of something crashing against the side of a stall, followed by the furious patter of running footsteps.

He reeled to a stop, quivering as his reason returned. It was all right. *Rose* was all right, he reassured himself.

He took a deep breath to calm his jumping reflexes. When he risked a furtive glance between the floorboards, he saw Hudson writhing in the straw, swearing and clutching his groin. Rose was nowhere in sight.

Still gasping, Hudson clambered to his feet and staggered out of the barn. "Mount up!" he bellowed across the yard. "We're going back to town. Pronto!"

A grim smile tightened Latigo's lips as he settled back into his hiding place to wait. He had been on the verge of tossing his life away to protect a white woman's virtue, a fact that shook him more deeply than he cared to admit. But in the end it had been unnecessary. Rose had proved quite capable of fending for herself.

Rose.

The name lingered in his thoughts like a caress as he remembered her strength. Her tenderness. Her fiery, passionate courage. She *had* been trying to warn him, he realized. He should never have doubted her.

Before the morning passed, for both their sakes, he would be gone from this place, Latigo resolved. He would never see Rose Colby again. But one thing he knew: for as long as he lived, he would never forget her.

Rose clutched Mason in her arms, her whole body shaking as the sound of hoofbeats died into the distance. It was all right, she soothed herself frantically. The posse was gone. Bayard was gone. She was safe, whatever "safe" meant in a world that was spilling around her like an upended churn.

Closing her eyes, she sank onto a chair, nestled Mason in the crook of her arm to nurse and tried to stop the room from spinning. She had been so afraid out there in the barn. Afraid for Latigo, afraid for her own safety. But she was all right now, Rose assured herself. Her home and her baby were safe. Even Latigo, as far as she knew, was safe.

But deeper instincts whispered she was wrong. Bayard was a man who always got what he wanted, and heaven help anyone who stood in his way. If he could not have her, he would look for a way to destroy her. As for Latigo…

But she could not allow herself to worry about Latigo now. She had seen no sign of him in the barn and, even with the posse gone, he had not shown himself. She could only conclude that he had left some time before dawn. By now, he would be on his way to Mexico.

Don't borrow trouble, her mother's gentle voice whispered in her memory. It was sound advice, lovingly given. But even as a child, Rose had been a rescuer of lost puppies, birds and kittens, a defender of the weak and the wronged. She had never been inclined to pay her mother's words much heed. And now there was Latigo.

But Latigo was not some poor wounded puppy she could nurse and keep. He was a man. An Apache. She had to remember that.

A passing ghost, gone with the first light of sunrise. That's how Latigo had answered when she'd asked him who he was. Only now did Rose understand what he was trying to tell her. She could demand nothing of him. He had gone silently, when she least expected it, leaving no trace of himself, nothing to remind her that he had ever passed through her life.

The plaintive two-note cry of a quail roused Rose from her musings. There were chores to be done, she reminded herself. There were pans to be scrubbed, chickens to be fed, cows to be milked. She would need to fill the feed trough in the corral, in case any missing horses got hungry and wandered in. There was the fence to repair, the laundry to be done, and the rest of the papers in John's office that could not wait a day longer.

Rose gazed into the buttery sunlight, crushed, suddenly, by the burden of her aloneness. The big house was oppressive in its silence. She missed Esperanza's womanly chatter and Miguel's quiet comings and goings. She missed the jokes and good-natured curses of the vaqueros. Heaven help her, she missed John's large, masculine presence.

The quail called once more from the hillside, beckoning her outside into the clear morning air. Mason had finished nursing and lay quietly in her arms. Fumbling with the buttons of her dress, she boosted him against her shoulder and walked slowly into the yard.

She had been outside earlier that morning, but only now, with time to stand and look, did Rose realize the destruction last night's storm had wreaked.

In every direction the land lay raw, as if scraped by giant talons. Rushing floodwaters, gritty with sand and boulders, had gouged bloodred gullies along the foothills. Where the desert lay flat, mud spread in naked fans, bare of life except for the towering saguaros that had managed to hold on beneath.

Rose's heart sank as she surveyed the muddy yard. Shingles blown off the barn were scattered everywhere, and the brush roof was gone from the *ramada,* leaving nothing but its supporting poles. The windmill, missing many of its slats, lay askew, creaking mournfully in the sunlit breeze.

The roads and bridges would be washed out everywhere, she realized. Horses, perhaps, could get through, but Miguel and Esperanza had taken the buckboard to Fronteras, and in any case, the plump, arthritic Esperanza was no rider. Days, even weeks might pass before they could return to the ranch.

She had no one to rely on but herself.

The chickens had emerged from their wrecked coop to peck for worms in the mud. Fussing hens and peeping chicks bustled to and fro as the speckled rooster kept watch from a peak of the battered roof. Life would go on, Rose knew, holding her baby close. *She* would go on, and somehow she would get through this morass of difficulty.

But as she gazed out across the ravaged desert, one emotion overrode all others, shadowing her spirit with the darkness of despair.

Never—not at any time since the deaths of her parents and sister—had Rose felt more alone.

Chapter Eight

Rose had not planned to climb the hill, but she found herself moving in that direction, clutching her son as she mounted the grassy slope. Mason lay quietly against her shoulder, almost too quietly.

Only as she neared the top did it occur to her that the graves might have been damaged in the storm. Anxious now, she plunged upward, all but sprinting the last few yards. She could see the low wrought-iron fence that surrounded the family graveyard, and then—

But the three low mounds were safe on the high, flat ground. The heavy rain had done little more than muddy the dust and scour the headstones. Still wet, the two modest alabaster slabs and John's imposing marker of polished black granite glistened in the morning sunlight.

Overcome with weariness, Rose sank to her knees in the damp yellow grass that bordered her husband's grave. John would want her to be strong, she told herself as she gazed out over the storm-ravaged ranch. He would want her to stride through life as he had done, carrying on the work he could no longer do, for his sake and for Mason's.

And she *would* carry on. She had disappointed John in life, but she would not let him down now, Rose vowed. If she could not find the strength within herself, she would draw it from the land. She would draw it from John's unseen presence and from the deep spiritual roots of her own father and mother.

Somehow she would do all that was expected of her.

She reached out to brush a bead of water from the sharply chiseled *C* on John's headstone only to pause, startled, as a shadow fell across her hand.

Her breath jerked as she looked up to find Latigo standing beside her.

His eyes darkened as he watched the apprehension flicker across her face. "It's all right," he said softly.

She lowered her gaze to hide a flood of warring emotions. Latigo had startled her, but the brief surge of fear had been washed away by a relief so overpowering that it brought tears to her eyes. He was safe. He was here. He had not gone away.

"Where were you?" she whispered, her throat tight and raw. "I was afraid."

"Afraid?"

"For both of us." She gulped back a little hiccup. "Bayard."

"I know. I was in the loft." A grim smile tightened his mouth. "I was about to charge to your rescue, but you managed that quite nicely by yourself." His gaze flickered to the missing button below her collar. "Did he hurt you?"

"No." Rose willed herself to speak calmly. "But Bayard isn't the kind of man to give up and walk away. He'll be back."

Latigo frowned down at her. "With all due respect, I suggest you lock him out of the house the next time he comes around. Just because he was your husband's friend—"

"Thank you, but I can take care of myself," she retorted, feeling like a reprimanded child. "You don't need to lecture me."

"In that case, I won't waste my breath." He turned away, his eyes glaring into the distance. A phoebe twittered from a battered creosote bush, its song piercing the uneasy silence that had fallen between them. Abruptly he swung back to face her. "Damn it, Rose, you didn't have to go into that barn alone with him."

"I realize that."

"But you took the chance."

"Didn't you know I was trying to warn you?" Rose asked tautly, breaking under the strain of the past hours and the scrutiny of his obsidian eyes. "Don't you realize how afraid I was that Bayard would just walk in and find you there?"

With a single liquid movement he lowered himself to a crouch, his dark gaze meeting her own. "I know it, Rose. But I would never have let you pay the price you almost paid. I would never have stood by and seen you raped on my account."

Rose looked away, shaken by his intensity. The thought that he would have sacrificed himself to save her was more than she dared to ponder.

His hand lay on the grass, his long brown fingers the color of the earth beneath. Her eyes could trace the veins and sinews under the smooth surface of his skin. She struggled against the frightening urge to reach out and touch him.

Nothing could be allowed to happen between them. Latigo was an Apache, a man on the run. To abandon all caution and to reach out to this man in her loneliness was a far greater price than she was willing to pay.

"I suppose you'll be going soon," she said.

"As soon as I can get my gear together. You'll be safer without me, I think."

"Yes. I'll manage fine." Rose fixed her gaze on a thread of mist that lingered above the mesas.

"Keep that big pistol close by. Something tells me you may need it more than I do." His gaze surveyed the yard below, the shattered windmill, the tumbled-down corral fence and the roofless *ramada*. Rose could sense his mind working in the morning stillness, his thoughts already moving away from her to the desert and to the freedom of Mexico.

"Will you be all right?" he asked her.

Rose nodded, knowing she could not let herself depend on him. Latigo was like an injured hawk she had once found. She had brought it home, splinted its broken wing and fussed over it for weeks, but it had given her no loyalty in return. As soon as it was strong enough, the bird had soared into the sky, never to return.

"I was all right before you came," she said. "There's no need for you to stay."

"I wasn't planning to."

"I know." Stung by his words, although she could not fathom why, Rose glanced down at the muddy red earth that covered John's grave. Her poppy seeds would grow with the rain, and, for a brief time, at least, there would be beauty here.

"I did promise you a meal," she said, forcing herself to sound cheerful. "The posse finished off the bread and eggs, but I don't make bad biscuits and gravy."

His eyes narrowed, then, slowly he nodded. "I'll take you up on that," he said. "But no more charity. Now that I'm able, I intend to pay for what I eat. I saw some tools in the barn, and that windmill of yours looks as if it could use some work."

"Your shoulder—"

"It still pains me some, but I'll manage." He stood, his lithe body rippling upward with easy grace.

"Are your parents buried here, too?" he asked.

"No," Rose answered softly. "John's company buried them where they died. Later that same day they found me alive in the desert, and John brought me here, to this ranch. I've been here ever since."

"Was he good to you?"

"In his way." Rose's eyes traced the precise letters the stonecutter had chiseled into the polished black granite. "John was a hard man, but he was kind and generous to a terrified young girl with no place to go. I was grateful."

"And that's why you married him?"

"My reasons for marrying John are none of your concern," she said, forcing open the distance that had narrowed too perilously between them.

"My apologies." Latigo exhaled and shifted his weight. Silence lay leaden on the air as he gazed out over the flat, making sure, perhaps, that the posse had truly left. "The day's getting on," he said. "I'd better find those tools and fix that broken windmill before you start running low on water."

"Thank you," she said, struggling to rise on her benumbed legs, with Mason in her arms. "I'm much obliged."

"I pay my debts." Without another word, he stepped behind her and boosted her up by the elbows, his touch so impersonal that Rose could not possibly read any meaning into it. "Careful going down," he cautioned. "It's slippery."

For a time neither of them spoke as they wound their way down the slope. Suddenly Rose's boots slid on a patch of muddy grass. Latigo gripped her elbow to steady her while she caught her balance; then, without asking, he reached out and lifted the baby from her arms. Mason had been fussing, but he settled contentedly against Latigo's chest, gazing up at him with wide violet eyes.

"You never had a child of your own?" Rose asked.

"No." Latigo's jaw tightened as he shook his head. "I don't suppose I ever will."

"That's a pity. Look how Mason takes to you. You'd make a good father."

"Mason's too young to know any better." Latigo shrugged, dismissing the whole idea. "And as for my making a good father, what kind of existence could I offer a family? Always on the move, always looking over my shoulder, no chance to put down roots."

"Maybe in Mexico, you could—"

"No. Not even in Mexico." Latigo's arms tightened around Mason as the slope steepened. "The border may stop the law, but it won't stop the bounty hunters. I'll be fair game for the rest of my life, for as long as it lasts."

"Then you may as well stay!" Rose heard her own voice saying. "Stay here and prove your innocence. I'd help you."

"Rose!" The name emerged as a groan. "Don't you know what you'd be risking? You'd be aiding a fugitive. You could lose your ranch, maybe even go to prison. What would that do to your boy? No, you mustn't even think about it!"

They had reached the bottom of the hill. Latigo paused long enough to ease the baby back into her arms.

"I'll get the tools and work on that windmill now," Latigo said, his manner distant. "As long as I'm at it, I may as well fix your corral fence. It shouldn't take long."

"I'll call you when breakfast is ready." Rose willed herself to turn and walk away from him. Latigo was right. No matter how desperately she might wish to help him, she could not risk her son's future.

She watched him stride across the yard. A proud man. A lone man, condemned to run like a hunted wolf, abandoning any hope of peace, comfort and love. Rose ached for him, but there was nothing she could do. Nothing except feed him, send him on his way and try to forget she had ever known him. As for any secrets hidden among the papers in John's office, she would be wise to forget those, as well. Any discoveries she might make would only put herself and Mason in danger. Forget the papers, reason shrilled in her head. Forget Latigo and his talk of the Indian Ring. She would go on as if the past two days never happened.

But even as she entered the house and closed the door behind her, Rose knew there could be no going back to her old innocence. Latigo's coming had raised hard questions about John and his past, questions that demanded answers.

And whether she found those answers or not, Rose realized, her view of life would never be the same again. A good man had been horribly wronged. To turn her back and walk away now would be to deny her father's legacy, her own principles, all she had ever valued and held dear.

Latigo strained against a broken support of the windmill, fighting to keep his balance on the rickety platform as he hammered a new timber into place. The task would have been easy if he'd had full use of his left arm. Working right-handed, however, was awkward and frustrating at best, especially when he wanted to do the best possible job for Rose.

From his high perch, he had a clear view of the ranch and the surrounding desert, as anyone approaching would have a clear view of *him*, he realized. But in every direction he looked, the landscape lay peacefully undisturbed.

The mouthwatering fragrance of fresh biscuits drifted up from the kitchen. Latigo's empty belly tightened in response, even as Rose's beautiful face materialized once more in his thoughts. He imagined her in the kitchen, glancing at her baby as she bent over the stove, her slim, delicate hands moving swiftly from one task to the next. He pictured her on the hilltop, gazing at the mountains as if she longed to fly away. He remembered the opaline fire in her eyes, the passion in her voice when she had urged him to stay and clear his name.

Lord, what he wouldn't give to stay with her, to fight her battles, to protect her, cherish her.

But he was only torturing himself now. Even if the past could be put aside, he had nothing to offer a woman but danger and despair. The sooner he cleared out and left Rose alone, the safer life would be for them both.

He was reaching for a nail when he heard the click of a latch. The kitchen door swung open to reveal her standing on the threshold, wearing a crisp white apron over her chambray gown. She looked fresh and young and innocent, he thought.

"Breakfast is ready anytime you want it," she called up to him. "Would you like it now? You can always finish the windmill after you eat."

"I'd just as soon finish the job before I climb down off this platform." Latigo picked up the nail and raised the hammer again. "This part's almost done. Replacing the vanes shouldn't take more than a few minutes."

"I'll keep your breakfast warm for you." She hesitated in the doorway. "Latigo?"

He glanced up from his hammering.

"When you get to Mexico," she said, and paused as if searching for the right words, "where will you go?"

"I won't know that until I get there."

"But what if I learn something? How will I be able to get word to you?"

"You won't." He scowled, touched and dismayed by her earnestness. "It wouldn't be a good idea, Rose. If a message can find me, so can a bounty hunter."

"But what if the real killers are exposed?"

"They won't be. They're too smart for that." Latigo hurled his bitterness into a volley of hammer blows, then paused to position the last nail. "Listen to me, I want you to stay out of this mess."

"Isn't it a little late for that?" she persisted. "If there's any chance that John was part of the Ring—"

"Don't be a meddling fool!" he snapped, desperate to keep her safe. "It's not worth it! The men who planned that ambush are ruthless. If you get in their way, being a pretty woman won't save you, and, believe me, lady, I don't want your death on my conscience."

"It's not your conscience I'm concerned about!" Rose retorted hotly. "It's your neck, and my husband's character."

"My neck is my own business," Latigo growled. "And your husband is dead. Let him lie in peace."

"It's not that simple," Rose persisted. "John has a son, and one day he'll need to know the truth. Don't you see? I can't let this rest."

The frayed thread of Latigo's patience strained and broke. "Blast it, Rose, I should never have told you any of this!" he snapped, whaling away at the nail. "You don't know when to back off! You have this way of getting inside a man and prying open his soul until—" The hammer glanced off the nail head, flew out of his hand, bounced off the platform and plummeted to the ground below.

Without a word, Rose bent and picked up the tool where it lay in the mud. Lifting her skirt, she ascended the rungs with precise steps. As her face came even with the platform, she thrust the hammer into Latigo's hand. Her eyes shot icy blue sparks.

"No one could ever pry open your soul," she said

coldly. "You've forged it shut with your own stubborn, cynical bitterness!"

Before he could answer, she was gone, scurrying down the ladder and whirling with a swish of lacy petticoats toward the house. He had been harsh with her, but that was a kindness, Latigo told himself. If Rose Colby viewed him as a surly, ungrateful bastard, she would be less likely to meddle in dark affairs that would only get her hurt. And she *could* be hurt, he had no doubt of that. She already knew too much, and the leaders of the Indian Ring would stop at nothing to protect their secrets. Not even the murder of a beautiful woman.

The thought of Rose in danger sent a surge of protective fury through Latigo's body. His wrist tensed, altering the angle of the hammer just enough to bring its head smashing down on the end of his thumb. He cursed roundly as the pain exploded up his arm.

Yes, he had to get out of here while he still possessed his reason. He had to leave soon, before this tender, vulnerable woman had time to throw any more chains around his heart.

Otherwise he would be torn, and his very desire to protect Rose Colby would plunge her deeper into peril.

Rose sat in awkward silence, watching the man across the table. Her own meal lay cold on her plate, scarcely touched, but Latigo's appetite did not seem to be affected by the tension between them. He ate purposefully, each bite of the rich biscuits and gravy fueling his body for the hard days ahead.

Rose had lived nine years with a man who gave her little of his private self. She had tolerated John's long, morose silences, his detached answers to her questions. But now, sitting across from this mysterious stranger, she knew she had outgrown her former patience.

"It won't work," she said, breaking the long stillness.

"What?"

"This performance of yours," she said. "Oh, I know what you're trying to do. You want to make me so angry that I won't care what happens to you. That way you can make a clean getaway, with no messy complications to leave behind."

"Rose." His black eyes flashed a warning, but she plunged ahead, ignoring the danger.

"Do you think I'm a child, that you can manipulate me with such a cheap trick? Can't you at least be open with me?"

Latigo exhaled sharply. Exasperation flickered across his lean, bronze face as he spoke.

"Don't you know there are some things better left unsaid?"

"I know you want to protect me," Rose persisted. "But I want to understand. I *need* to understand everything. You. John. The Indian Ring."

"I've told you what I know."

"But is it *all* you know? You told me about the murders. You told me you suspected the Indian Ring, and you intimated that both John and Bayard might have been involved. That can't be the whole story. There has to be more."

Latigo did not reply. He sat studying her, waiting for her thoughts to find their own way. Rose stared at him, trembling as the shadows shifted in her mind, revealing subtle glints of truth.

"You never would have come here," she whispered. "You would never have taken a chance on asking John for help if you hadn't known."

"That's where you're wrong, Rose." A vein throbbed lightly along the taut brown curve of his throat. "I was taking a big gamble. I didn't know. I only suspected."

"That John was working against the Ring?"

"Yes."

Rose's hands unclenched in her lap. A strange giddiness swirled up in her body, held in check only by her own fear. She stared at Latigo, her silence demanding answers to questions she did not know how to ask.

"More than a year ago I served under Major Henry Scott, head of army intelligence at Fort Grant," he said. "Scott was working to break the Ring, and he had an inside contact, a man known only to him."

"John?" The name emerged as a whisper from Rose's aching throat.

"I never knew for sure. Whoever it was, the major was very protective of his contact's identity. Only a few things he mentioned—a cattle ranch, the old Tucson militia—led me to believe it might be your husband."

"Then why couldn't you have gone to Major Scott after those government men were killed? Why couldn't you have asked for his protection?"

Latigo's throat quivered as he swallowed. "Henry Scott died last summer on patrol in the Chiricahuas. His men found him in a ravine, thrown from his horse, with a broken neck."

"Murdered?" Rose whispered in horror.

"No one thought so at the time. But the major was a cautious man. It seemed an unlikely accident, and whoever his informant was, Scott took the secret to his grave."

"How could you keep this from me?" Rose felt a tide of hot outrage flaming into her cheeks. "You told me the ugly things about John—the militia's reputation, the massacres of Apache women and children! Were they true?"

"Yes. I saw the evidence myself."

"Then why didn't you tell me *this?*" She was on her feet, startling her son where he lay in his basket on the far end of the table. "You could have spared me two days of anguish! Why didn't you tell me that John was fighting this evil, that he was really a hero?''

"Sit down, Rose.'' Latigo's black eyes glinted dangerously. Mason had begun to cry. Rose scooped him into her arms and, after a defiant pause, lowered herself to the chair.

"I'm waiting for an explanation,'' she said.

"Then be quiet and listen to me.'' He pushed his plate aside and leaned toward her, his forearms resting tautly on the edge of the table.

"First of all, I couldn't be certain your husband was Scott's secret informant,'' he said. "I didn't want to tell you something that might not be true.''

"I see.'' Rose regarded him coldly. "And what else?''

"You. Your safety.''

"You're treating me like a child again!''

"Listen.'' His voice and eyes held her in check. "When we first talked about the Ring, I realized you knew nothing about your husband's activities. That innocence was your protection. As long as you were no threat to the Ring, they had no reason to harm you. But now that you know…'' His mouth tightened as he shook his head. "Rose, you should have left well enough alone. Now I've put you in more danger than you can imagine.''

"But how could I have chosen *not* to know?'' she asked, her arms clasping her baby. "You're talking about Mason's father, about his legacy of—''

"What I'm talking about is your life,'' he said quietly. "Before long, I'll be on my way to Mexico, and you'll be on your own. Take my advice and forget everything I've told you. If you're fool enough to act on what you've learned, I can't be responsible for what happens.''

Rose glared at him across the table, seething with anger at this stubborn man who could not, *would* not, see her desperate need to put things right. He had made up his mind to leave, and nothing she could say or do would move him.

"Go, then!" She pushed back her chair and rose on trembling legs. "Turn your back on justice and honor! Turn your back on me and my son! Slink off to Mexico like a coward and save your own precious skin!"

The silence in the kitchen was broken only by the sound of Mason snuffling against Rose's neck. A cold mask had slipped over Latigo's features.

"That, my dear Mrs. Colby," he said in a blade-thin voice, "is exactly what I intend to do. If you'll allow me a few more hours to finish the chores and scout the hills, I'll be on my way, and I won't trouble you again."

Without another word, he got up from the table, walked calmly across the kitchen and out the door.

Rose stood rooted to the floor as the latch shut behind him. For a long moment she stared at the closed doorway. Then, slowly, she crumpled back onto the chair.

So be it, she thought angrily. She had asked, demanded, all but begged for Latigo's cooperation, and he had refused. Now she had no choice except to carry on her quest alone.

It would be a dangerous quest. Latigo had told her so, and she believed him. But whatever the peril, she could not turn away from this compelling key to John's past.

From the corral, the sound of hammering echoed across the yard. Latigo was already fixing the fence, as he had promised. Beyond that, she knew he would not stay long. He had made his decision, and he was not a man to be cajoled against his will.

But she had made a promise, too, Rose reminded herself as she stood up and eased the drowsing Mason back into his basket. She had promised Latigo supplies for his journey, and he would have them.

Jerking her loose apron strings tight, she set to work. The sporadic rain of hammer blows from outside punctuated her movements as she wrapped the leftover biscuits in a napkin, added some smoked beef, beans and flour from the pantry. Latigo would be on foot, she reminded herself as she arranged everything in a laundered flour sack. He would only be able to carry so much.

All the same, Rose could not resist adding a small jar of blackberry preserves, a half-pound tin of Arbuckle coffee, some sugar, some rolled oats, a tiny bag of salt and a spare pot for cooking. What he preferred not to carry, he could give away or trade, she reasoned as she knotted the top of the sack and placed it on the back stoop where he would be sure to see it.

He would need water, but she had noticed a canteen looped over the horn of his saddle. He could fill it himself from the outside pump.

Clothes. Here again, there were limits, not only on what he could carry but on what Latigo would accept. He was, after all, a proud man. But surely he would not refuse extra wool stockings, and there were several good pairs in the chest upstairs. With a quick glance at Mason, Rose hurried to the front hall and up the long staircase, the hammer blows still ringing in her ears.

Only as she was returning by way of the dining room did she pause, suddenly, before the open door to John's office. Her eyes wandered over the half-open drawers, the papers piled on the desk. Her thoughts churned and tumbled like rocks in a spring flood, only to crash to an abrupt halt.

For a long moment Rose stood as still as glass, her hands clutching the bundled socks as new revelations settled in like pieces of a giant puzzle. The ransacked drawers. Yes, in light of what she knew, the whole thing made a horrifying kind of sense. Someone had known John was gathering evidence against the Ring; sometime after his accident, someone had come looking for it.

Rose's chest quivered as she willed herself to breathe. She remembered Bayard and his overeagerness to help her go through John's papers. Had it been just another of his schemes to get her alone, or was there some purpose so dark and convoluted that the thought of it left her numb with disbelief?

Then there was the death of Major Scott, so close to the time of John's accident, and so similar in its nature.

She had to tell Latigo about the papers and her suspicions. She had to persuade him to help her search. They both needed answers. Neither of them could unlock those answers alone. But working together, perhaps...

She raced through the kitchen and out the back door. Latigo was nowhere in sight, but she could hear the sound of hammering from the far side of the barn. He had evidently finished the corral fence and moved on to the damaged chicken coop.

Rose had taken a half-dozen strides in that direction when a piercing wail from the kitchen stopped her like a blow. The baby! Something was wrong—

She whirled back toward the house and burst inside. Mason was lying in his basket, his tiny pink fists flailing the air as he screamed. Rose snatched him into her arms, rubbing his rigid little back in an effort to soothe him. Maybe he'd been stung by a bee or a wasp, or—God forbid—

Frantic with fear, she used her free hand to pick up each of his blankets and shake it hard over the floor. There were scorpions in this part of the desert, vile-tempered little creatures whose sting could easily kill a child.

But nothing fell out of the blankets. Nothing, even, from the empty basket itself; and by the time Rose had finished checking, Mason's wails had subsided to snuffling whimpers. Laying him on the table, she lifted his nightgown, removed his diaper and checked every inch of his delicate pink skin for a spot of redness or swelling. She found nothing.

Dizzy with relief, she snuggled him against her shoulder and climbed the stairs to her bedroom. Mason would fall asleep after his feeding. Then she would hurry outside and find Latigo. She would tell him everything, and she would demand the same from him, everything he knew about the Indian Ring and Major Henry Scott's so-called accident. Getting the taciturn half-Apache to talk would be like forcing water from a stone, but whatever it took, Rose vowed, she would not give up. She needed answers, needed them desperately, and there was no other way to get them.

Mason nursed restlessly, stopping every minute or two to fuss and twist his small dark head from side to side. At last his little body relaxed in sleep. With exquisite care, Rose eased him into his cradle and tucked the blue lambs-wool coverlet around him. His breathing was light and even. She paused to lean down and brush a kiss across his forehead. Then, holding her breath, she cat-footed out of the room and hurried downstairs to find Latigo.

Only as she reached the landing and pivoted into the front hall did she realize that the sound of hammering had stopped. In the silence, a small knot of anxiety tightened in the pit of her stomach.

She plunged through the kitchen and flung open the back door. The bundle she'd prepared lay untouched on the stoop. Her knees weakened with momentary relief. Surely Latigo would not leave without supplies.

Would he?

She raced into the yard, searching the corral, the shed, the barn. She found Latigo's saddle where she herself had hidden it. The canteen, however, was gone.

Only as Rose turned dejectedly back toward the house

did she remember what he had said about scouting the hills. Latigo would be back, she told herself, her heart lifting. Surely, after all they'd been through together, he would not just go off and leave her without a word.

Not unless this was his way of saying goodbye.

Chapter Nine

The house had never seemed larger nor more silent. Rose flung herself into a frenzy of housework, clattering dishes and pans in the kitchen to drown out the slow dirge of the grandfather clock. She gathered the eggs, milked the cow, checked Sundown's leg and fed him some oats.

Everywhere she went, her eyes strained for a glimpse of Latigo's tall, rugged frame emerging from the shadows or looming dark against the sun. But as the hours passed, she began to lose hope. He was gone like smoke on the wind, unavailable to argue with her or tantalize her with fragments of the puzzle she was so desperate to solve.

Mason was still asleep when Rose finished the chores. She stood for a moment, gazing at him, then walked slowly back down the stairs to stand in the open doorway of her husband's office, gathering her resolve.

Her first search of John's papers had revealed nothing. Maybe there was nothing to find, and never had been. Or maybe the intruder had already found what he wanted and taken it away. But she could not assume any of those things. She needed to look again, more closely this time. Bayard had been too eager to help her. She had to believe there was a reason.

As she opened the first drawer, Rose resisted the urge to thrust Bayard's image from her mind. He had behaved oafishly this morning, but she knew better than to dismiss him as an ill-mannered fool. He had too much power and influence to be a stupid man. Everything Bayard Hudson did was driven by a purpose.

Even his pursuit of her.

Why? she asked herself as her finger inched down the tedious columns in a ledger book. There were beautiful, sophisticated women in Tucson who would be his for the asking. Her own mirror showed her a thin, careworn face; sunbleached hair, hastily twisted up and pinned: a wardrobe of faded chambrays and calicos more suitable for rubbing down a horse than dancing a quadrille. The notion that Bayard was bewitched by her beauty was almost enough to make Rose laugh out loud.

And if it was a family he wanted, her shortcomings on that front were no secret, either. For all she knew, Bayard could even be aware of the news the doctor had given her after Mason's difficult birth—that she could have no more children. Men did talk, after all. Even doctors.

So what was Bayard really after? The ranch?

That, too, seemed unlikely. Bayard's freight and mercantile business had made him one of the wealthiest men in the territory. Moreover, she had never known him to profess any love for land and cattle. No, it had to be something else, and unless the man was so blind and feebleminded as to be truly infatuated...

Rose shoved the whole question of Bayard aside and focused her attention on John's papers.

Half an hour later, she finished her fruitless inspection of the first drawer, closed it with a sigh and opened the second. At least she was learning about the operation of the ranch, she consoled herself.

The clock struck three just as she opened the third

drawer. As if roused by the sound of the chime, Mason woke up and began to fuss. The thin, fragmented cry, so unlike his usual hungry wail, echoed down the silent stairwell, startling Rose like a gunshot. In a heartbeat she was racing up the stairs, all her mother instincts shrilling that something was wrong.

The air in the bedroom was too warm, and permeated with a subtle sickly odor. Mason was thrashing in his crib, his face flushed, his cries oddly pitched, like a small, lost bird's.

"What's the matter, little love?" Rose struggled to sound calm and cheerful despite the cold lump of fear that blocked her throat. "Don't worry, now," she murmured, reaching down to gather him into her arms. "We'll get you changed and fed, and you'll be feeling better in—"

Her whole world came to a shattering halt as her fingertips touched his skin. It was dry and terrifyingly hot.

Her son was burning up with fever.

Latigo squatted Apache-fashion under the lip of a rocky outcrop, his eyes squinting into the sunset. His fingers toyed with a long strand of grass, twisting it restlessly. The vast Colby ranch spread below him, the barn and house within easy view. He could have spent the rest of the day down there. Maybe he should have. Rose could have used more of his help.

But no, he had needed to get away for a few hours. He had needed to make certain no one was lurking in the hills to menace Rose when he was gone. And he had needed time to be alone and think.

While the sun crawled across the sky, he had climbed the hills and prowled the rocky arroyos, his mind churning. And always, no matter how convoluted his reasoning, his thoughts had returned to the same point. For Rose's sake and for his own, he would have to leave at once.

As the land cooled, Latigo could feel life stirring around him. A tiny flycatcher flashed through the underbrush, its song a bright note in the shadows. A cicada whirred up from the damp yellow grass to disappear in the twilight. A red-tailed hawk winged its way home against the purple sky. Soon, Latigo knew, it would be dark enough for him to set out.

A fresh breeze struck his face, blowing back his hair and filling his nostrils with the richness of sage and fresh, damp earth. Latigo's senses recalled the fragrance of lavender, the warmth of Rose bending over him, her corn-silk hair skimming his bare shoulder, her eyes the color of twilight.

No, he lashed himself, he could not stay at the ranch another hour or he would be pulled into her world and lost. He would stay until his presence doomed them both.

He would say goodbye now, and he would go.

As he rose to his feet, Latigo suddenly noticed a movement in the yard—a dark, blurred shape, then another and another, flowing like ghosts through the long blue shadows. He leaned forward, every nerve tingling, eyes straining through the dusk.

Horses.

Some of Rose's horses, scattered by the storm, were returning to feed.

Heedless of any danger, he started down the hill at a lope. There was plenty of feed in the corral. He had seen Rose leave hay and oats there that morning. But unless the open gate was closed behind them, the skittish mustangs would be gone as swiftly as they had come.

As he ran, Latigo thought of the saddle he had left in the barn, buried under a heap of straw. He would have a use for it now. Mounted, he could cross the desert swiftly. By tomorrow morning, with luck, he would be halfway to the border.

Now he could hear the muted thud of the horses' hooves against the packed earth and the soft, wet snorting sounds they made as they crowded through the corral gate and began to feed. Rose would hear them, too, he reasoned. Any second now, the door of the house would open, and she would come flying out into the dusk, flushed with excitement at the return of her precious animals.

His throat was tight with anticipation as he raced into the yard. But Rose did not appear, and after a few minutes he realized she was not coming. Telling himself it was for the best, he closed the corral gate to keep the horses in. Then he slipped into the barn to get his saddle.

Returning a few minutes later, he paused to stand with one boot on the lower fence rail, his narrowed eyes studying the half-dozen horses that milled in the gathering darkness. His own mustang had not returned. He would have to take one of the others. If the time ever came when he could get his hands on the pension fund he'd accumulated at Fort Grant, he would repay Rose with interest for all her trouble, Latigo vowed. For the past ten years, he'd been putting most of his army pay aside, with the idea of buying some land south of the border and starting his own ranch.

But why dwell on that now? News traveled fast, and the money had probably vanished into somebody's pocket as soon as word of the murders reached the fort.

Latigo glanced up at the pale rectangle of Rose's window, gathering his resolve to knock on the door and say goodbye. He took a moment to pile his gear in the shadow of the barn. Then he mounted the front steps, raised the heavy bronze knocker and rapped sharply.

The sound echoed into a silence so profound that Latigo could almost hear the beating of his own heart. He waited, and as seconds became minutes, he began to worry.

He knocked again, an urgent pounding this time that

rang into the same stillness as before. If anything had gone wrong, he would never forgive himself for leaving her alone.

He was about to hurl himself against the double doors when he heard the familiar patter of Rose's running foot-steps across the tiles of the front hall. His shoulders sagged with relief as he heard her voice through the needle-thin crack.

"Who's there?" The words quivered with strain.

"It's Latigo, are you all right?"

She did not answer, but he heard the groan of the massive bolt sliding along its track. Seconds later the door swung open to reveal her standing like a wraith in the darkness of the hall, her agitated hands twisting the hem of her apron.

"Your horses are back," he said. Then she took a step toward him, and the dying light from outside fell across her tear-ravaged face.

"It's Mason," she said. "I can't stop the fever. I've tried everything I can think of…" Her body sagged, then jerked painfully upright as she fought for self-control. "He's been sick all afternoon. I don't know what caused it—maybe something I did."

She swayed slightly and stared at Latigo. "His body is on fire. I've bathed him in cool water. I've wrapped him in blankets. I've prayed and prayed!" She shook her head in helpless despair, her pale hair tumbling unheeded around her face. "He's only getting worse. Please, if there's something you can do, anything—"

Latigo strode across the threshold and closed the door behind him. He knew all too well that he could be sealing his own doom, but he could no more walk away from Rose in her need than he could sprout wings and fly like one of Reverend Ezekiel Packer's angels.

"Show me your son," he said. "I'll do whatever I can."

* * *

Rose led him up the stairs, scarcely noticing when her tired feet stumbled over the hem of her gown. From the bedroom she could hear Mason's plaintive little cry. The sound was weaker than she remembered earlier, and she knew the fever was burning the life from his tiny body.

"Hurry," she urged Latigo, senselessly, she realized. Latigo was neither a doctor nor a miracle worker. His being here would make no difference.

At the top of the stairs, he moved ahead of her, striding down the hall. By the time Rose reached the bedroom he was bending over the cradle, lifting away Mason's blankets.

"What have you given him?" he asked, glancing back at Rose. "Food? Medicine?"

"Nothing since midday. He won't nurse, and there's nothing in the medical box but whiskey, iodine and bitters."

"He needs fluids and something for the fever. I've got some dried sage in my saddlebags that makes a good tea. Willow bark is better, but there's no time to fetch it."

Rose did not realize she was staring at him until he spoke again. "My Apache grandmother was a healer. What little I know, she taught me."

"I'll start some water boiling." Rose fled from the bedroom and hurried downstairs. She had spent the afternoon rocking her baby, crying tears of frustration and anguish as she struggled to cool his burning skin. Just to move, to act with purpose, was a blessing in itself.

Still, her hands shook as she shoved sticks of kindling into the stove and watched the embers spark to life, their blue-tipped flames licking the dry wood. As she lit the lamp and filled a kettle with water, she heard Latigo's boots on the stairs. The front door opened and closed as he hurried outside.

She could not expect a miracle from the tea, Rose reminded herself. Apache medicine was primitive at best. Apache children died, just as white children died, innocent in their suffering. She had waited so long for Mason, and he was all she had. Dear heaven, if anything were to happen to him, her life would be over.

Rose turned, startled, as Latigo appeared in the kitchen doorway. In one hand he carried a small, fringed deerskin bag.

"Sage," he said. "I can make the tea if you want to go back upstairs."

Rose set the kettle over the fire and moved away from the stove. "Thank you," she said wearily.

He hesitated where he stood, lamplight playing on his sharp, bronze features. His eyes were dark and guarded. "Rose, your boy is very sick. I can't promise anything."

"I know," she whispered, staring down at her hands. "I know."

He stepped to one side, an awkward, silent invitation for her to leave. Rose lifted her chin and walked swiftly out of the kitchen, only to turn abruptly back to face him. "I thought you'd gone for good," she said.

"You know I wouldn't leave without telling you good-bye."

"Is that why you came back?"

He stared down into the open kettle, where the aromatic sage was already beginning to simmer. "Yes," he said, "for that, and to help myself to one of the horses in your corral."

"Horses?" Rose had turned to go once more, but she froze with her hand on the door frame. "My horses are back?"

"A few. They came in at dusk to feed, and I closed the gate behind them."

Hope swirled up in her, dizzying in its power. "But with

a horse someone could ride to Tucson for the doctor..." Her voice trailed off as her eyes met Latigo's, and she knew they were both thinking the same thing. Tucson was three hours away and at least three hours back. Even if Latigo was willing to risk the ride, and even if the doctor was willing to come, the small, frail candle of Mason's life did not have six hours left to burn.

Despair slammed into Rose like a blow. She sagged against the door frame. Then, seized by an irrational fury, she suddenly flew at Latigo, her fists flailing the air, glancing off his chest. "You were out there!" she gasped, beating at him in helpless rage. "All the time I was holding him, praying my heart out, frightened to death—you were out there, minutes from the house! If you'd been here, maybe you could have done something sooner, you stubborn, coldhearted Apache bas—"

His arms caught her close, holding her like a steel vise against his chest so that she could not move.

"Don't, Rose." His throat quivered against her hair as he spoke. "We can't change anything that's happened. We can only go on from here and do the best we can!"

Her body jerked with tearless sobs. "If Mason dies, I'll never forgive you—or myself!"

"Don't talk like that." His arms had softened, but he still held her fast, his heart hammering in her ear. The fresh cedar aroma of his shirt mingled with the warm, smoky scent of his skin. "Don't even think like that," he said. "Thoughts open paths for things to happen. That's what my grandmother used to tell me, and I still believe it. Think about getting your son well, nothing else."

She was trembling now, so hard that she feared, if he let her go, her legs would give way and she would crumple to the floor. "I'm trying to," she whispered. "But I'm not strong, Latigo. I can't say that I ever was. And I've lost everyone who ever meant anything to me, everyone except Mason. I can't lose him, too."

"You're stronger than you think, Rose." His arms had grown tender. His breath stirred her hair as he spoke. "You will be strong for your son."

Rose closed her eyes, stealing a moment of refuge as she regrouped her shattered emotions. "I picture Mason growing up," she whispered. "I think of him learning to walk, to ride, to manage the ranch. I see him bringing his bride home, their children growing up here, filling this gloomy house with laughter and noise. And I see me, the happy old grandmother, looking after them all." She stiffened in his arms. "I'm all right now. Let me go back to him."

A tremor passed through Latigo's body as he exhaled. His arms dropped to his side, releasing her. "Go," he said, turning away at once. "I'll find what I need and be up with the tea in a few minutes."

Rose could hear Mason fussing as she hurried upstairs. He lay on his back, his legs thrashing feebly beneath his blue blanket. Rose gathered him up, laid him against her shoulder and sank into the rocking chair. His head lolled like a rag doll's against the curve of her neck. His forehead was hot and dry against her skin.

Thoughts open paths for things to happen. Latigo's words were nothing but superstitious Apache nonsense, Rose lashed herself. Mason was so ill, so helpless. She could not allow herself to believe her thoughts could make any difference. Even her prayers, she sensed, had not traveled beyond the walls of the room. They lingered on the air, the unheard ghosts of the faith she had abandoned at her marriage. Like her parents, like John, her precious child was slipping from life. Even now she could almost feel him growing weaker in her arms.

You will be strong for your son. Rose clasped Mason

tighter, struggling under the crush of her own fear. "When you're well," she whispered to him, "I'll take you outside and show you the spring flowers...blue lupines and Indian paintbrush and Mexican poppies, so beautiful, as far as your eyes can see. We'll chase jackrabbits and look for lizards, and we'll have such a wonderful time..."

Slowly Rose became aware that Latigo was standing at her shoulder, one of her china cups almost lost in his large, brown hand. "It should be cool enough," he said, swirling a teaspoon in the sharp-smelling liquid. "You don't have a baby bottle, do you?"

Rose shook her head.

"Hold him, then." Latigo crouched beside the chair and lifted the brimming spoon. "It's bitter. He's not going to like it."

Rose braced Mason's head against her breast and tilted his mouth open. At the first taste, he gagged, spat and thrashed. The tea ran down his chin and dribbled onto his nightgown.

"Here." She took the cup and spoon and thrust her crying son into Latigo's arms. "Sit down with him. I'll see what I can do." She took a tentative sip of the tea in the cup. Her throat jerked spasmodically as she swallowed. As Latigo had warned her, it was bitter, worse than bitter. How could anyone, let alone a tiny baby, be expected to drink it?

Latigo had sunk into the chair with the sobbing Mason cradled awkwardly against his chest. The yellow lamplight etched stark black lines at the corner of his eyes. He looked drawn and weary.

Drained of words, Rose walked out of the bedroom and downstairs to the kitchen. She stood in the doorway for a long moment, her desperate gaze sweeping the shelves and counters.

Suddenly her eyes fixed on a pot of honey that Esperanza had left next to the bread box. Wrenching off the lid, she drizzled a thread of the golden liquid into the tea, stirred it and took a sip. Better, yes. But it would still be too strong for Mason. Rose added a few spoonfuls of milk from the crock in the pantry. Then, knowing she could spare no more time, she hurried back up the stairs.

From the bedroom, the lamp cast a pale rectangle onto the polished floor of the hallway. Rose moved into its light, only to pause on the threshold of the room, transfixed for an instant by what she saw.

Latigo sat in the rocking chair with Mason nestled in the crook of his arm. Lamplight gleamed on his thick, black hair as he bent over her whimpering son, singing to him in a whispered, tuneless chant. Rose's breath stopped as she realized what she was hearing.

For the space of a heartbeat the past crashed in on her. Paint-streaked Apache faces. Bloodcurdling screams. And now, in the sanctuary of her own bedroom, brown Apache arms holding her son—the same arms that had held *her* in the kitchen as she cried and trembled.

Rose's knees went weak beneath her skirt, but only for the space of a breath. Her son's life was at stake, and this was no time for memories. If anything could save him, even Apache medicine—

Latigo glanced up, his obsidian eyes reading her thoughts. "A lullaby," he said in a soft, thin voice. "The only one I happen to know."

"I've sweetened the tea." Rose moved toward him, forcibly numbing her emotions. "Hold him," she said.

Latigo propped the baby in his arms as Rose sank to a crouch beside the chair. She could feel his eyes on her as she lifted the teaspoon and crooned tender, comforting words to Mason. "Here, little love, it won't be so nasty now, I promise."

But Mason would not be lulled. At the sight of the spoon, his small red face crinkled into a grimace, and he began to struggle.

"*Hold* him!" Rose thrust the spoon into his open mouth and forced the tea down his throat. This time he did seem to swallow a little, but he choked and spat and fought, wasting a perilous amount of his strength.

"Again." Rose's gaze flickered upward to meet Latigo's as she refilled the spoon. He braced Mason in his arms, cradling the small head with one hand.

What if the tea didn't help? The question tortured Rose as she poured one spoonful after another into Mason's screaming, choking mouth. What if the brew was too strong or too weak to do any good? What if it wasn't meant for babies at all, especially white babies? She could be hurting her little son. Dear heaven, for all she knew, she could be killing him!

But she dared not stop.

Latigo said little during the ordeal, but his eyes followed her every movement, measuring her fear as the tea dwindled in the cup. His silence seemed to plead for her trust in a man of the same blood as the savages who had murdered her family. Did he understand what he was asking of her? Could he imagine the things she saw when she closed her eyes in sleep at night?

Rose veiled her emotions behind an impassive mask. She willed herself to see only her sick child.

Mason had exhausted himself. He took the tea more and more passively. His quiescence worried her. The hazy, far-away look in his periwinkle eyes frightened her even more.

As she tipped the cup to spoon out the last of the tea, Latigo's restraining hand fell across her wrist. "That's enough," he said. "Wrap him up and keep him warm. The tea should make him sweat."

Rose exhaled wearily as she set the cup on the floor.

She had been crouching for so long that her legs had gone numb. Latigo's face blurred in her vision as she stumbled to her feet and lifted Mason into her arms. His hot little body jerked, then relaxed again to settle against her breast.

Rose sensed Latigo's eyes following her as she crossed the room to the cradle, gathered up Mason's blue blanket and laid it flat on one corner of the bed.

"He should sleep for a while," Latigo observed as Rose lowered her son to the blanket and wrapped it snugly around him. "You look as if you could use some sleep yourself."

"No, I'll be all right. I just want to hold him." Rose sank onto the edge of the bed with Mason in her arms. The familiar walls and furnishings seemed to swim in the warm, golden air. Her limbs were leaden with fatigue.

Mason's eyelids fluttered and drooped. Then his silky lashes settled onto his fever-flushed cheeks. His breathing was ragged and shallow.

"Sleep and warmth, that's what he needs now," Latigo's voice droned from the periphery of her awareness. "So do you. Rest now. Let the tea do its work."

Rose could feel her own eyelids growing heavy. Her head drooped, then jerked sharply erect. "No," she whispered. "I can't sleep until I know Mason is all right. If he should wake up and need me—"

Or if he should die, she thought.

"Take the chair, then. It'll be easier on you." He eased his long body out of the rocker, walked to the window and opened it wide. A freshet of cool night air struck Rose's skin, shocking her awake.

"The baby!" She arched protectively around Mason, tugging a fold of the blanket over his face. "Close that window! Don't you know what drafts can do to a sick child?"

"Fresh air is good for sickness. That's what my grandmother used to say.'' Latigo closed the window to a hand-breadth, then deliberately turned and walked across the room.

With a sigh, Rose swung the back of the rocker toward the offending draft, shielding Mason with her own body as she settled into place. The night breeze ruffled her sweat-dampened hair, cooling the nape of her neck and clearing her foggy mind.

Latigo lingered pensively in the open doorway, his black Apache eyes cautious, as if awaiting some signal.

"You can go now," Rose said softly. "Take one of the horses. Take whatever provisions you need. Only leave me a little of your sage, in case…"

Her gaze dropped to Mason's small, flushed face. He was so tiny and so ill. The next few hours, she knew, would determine whether he lived or died. Either the fever would break, or its heat would, at last, burn the life from his fragile body. There would be no need for more sage.

She saw Latigo hesitate in the doorway. Shadows flickered across his face as he stepped back into the room, paused again, then walked across the braided rug and sat down on the edge of her bed.

He would stay.

Chapter Ten

They waited in a torment of silence as the night deepened. Rose kept anxious eyes on Mason, measuring every breath, watching every nuance of expression that flickered across his tiny, sleeping face. Latigo spent his time listening, his eyes narrowed to alert slits, his body tensing at the snort of a horse or the cry of a coyote.

They both stirred as the lamplight began to wane, the flame sputtering on a wick that had burned too low. "No, there's a trick to it," Rose murmured as Latigo made a move toward the dressing table. "Hold the baby. I'll take care of it."

Rising swiftly, she eased her son into Latigo's waiting arms and glided to the lamp. In a moment her fingers had cranked up the wick, flooding the room with amber light and leaping black shadows.

When she turned back toward Latigo, she saw that he had loosened Mason's blanket and was probing cautiously beneath it with his fingertips. The eyes he raised to hers were bleak as the white moon that hung in the darkness outside.

"No change?" she whispered, knowing what his answer would be.

He shook his head. "Lie down and get some rest. I'll wake you if there's any need."

"No." She reached down and lifted her son from Latigo's arms, cradling him against her swollen breasts. If the next few hours were to be Mason's last, she would not miss one precious breath.

"The sage takes time," Latigo said.

"Yes, I suppose it does." Rose sank wearily into the chair.

Downstairs, the clock began to strike. She closed her ears to the sound, fearful of counting the hours that had passed. The night had been too long and filled with nightmares that had nothing to do with Apaches.

She glanced at Latigo, needing the sound of another voice in the room. "You never told me the rest of your story," she said.

His only response was a recalcitrant scowl.

"Please. It's so quiet."

He sighed, and she sensed the struggle in him as he gathered his thoughts. Latigo was not a man who revealed himself easily, she sensed, especially to a woman.

"You told me how the white soldiers found you," she prompted him. "You said they turned you over to a missionary couple at Fort Grant."

"Oh, yes." His razor-edged laugh startled her. "The Reverend Ezekiel Packer and his good wife. I should be grateful to them, I suppose."

"But you're not?"

"Gratitude is just one of the virtues Reverend Packer tried to beat into me with his brass-buckled belt," Latigo said in a cold voice. "He never quite succeeded."

Rose stared at him, askance.

"Am I shocking you?" His eyes glinted like black ice.

"No." Rose met his gaze boldly. "I'm just wondering how a man can walk around with so much anger bottled up inside him. 'Resentment poisons the soul,' that's what my father used to say.''

"Maybe I have no soul to poison. That's what the reverend believed about Apaches, that they had no souls. He would never have taken me in if I hadn't been part white."

"But he didn't have to take you in at all," Rose argued softly. "There must have been some goodness in him."

"That's what I kept telling myself, even when I couldn't sleep for the pain of the welts on my back." Latigo had risen to his feet, his shadow looming across the bed. "You see, Rose, I wasn't always the stubborn savage you think I am. For a very long time, I tried my best to be a good little white boy."

"Why? To please your new parents?"

"Lord, no!" He made a hollow, bitter sound. "A few months after taking me in, Reverend and Mrs. Packer moved to Prescott. They sent me to school for the first time. I was twelve, and the teacher made me sit with the six-year-olds. For the first few weeks it was humiliating. And then, suddenly it didn't matter. It was as if a window had opened on the whole world."

Rose's lips parted as she gazed at him, transfixed by the wonder that, even now, illuminated his lean, bronze face. It was as if Latigo's bitter shell had fallen away.

"Within a year I was reading everything I could get my hands on," he said. "Dime novels, the reverend's Bible, Twain, Dickens, Dante, the history and geography and science books from the classroom." A shadow fell across Latigo's face. "I was so caught up that I did a very foolish thing. I began to dream. College, travel—I would do it all, I promised myself. Then I would come back to Arizona and do something to help my people. I thought about becoming a teacher, then a doctor, then a writer—a voice for those who had no voice. I imagined writing the whole history of the Apaches, everything, so there would be a record.''

The words ended in silence, and when Latigo turned back toward her, Rose saw that his features had hardened once more. The vulnerable young man she had glimpsed was gone.

''I stayed because of that dream,'' he said. ''I put up with the reverend's whippings. I put up with being taunted by the children at school because of my dark skin. I stood it all because it was the only way to get what I wanted.''

''What happened to all your plans?'' Rose asked, risking another blast of bitterness. ''Where did things go wrong?''

''You mean, how did I become a washed-up army scout on the run?'' His laugh was a raw wound. ''I left, that's all. I was sixteen years old when I walked out of the reverend's house and struck out on my own, and I never looked back.''

''But why, with so much promise?''

''The reason doesn't matter any longer. I had no choice.'' He stalked to the open window, every muscle taut as he listened to the sounds of the night outside.

''I headed south to the Chiricahua Mountains to find my mother's people,'' he said. ''Cochise's band treated me well enough, but I knew that if I stayed, sooner or later I'd be expected to paint my face and join my cousins on the warpath, and I knew I could never do it. So did they. I left after a season—for good.''

Latigo stretched his long frame, his face in shadow. ''For the next few years, I knocked around from ranch to ranch wrangling horses. Then the Apache wars broke out and the army needed scouts.'' He shrugged, dismissing his own motives. ''The pay was better than breaking mustangs.''

''But you were fighting against your own people.''

''Not against Cochise. I made that a condition when I

signed up. And I did a lot more tracking and interpreting than fighting.'' His throat moved as he swallowed. ''I also did a lot of rationalizing. I knew the Apaches would lose in the end, and I told myself I was saving lives on both sides by working to bring an end to the resistance. It made sense, but by time the worst was over, I didn't like myself much.''

''And the reverend never tried to find you?'' she asked, hiding the sympathy she knew he would detest.

''No.''

''What about the reverend's wife, your adoptive mother? Surely she must have cared enough to—''

''No.'' The undertone of tightly reined vehemence in his answer warned Rose that she had probed too deeply. He turned away from the window, his expression lost in the leaping shadows that played across his features. ''That's enough talk about me. My past is my own, and I don't make a practice of opening it up to be read like some cheap novel.''

Rose recoiled as if he'd slapped her with the flat of his hand. ''You don't need to stay,'' she said coldly. ''Maybe you should leave now, while you have a few hours of darkness left.''

He hesitated, then settled back onto the edge of the bed, as if in stubborn defiance of her words. Rose toyed with the folds of Mason's blanket for a moment, shifting his birdlike weight from her left side to her right. Her left arm was soaked from the heat of his tiny body, but the sweat was her own, not his. The fever had not broken.

She glanced up in despair and met the unveiled impact of Latigo's gaze. A grave concern, bordering on tenderness, flashed in the liquid depths of his eyes only to vanish at once like an illusion kindled by the flickering lamplight.

Rose's throat tightened as the stony mask slid back into place, shielding them from the peril of emotions too deeply hared. He had kept himself aloof, revealing only brief flickers of his true nature, like images glimpsed through the window of a fast-moving train.

He stirred restlessly, moving forward on the edge of the bed. "I'm going out to check on your horse," he announced, his lean, sinewy body straightening to its full height. "I won't be long."

Rose watched in silence as he strode toward the doorway, then turned for an instant to look at her. "I'm not leaving, Rose," he said softly. "I won't go without telling you."

His going left a void in the room, a bleak, frightening emptiness that had already begun to eat her alive. Agitated, she pushed out of the rocker and walked to the window with Mason in her arms. He slept fitfully. Rose clasped him protectively, as if defying death to take him without taking her first.

Feeling dizzy and light-headed, she gulped the thin draft of night air that drifted through the narrow opening. She had to stay awake for Mason. She had to fight for him as he could not fight for himself.

Her thoughts froze as her tired eyes caught a movement in the yard below. For the space of a breath her mind spun into denial. It was a trick of light and shadow, that was all. Some object blown by the night wind. But when she looked again, eyes straining into the darkness, her blurred gaze told her it was a human figure she was seeing, creeping with a fluid, catlike motion toward the barn.

Gulping back a scream, Rose pivoted away from the window and flattened herself against the wall. Shouting would do more harm than good, her spinning mind reasoned. Latigo might not hear her from inside the barn, and if the intruder had a gun and meant to shoot or capture him, a scream from the house would only hasten the attack. She would have to shoot.

John's Peacemaker lay underneath her pillow. Ros
paused to lay Mason carefully in his cradle, then seize
the weapon and darted back to the window.

The rising moon cast pools of shadow over the mudd
yard. Rose glimpsed the intruder moving between light an
darkness. Her vision swam. Her hands shook uncontrol
lably as she thumbed back the hammer, thrust her arm
out the window, and, without bothering to aim, squeeze
the trigger.

When Latigo heard the shot he was in the loft, forkin
down some hay. He froze, then, still clutching the pitch
fork, he scrambled down the ladder and made a dive fo
the barn door.

For a moment he crouched there, his breathing tense an
shallow as his eyes scanned the trampled yard, seein
nothing amiss. A glance toward the house showed Ros
silhouetted in the upstairs window. She was still grippin
the pistol.

Bewildered, he plunged across the yard, mounted th
front porch and bolted into the front hallway, pausing onl
to brace the pitchfork in a shadowed corner. Rose stoo
on the landing above him, ghostly pale in the darkness.

"Are you all right?" she whispered, her voice echoin
down the stairwell. "I saw something, someone, in th
yard."

"I didn't see a thing. Are you sure?"

"I don't know." Strain threaded her voice. Her rigl
hand slid along the banister as she moved unsteadily dow
the stairs toward him. "It looked like a man, but it ma
have been a shadow or an animal. I fired the gun to war
you."

"You should have been more careful," Latigo growl
as the fear he had denied too long came crashing in c
him. "What if it had been a man with a gun? He cou

have shot back and hit you. You made the perfect target, standing there in the window like that. Blast it, don't you know better than to—''

The words died in his throat as Rose began to crumple. Collapsing softly, like a blossom dropping from its stem, she slid to his feet in a tangle of chambray skirts and muslin petticoats.

With a muffled curse, Latigo scooped her off the floor. She whimpered as he hefted her against his chest, her head rolling back over his arm. Her eyelids were closed, the lashes dark gold where they lay in the violet hollows that shadowed her eyes.

She lay in his arms as he mounted the stairs, soft and light and precious. Her face was pale, her throat a soft ivory curve in the darkness. Latigo struggled against the warm tendrils of emotion that curled through and around his spirit, binding him like a helpless captive. He had stayed too long with this woman—long enough to put them both in danger. But he could not leave her now.

Rose moaned softly as he strode into her bedroom and lowered her gently to the bed. He managed to avert his eyes from her delicate ankles and lace-edged drawers as he pulled her rumpled skirts down over her legs. But something warm and aching melted inside him as he bent to unlace her high-topped shoes and work them gently off her small, almost childlike feet. He battled the urge to cradle those feet in his hands, to caress the exquisite contours of flesh and bone with his fingertips.

With each shallow breath, her swollen breasts strained the tiny buttons that held the bodice of her gown. Two quarter-sized circles of moisture stained the blue fabric where her milk had begun to seep. Latigo swallowed the dryness in his throat and forced himself to glance away. He had no right to look at this woman and feel what he was feeling at this moment.

Resolutely he strode to the window and opened it wide
The cool, earthy scent of a desert night swept into th
stuffy room. No wonder Rose had fainted, he groused a
he checked her snugly wrapped infant in the cradle and
found him sleeping quietly. White women did not know
how to breathe! They shut themselves up in closed house
where the wind could not blow its cleansing breath. The
they squeezed in their middles with those infernal corset
so that their lungs had no room to fill with fresh air.

And fresh air was exactly what Rose needed right now

Steeling himself, Latigo walked back to the bed and
scowled down at Rose's hand-span waist. This was a
emergency, he told himself as he bent over her. Those
tightly constricting stays would have to be loosened a
once.

Holding his breath, he began.

The top button was missing, torn away by Bayard Hud
son, he remembered darkly. The second, impossibly tiny
and covered with fabric that matched the gown, resisted
his unsteady fingers, sparking a whispered curse before i
finally slipped through the buttonhole. The third and fourth
were easier, but even in the cool night breeze, Latigo wa
perspiring lightly beneath his shirt.

He took excruciating care not to touch her flesh with hi
fingers, but he could do nothing about his other senses
Her subtle woman-scent crept into his nostrils as he leaned
close. Coupled with the sight of her creamy breasts swell
ing over the embroidered edge of her camisole, it triggered
a release of hot sensation that rocketed downward, with
the exact result nature had intended. Latigo clenched hi
teeth, struggling to ignore the firestorm raging in his vitals
Rose needed air. That had to be his only concern.

An eternity seemed to pass before he freed the last but
ton, opening her gown to the waist. The busk of her corse
lay exposed below the finely puckered muslin that veiled

her breasts. It was held together by a witch's gauntlet of minuscule steel fasteners. Dismayed, Latigo paused for a moment to unkink his back and collect his scattered reason.

Rose's eyelids were still closed. Lamplight played across the tiny, tired lines at the corners of her eyes. Latigo battled the urge to lean close and brush them with his lips, then trail small secret kisses down the curve of her cheek, all the way to the lovely, full-blown flower of her mouth.

But what was he thinking?

Battling the tortures of hell, he bent to tackle the first ant-sized hook at the level of her waist. It was even more stubborn than the buttons had been, and so tight that he could not hope to loosen it without pushing in on her waist. He was still fumbling, muttering half-voiced curses, when Rose suddenly opened her eyes.

"What in heaven's name are you doing?" she whispered, shrinking back against the pillows.

Latigo stepped back from the bed, his cheeks blazing with color. "What do you think I'm doing?" he growled. "You fainted on the stairs. I was trying to loosen that infernal device around your waist so you could get some fresh air into your lungs!" His irritation mounted as she continued to stare at him with bewildered eyes. "Believe me," he snapped, "if I were bent on ravishing you, I'd have chosen an easier route!"

She groaned foggily. One hand fluttered to the front of her bodice. As she discovered its state, her eyes shot wide open. She fumbled with the fabric, tugging it furiously together and managing to get two critical buttons back into their holes.

"I take it you don't want to finish the job without my help," Latigo commented dryly.

She glared at him as she struggled to sit up. "That won't be necessary. I'm perfectly all—" The words ended in a gasp. "My baby!" Her gaze darted frantically around the room. "Where is he?"

"It's all right, Rose." He clasped her shaking shoulders, easing her back onto the pillow. "He's asleep in his cradle, right where you left him."

She twisted her body away from him, pushed herself partway up with her arms, then collapsed dizzily back onto the coverlet. "Bring him to me," she whispered.

Latigo crossed the room and leaned over the cradle. Rose's son was lying awake on his back, gazing up at him with calm, alert eyes—her eyes. Something hardened in Latigo's throat as he eased his large, callused hands beneath the tiny blue bundle and nestled it against his chest.

"Is he all right?" Rose's anxious question blended worlds of fear and love.

"See for yourself." Latigo strode across the room, hesitated, then lowered the baby carefully into her outstretched hands.

"Oh," she whispered, gazing down into the small, alert face. *"Oh…"*

Cradling her infant in the hollow between her knees, Rose began to peel back the tightly wrapped layers of blanket. She performed the task slowly, almost fearfully, as if she were unwrapping a fragile gift. Latigo stepped back to watch her, masking his own anxiety as she tugged away the fuzzy blue wool and began unfolding the soft flannel underblanket.

She glanced up, as if for reassurance, her wet eyes glittering with pinpoints of reflected lamplight. For an instant her gaze held his, then she bent over her son again, crooning half-heard endearments as her fingers worked.

Latigo felt his heart leap as she laid aside the last fold to uncover her baby's perspiration-soaked nightgown. A little sob of relief escaped her throat.

The fever had broken.

Rose lifted her son in her arms and clasped him fiercely against her shoulder, her eyelids tightly shut, her body quivering. Seconds passed before she opened her eyes and glanced up at Latigo.

"Close the window, he'll get a chill." She was in command of herself once more. Only a single tear trickling down her cheek betrayed the depth of her emotions. "And I'd be grateful if you'd get me some dry clothes for him."

Latigo strode to the open window, scanned the yard below and, seeing nothing, closed and latched the panes.

"Clothes?"

"The chest, the reed one." She spoke in small, breathy bursts. "His things are in there."

Latigo opened the chest and found the baby clothes, washed and folded in sweet-smelling stacks. Feeling large and clumsy, he selected a delicate muslin nightgown embroidered with violets from the top of the pile, then found a tiny undershirt and a thick flannel diaper. Closing the top of the chest, he walked slowly back across the room.

"Thank you." Rose had undressed her baby. He lay covered by a fold of the blue blanket, chomping hungrily on one puckered little fist.

Latigo laid the clean clothes on the bed, then crouched beside her for a closer look. "I'd say your little one might want to eat," he said, his voice emerging as an odd, husky rasp.

"Yes, I know." Rose's eyes flickered downward to her swollen breasts and the two unmistakable wet spots where her milk had seeped through her gown. Color rose in her cheeks, staining them a radiant pink. "As soon as he's dressed," she muttered, fumbling with the diaper as her son kicked energetically. Her hands were shaking so hard she could barely manage the pins.

Latigo stood up, clearing his throat. "I'll stay the night

to make certain you're safe,'' he said. ''Then, come morning, I'll be on my way.''

''You don't have to go.'' She glanced up at him again, the warm directness of her gaze tearing at his heart.

''Don't—'' he began, but she cut him off.

''Please, Latigo. There are so many questions, so many missing answers neither of us will ever find alone. As long as you stay out of sight, you'll be safer here than out there in the desert, or even in Mexico. I owe you for Mason's life! Let me help you.''

''No.'' He forced the words, syllable by syllable. ''I can't stay, Rose. And we both know the reason why.''

Her hands had stopped moving. They lay like fallen petals against her skirt. Her full, moist lips were parted, her blue eyes as innocent as a child's. ''I don't understand.''

''I think you do.'' Latigo's voice roughened as he felt himself stumbling ever deeper into a trap of his own making. ''You understand as much as I do, however little that may be.''

''Please.'' Her fingers reached out and clasped his wrist, their light, insistent touch all but undoing him. ''You and I have been dueling like two enemies ever since you came here, thrusting and parrying, speaking in evasions and half-truths. We can't afford to be enemies any longer, Latigo. Go if you must, but leave me with one thing—your honesty!''

She was gazing up at him, the baby lying quietly in her lap. Latigo felt the pressure of her fingers against his flesh. He felt the ache, the longing that surged through his wretched, solitary soul, and he knew, with tragic certainty, that she felt it, too.

''Honesty?'' he rasped, his free hand catching her behind the shoulders as he loomed over her. ''I'll show you honesty, Rose!''

He felt her straining upward, clutching the baby with

one arm. Then the earth moved as their lips met, crushed and clung in a shattering explosion of need.

Latigo arched her against him, his pulse igniting as her soft, moist mouth opened to his kiss. The taste of her was wild honey, sweet and warm on his tongue. He felt her free hand in his hair, her breath on his face as he lost himself in holding her, in feeling her need, her fire, her tenderness. He knew that in the last moment of his life, whenever it might come, this was what he would want to remember.

They broke apart awkwardly as the baby began to whimper between them. Latigo stepped back from the bed, his mouth still burning as he watched Rose tending to her son. Her cheeks were flushed, her lips damp and swollen. Her beauty, as she glanced up, stunned him, leaving him as tongue-tied as a schoolboy.

"You'll be wanting to feed the little one," he murmured. "I'll finish seeing to the stock and make sure our visitor isn't still slinking around."

"Latigo." Her voice caught and held him as he turned away.

"I have to leave here, Rose," he said quietly. "For both of us. You know that as well as I do."

"Yes, I know." She glanced down at the baby, then looked up at him, her eyes warm and direct. "And, yes, I know why. But, please, we need to talk first. Promise me you won't go now."

"I promised earlier. And I keep my promises." He turned again to go, quickly, before the sight of her could cloud his mind and bind his heart. He needed time alone to think clearly about his plans. It would make things easier when daylight came, and he had to leave her for good.

"Latigo." Again her voice stopped him. He paused in the doorway.

"The pistol, it's on the dresser. Please take it outside with you."

He hesitated, remembering how vehemently she had insisted on keeping the Peacemaker from him. Then he walked over and lifted the weapon from the dresser. An iron ring containing the keys to the house lay on the dresser scarf, beside a small porcelain music box. Latigo picked up the keys. If anyone was outside, he would be wise to lock the house while he checked on the animals.

"Call when you're ready for me to come back up," he said.

"Yes. I'll call you."

Downstairs, Latigo cocked the pistol as he stepped out into the night. For the space of a long breath, he stood on the porch, watching and listening. But the shadows were peaceful, the darkness rich with the familiar sounds that told him all was well. Locking the door behind him, he made a circuit of the yard and its brushy fringes. He checked the barn, the corral and the bunkhouse, but nothing had been disturbed. Maybe Rose had fired at a shadow or a wild animal, and sent it bolting into the night. In the morning he would look for tracks.

By the time he returned to the porch, the crescent moon had risen well above the mountains. Should he forget his word and go now? That would be the sensible thing to do. He had the pistol. He had his choice of mounts. He had enough darkness left to cover a good fifteen miles before the sun came up.

Latigo settled onto the top step with a sigh. He had made Rose a promise, and he cared for her too much to break it. He would give her a little more time to finish with the baby. Then he would return to her.

He would sit beside her and watch her as they talked. And he would feel her tenderness tearing at his heart until there was nothing left.

Chapter Eleven

The tears came freely now. Rose leaned back against the pillows, letting the scalding streams spill down her cheeks as Mason nursed hungrily.

Was it Latigo's tea that had saved her son's life, or only the mercy of God? She could do no more than thank both God, with her prayers, and Latigo, with whatever help he would accept from her.

An iridescent, sensual warmth shimmered through her body as she remembered his kiss—*her* kiss, too, because she had wanted to kiss him. She had raised her face when he leaned close. She had reached up with her hand and pulled his dark head down to hers, aching to know the wild, forbidden taste of him. She had allowed herself to feel every breathless, blistering second of that kiss.

Heaven help her.

What kind of wanton had she become? Rose asked herself, staring into the low, flickering flame of the lamp as she struggled to understand. John had seldom kissed her. Kissing was not essential to procreation, she supposed, and the few kisses he did give her had been brusque and awkward. As for Bayard's wet, lustful kisses, they had done no more than fill her with rage and panic.

Yet she had willingly and passionately kissed a man of a hated race, a bitter misfit, a fugitive. *An Apache.*

She had kissed him and felt her soul catch fire.

Fire burned and destroyed, Rose reminded herself. Whatever she might feel for Latigo, she could not be foolish enough to let such a kiss happen again. She was too lonely, too vulnerable to bear the consequences of a fire blazing out of control.

Latigo would leave, that much she knew. He would pass out of her life like the shadow of a hawk gliding over the ranch, leaving nothing behind but the memory of dark eyes, strong arms and a single stolen kiss.

She would be wise, Rose promised herself. She would accept Latigo's going as something meant to be. She would bid him farewell and go on with her life as if she had never known him.

She would be calm and sensible, for the good of everyone involved.

Mason belched as she lifted him to her shoulder, then snuggled against the curve of her breast and dropped almost at once into a deep, contented slumber.

Rose slipped off the bed, tiptoed across the room and eased him into his cradle. Then she walked softly toward the washstand, where she splashed her tear-streaked face, hastily buttoned her bodice and repinned her hair.

Latigo had asked her to call him when she was ready. But the night was cool and inviting, the bedroom suddenly too warm, too intimate. It would be far wiser, she reasoned, to go downstairs, find Latigo and talk with him on the porch.

Leaving the window open so she could listen for Mason, she snuffed out the lamp and moved downstairs in the darkness.

The tiles clicked lightly as she strode across the front

hall and pushed at the front door, only to find it locked from the outside.

Panic, fueled by exhaustion, flared like tinder as she remembered that Latigo had taken both the gun and the keys. Was this his way of leaving? Locking her in the house, unarmed and alone?

She rapped, then pounded the thick, carved wood with both fists, bruising her knuckles in an outburst of frustrated rage. "Latigo!" she rasped, not wanting to shout and wake the baby upstairs. "Latigo! Blast your soul, if you've gone and—"

The key rattled in the lock, and in the next instant, the door swung open and he was there. Caught off balance, Rose stumbled across the threshold and into his arms.

Still wild with fury, she fought him for an instant, landing a single-fist blow on his rock-hard chest before she sank against him with a little gasp, overwhelmed by an avalanche of emotions.

He cradled her fiercely, holding her arms to her sides. "It's all right, Rose," he murmured. "I know what you must've been thinking. But I was waiting for you to call me, that was all. I wouldn't have left. Don't you know me better than that?"

"I'm not sure I know you at all," Rose meant to say, but suddenly the effort seemed too great. She felt her cursed tears again, stinging her eyes as worry and sleeplessness took its toll. She found herself trembling uncontrollably, her breath emerging in tight little sobs.

"It's all right, girl." Latigo rocked her gently, surrounding her with the subtle aromas of wood smoke, cedar and her own homemade soap. "You've been strong, Rose, stronger than any woman should ever have to be. But it's all right to bend a little, like the willow. Sometimes that's the only way to keep from breaking in a storm."

His throat moved lightly against her temple as he spoke.

Rose could not remember being comforted in a man's arms since her father's death, and the sweetness of it recalled early springtime in the forgotten country of her youth, soft, green and vibrant with awakening life.

This man was nothing like her father, Rose reminded herself. Latigo was as wild and dangerous as the desert, and no woman who valued her heart or her reputation would let herself get so close to him.

But it was already too late for a lecture on common sense. His nearness unleashed freshets of warmth that surged through her body. Her emotions pinwheeled out of control as she melted against him, stunned by the power of her own response. After nearly a decade with John, she thought she had learned all there was to know about the male sex. But in Latigo's arms she felt confused and uncertain. How could one man render her furious, miserable, ecstatic, tender and wanton all at once?

He bent his head and his lips found hers, cool and hard in the darkness. She opened to him with a little shudder, ravenous, suddenly, to know the taste and smell and touch of him. She moaned as the rough, wet, velvet tip of his tongue invaded her mouth to tease and explore, igniting flame points of new sensation where it grazed her sensitive flesh. Never in her life had she known anything so exquisite, so intense.

Dizzy with need, she clasped his lean waist, her fingers flexing as she bound him against her. Waves of forbidden heat rippled through her body to coil deep in its wet, burning core.

A voice in the back of her mind shrilled that this should not be happening, but Rose was beyond hearing it. This *was* happening, and the will to stop it was gone, burned to a wisp of ash by her own desire.

Latigo's abandon matched her own. His breath rasped as he edged her backward, step by step into the shadows against the house. She strained against him, wanting him to touch her throat, her breasts, to touch her everywhere. "Yes," she whispered as his fingertips stroked her breasts through the thin muslin. "Yes."

Rose whimpered with need as his body pressed her back against the cool adobe wall and she felt the long, hard ridge of his arousal along her belly, unmistakable even through the thickness of her skirts. He groaned softly as she arched against him, the pressure an exquisite torment. Tomorrow she might pay with her immortal soul, but right now she wanted every part of this man. She wanted him to love her as she had never been loved in her bleak and lonely life.

Her fingers raked his thick black hair as she pulled him down to her. "Please, Latigo," she whispered as his frantic lips grazed her cheek, her temple, her closed eyelids. "Please, I need you so."

Weighted by desire, they sank into the deepest shadows of the porch. Esperanza had left a quilt on the old rocker where she liked to sit. Latigo seized one of its corners and, in a single motion, flung and spread it over the tiles. Rose felt him tremble against her as he lowered her to the padded surface, and then he was beside her in the night, his dark head haloed by the stars.

His kisses were rough and hungry. Rose was on fire. Her legs parted beneath her skirts, pleading for the touch that would set her free, the healing love that only he could give her. His hand—yes—she gasped with need as he found the path. She was ready for him, wet, swollen and aching. Exquisite little spasms rocked her body as he stroked her with quivering fingers, touching her as she had never imagined she could be touched.

His own desire lay hard against her hip, straining at the seam of his trousers. She groped at the fastenings, wanting him, all of him.

He gasped as her fingertips brushed the marble hardness of his flesh. "Rose."

"Love me, Latigo," she whispered. "Take me. Here. Now."

She felt him hesitate. Then a long, slow shudder passed through his body. Gently he removed her hand and sat up.

"No, Rose," he said, looming above her in the starlight. "I know what you want, I know what we both want. But I can't do this to you."

She stared at him, disheveled, hurt and bewildered. "Why?" she whispered, the useless question ripping from her like the cry of a wounded bird.

He shook his head, then reached down and drew her up against him, very tenderly this time. Rose sat like a dresser's mannequin in his arms, rigid with the humiliation of a woman scorned.

"Damn it all, Rose," he murmured, stroking her tumbled hair. "I want you more than air and food and water. I want you so much it makes my gut ache. But when I think of the chance that I could go off and leave you carrying a part-Apache baby—"

Rose forced a bitter laugh, knowing that the truth would make no difference now because the moment had passed. "Put your mind to rest on that score," she said. "Mason is my last. I don't know exactly what went wrong, but after he was born, the doctor said that even if I were to remarry, I'd never be able…to conceive another child." Her shoulders sagged as she slumped against him, drained by her own truth. "But that isn't your real reason, is it? I'm beginning to know you, Latigo."

His lips grazed her hairline, half-distractedly, as if his mind were somewhere else, but he did not speak. Rose could feel the subtle tightening of his chest muscles as he held her.

"I just told you the most painful secret of my life," she said. "Don't you owe me as much?"

Still he resisted, defying her to breach the wall of his silence. Suddenly Rose remembered what he had told her upstairs or, more precisely, what he had *not* told her. Then, all at once, she knew.

Her hand darted up to capture the curve of his jaw, forcing him to look down into her face. "Tell me the truth, Latigo," she whispered. "What did she do to you, the reverend's wife? What did she do to make you run away and leave your dreams to die?"

Latigo pulled himself away from her, rising to his feet. He strode to the edge of the porch and stood glaring into the darkness.

"White women!" he said in a voice she had never heard before. "Why do they think they need to know everything? Why do they have to rip open the past and pick it apart like buzzards on a rotten carcass?"

Rose's breath jerked as if he had struck her. Latigo was deliberately trying to hurt her, she realized. He wanted to drive her away before she could open the festering wound he had carried for so long.

But she could not let that happen. Not if there was to be any understanding between them before he vanished into the desert.

She rose to her feet and moved out of the shadows to stand behind him, her hands clasping his rigid shoulders. "It's not going to work, Latigo," she said softly. "Not with me."

She felt him slump as his breath exploded in a long exhalation. "I've never told anyone," he said. "And I'm not at all sure I want to tell you."

Rose's grip softened on his shoulders. Her fingers began to massage the tightness from the rock-hard muscles, avoiding the tender area of his bandaged wound. He moaned out loud. "Sweet heaven, but that feels good," he murmured.

"Sit down, and I can make it feel even better, for the price of your story."

He sank onto the edge of the porch with a mutter of defeat. Rose knelt behind him, her strong hands expertly working the broad planes of his shoulders. The fire inside her had burned down to a low, simmering ache.

"Mrs. Lucinda Packer," he said, speaking the name of the reverend's wife as if every syllable were a vile taste in his mouth. "She was younger than her husband and not bad looking, not that it made any difference to a lonely boy who missed his mother. She was kind to me, at least behind her husband's back. When he beat me, she would stand by and never do a thing to stop him. But afterward she'd sneak up to my room and bring me a sweet and rub liniment on the welts. It was good to have somebody, anybody, who cared about me. Or so I thought."

He fell into a brooding silence. Rose's hands paused, then slipped down his back to drop quietly to her lap as she waited for him to continue.

"Things went on as usual until—" He cleared his throat, ill at ease, even with the memory. "Until I started growing up. The first year I was taller than she was, and my voice began to change, I began to notice her looking at me."

Rose gazed at the back of his dark head, mute with dismay as she sensed what was coming next.

"Not that I thought much about it," he added, forcing every word. "I was young and had other things on my mind. But when she came to my room with the sweet and the liniment, she began to stay longer. She'd stroke my back, curl my hair around her fingers—"

He broke off, shifting his buttocks on the steps so that he was looking directly at Rose. His eyes were veiled by pools of shadow. "Tell me you don't want to hear the rest of this," he said.

Her fingers stole out to lie on the back of his hand. Her sensitive palm felt the cool, leathery skin, the veins and sinews, the trembling pulse beneath. "I think I need to hear it," she said softly.

A shudder passed through his body. "One night when I was about sixteen, I was in my room, taking a bath in the big tin washtub I'd hauled up there. I heard the door open. Mrs. Packer walked in, wearing nothing but her robe, and she asked me if I wanted her to scrub my back. I said no and tried to hide myself in the water, but she came close and started…washing me."

He gazed down at their joined hands. "I was innocent," he said. "None of the girls in the town, not even the easy ones, would let a half-breed Apache touch them. But I was no saint, Rose. I glanced around and saw that she'd dropped her robe on the floor." His face darkened as, once more, he fell into an awkward silence.

"You were only a boy," Rose protested gently. "You can't be blamed if an experienced woman seduced you."

"*Seduced* me!" His laugh was raw edged as he withdrew his hand from hers and balled it into a bitter fist. "If only it had been that simple!

"I'd heard the old Bible story about Joseph and the wife of Potiphar, and I knew it was time for me to cut and run for my life. But when she reached around me and put her hand in the water, it was as if—" He stared up at the moon, then down at his boots, everywhere except at Rose, as he spoke around the knot in his throat.

"Right about then, we heard the front door open downstairs and realized it was the reverend coming home early from his church committee meeting. There was no place to hide, but Mrs. Packer found a way out. As her husband came up the stairs, she started screaming like a banshee and ripping at her robe.''

"And you were blamed for attacking her," Rose whispered.

"I didn't wait around to find out. It took me about two seconds to weigh the odds against my being believed, throw my clothes and boots out the upstairs window and disappear after them. I didn't stop running for the next nine days.''

"Just like you're running now?" Rose stood up and brushed the dust from her skirts.

"Just like I'm running now." He leaned forward with his elbows braced on his knees, staring stubbornly across the yard at the corral.

"And you think I'd betray you the way that terrible woman did?''

He glanced up at her, his eyes hard, black sparks in the moonlight. "It doesn't make any difference, Rose. Either way, there's no justice for an Apache in a white man's world.''

"But it's not fair!" Rose fought the urge to seize his shoulders and shake him. "You were innocent then! You're innocent now!''

His eyelids narrowed, shutting away the emotion in his gaze. "Rose Colby, you're a rare jewel of a person," he said in a razor-thin voice. "You're honest and fair and trusting, and you expect others to be the same. But you're an innocent little fool, because the world isn't like that. People are cruel and treacherous, justice is a mockery, and the only sensible men are cowards!''

"My husband was no coward!''

"Your husband is dead.''

Rose stared at him for the space of a long breath, then turned toward the door, weary from the strain of the past hours. "It will be morning in a few hours," she said. "I'll make us some coffee in the kitchen.'' She paused with her hand on the latch. "I won't try to stop you from going, Latigo. But I want to hear everything you know about the Indian Ring and John's involvement in it. I think you owe me that much.''

Latigo sighed and nodded as he eased himself to his feet and followed her into the house. Leaving him to light the kitchen lamp and stoke the fire, she went upstairs to check on Mason. She found him fast asleep, his breathing even, his skin cool and sweet.

Crossing the room again, she caught a glimpse of herself in the large oval mirror that hung above her dresser. She paused, transfixed by the face staring back at her, pale in the moonlit darkness. It was a passionate face, the eyes large and intense, the lips full and damp, the sharp cheekbones heightened by shadows. A sensual face, flickering with hidden fires. A stranger's face, disturbing, frightening, intriguing. A face she could barely recognize as her own.

Night was the time of ghosts, a time when the Apaches, even the bravest warriors, kept close to their fires and did not hunt or fight. Even after years in the white man's world the old tales of owl spirits and monsters stirred in the corners of his mind, whispering to him in the darkness.

But it was no Apache ghost that troubled him tonight, Latigo noted as he started the coffee. It was his own ghosts—his emotions, his desperate acts, his past and his future, swirling around him on the fringes of the lamplight.

He had spent most of his life on the run, running from trouble, from involvement, from injustice, and from the fact that he had turned his back on his own people. But here on this ranch he had suddenly been brought up short. The passion, courage and persistence of one beautiful woman had forced him to stop and face the man he was.

His cheeks flamed as he remembered the electric feel of

Rose in his arms, the sweet, moist fire of her mouth and the eager arch of her body, straining against him in womanly need.

Still wanting her, he cursed his own restraint. How easy it would have been to take her right there on the porch, to fill her with his hard, aching flesh and love her as she had begged to be loved. As he had burned to love her from the first moment he saw her.

Perhaps she was still willing.

But no, he had done the right thing, stopping the blaze before it could consume them both. He cared deeply for Rose, but the love of an outcast Apache, a hunted man, could bring her nothing but anguish.

He could hear her coming back to the kitchen, the familiar light cadence of her steps moving down the stairs and across the tiles. His pulse quickened as she entered the kitchen, her hair framing her face in sweat-dampened tendrils, her eyes luminous in the soft golden light.

His gaze followed her as she flashed him a swift glance, then hurried to the stove to check the boiling coffee. He did owe this woman something. He owed her exactly what she had asked of him—everything he knew about John Colby and the Indian Ring. He would give her that much. Then, for her sake and for his, he would ride out of here and never look back.

Leaving the coffeepot to simmer a few more minutes, she sank onto the edge of the chair across from him. Her hands toyed with the empty cup, balancing it lightly between her fingers as she spoke.

"One thing puzzles me," she said, plunging into the matter at hand. "I can understand John's having been part of the Ring. He hated Apaches. He profited from business with the army. And he had some powerful friends. What I don't understand is why he would turn his back on those friends and work against them."

"You're assuming your husband did turn against the Ring. I told you, there's no proof either way."

"But let's suppose he did," she persisted. "Do you think he could have been informing on the Ring all along?"

"I doubt it. If he had, Henry Scott would've had more to go on than he did." Latigo leaned back in his chair, wishing he had all the answers she needed and deserved to know. John Colby had been a heaven-blessed man to know the devotion of such a woman.

"What would have driven him to do it?" Her gaze held his across the table. "What would he have to gain? Vengeance? The hope of redemption?"

"I was hoping you might be able to answer that question."

She shook her head, her long lashes shadowing her pale cheeks. "Some husbands confide in their wives. John was like a closed book. He told me nothing."

"Did anything happen that might have turned him against his old friends?" he asked. "Maybe a quarrel? A loss?"

"Nothing I was aware of, except—" She paused, then shook her head. "No. That doesn't make sense."

"What doesn't?"

"I was thinking of the Rooney family, poor people. They were homesteading a piece of land just outside the ranch boundary, the parents, two boys in their teens from Mrs. Rooney's first marriage, I think, and two younger— oh, why am I telling you all this? It's leading nowhere!"

"It's all right. Go on." Latigo had not moved, but he felt the sudden kick of his pulse.

"They were so poor they barely had rags to wipe the little ones' noses," Rose said. "I took them some food and clothes, and John promised the big boys work if they wanted it. They were on the porch the next morning, ready to start." She took a tentative sip of her coffee, her eyes closing wearily as she swallowed. "They were good boys. John took a real liking to them. He took them riding, taught them how to rope and shoot. She forced the words. "I suppose they were a substitute for the sons I had never been able to give him.

"One Monday morning, the boys didn't show up for work. John rode over to their homestead to see what had happened to them." Her hands had begun to shake so hard that hot coffee splattered onto the table. "He found them— all of them, the whole family—"

Latigo reached across the table and gently lifted the cup from her hands. "It's all right, Rose," he said softly. "I know what your husband found. I worked with the army commission that investigated the massacre of the Rooney family."

"Then you saw what happened."

"Yes." Latigo had dealt with more than his share of nightmare scenes, but the brutality of the Rooney murders had shaken him deeply. All of them had been scalped, the small children shot full of arrows, the man and boys lanced and hacked to pieces, the woman—

"Apaches." The undertone of horror in Rose's voice struck Latigo like an icy slap.

"No," he said.

She stared at him.

"It wasn't Apaches. Someone tried to make it look that way, but we found plenty of evidence to the contrary. We knew the attack had taken place at night, because a burning lamp had been knocked over. Apaches almost never attack after dark. There were no prints of moccasins or unshod horses anywhere in the yard. The army kept their findings quiet in hope that the real killers might lower their guard. Unfortunately, nothing came of it."

Her agitated fingers twisted a loose button at the neck

of her gown. "You're saying that awful massacre was the work of the Ring?" she whispered.

"More likely some hired thugs, and they would have hightailed it for the border as soon as they picked up their pay. That was my guess, and Major Scott's, as well. The Rooneys were newcomers without many friends, and their homestead was isolated. They were a natural choice for a massacre that could be blamed on the Apaches and used as an excuse to bring in more troops and delay the railroad."

"And John?"

"Your husband was one of several people Major Scott interviewed afterward." Latigo kept his voice flat and emotionless. "But I was gone by then. Some trouble had flared up on the San Carlos, and I was called back to help deal with it. It turned out to be nothing more than a few old women brewing *tizwin,* but it took me away from the Rooney investigation, and I never made it back."

"But if it was the Ring, and if John was part of it, why wouldn't he have known ahead of time? He cared deeply for those boys. He would never have allowed them to be murdered like that."

Rose realized she had just answered her own question. She leaned toward Latigo, her eyes widening. "It's beginning to make sense. John came back from the Rooney place so angry, so bitter."

"It might make sense, Rose. But it isn't proof."

"What if I told you I might have proof?" Her voice was husky with suppressed excitement. "Somebody ransacked John's office after his accident. They—" She broke off, her soft lips parted. "Latigo, why are you looking at me like that?"

"Tell me exactly what happened to your husband," he said, feeling as if a trapdoor had opened beneath him.

She sighed, cradling the porcelain cup between her

hands. "It was an accident, as I told you. A fall from his horse."

"But no one saw it happen?"

"No. The vaqueros found him later that day. He was lying facedown in a wash, they said, with the back of his head smashed and bloodied." Rose's shaking hand splattered coffee into the saucer as the color drained from her face.

"Merciful heaven, I never thought of it," she whispered. "If John had fallen on the back of his head, the wound would have been caked with dirt and sand. Latigo, it wasn't! I dressed it myself, and it was clean! Someone hit him!"

"When did the accident happen, Rose?" Latigo asked quietly.

"July, the twelfth of July."

"Henry Scott died in mid-July." He walked to the window and stared out into the darkness, feeling as if a crushing weight had descended onto his shoulders. "There has to be a connection, Rose, and I can't ignore it any longer. I've no great regard for soldiers, but the major was one of the finest men I've ever known."

Rose had slumped over the table, her hands clasped tightly. "Whoever hit John must have left him for dead," she said, speaking with great effort. "They didn't realize how strong he was. But he might as well have died then and there, for all his life was worth afterward."

Latigo stood beside the window, watching the play of anguish across her pale, tired face. Rose Colby did not deserve any of this, he thought. She deserved a life brimming with love, warmth, security and happiness, all the things a man like him could never give her.

"When your husband died, how did it happen?" he forced himself to ask.

"He just slipped away," she said. "Alone, in his sleep.

It was strange, now that I think of it, because in his last few days, he'd begun to rally a bit. He didn't speak, but his eyes seemed brighter, more alert, almost as if he recognized me and knew what was going on. We'd begun to hope, both Bayard and I—''

''Bayard Hudson was there?''

''I told you, Bayard was devoted to John. He rode out from Tucson every few days to sit with him. John didn't know him either, of course, but at least he—'' She stared at Latigo, sensing the growing darkness in his expression. ''What's wrong? What are you thinking?''

''Tell me exactly how it happened.''

''There's not much to tell. Bayard had been with him for a while that afternoon, but he had to go back to Tucson. He told me—''

Rose gasped softly, then continued in a strained whisper. ''I was in the parlor, knitting an afghan for the baby. Bayard came downstairs from the bedroom. He told me John was sleeping, and that I should let him rest awhile because he'd seemed unusually tired. About an hour after he left, Esperanza went up to tidy the room. I heard her scream.''

Rose pushed her chair away from the table. ''No,'' she said, rising shakily to her feet. ''It can't be true, what we're both thinking. Heaven knows, Bayard is capable of some mean, underhanded tricks, but not *this,* Latigo. Not the cold-blooded murder of his best friend!''

Latigo rubbed his eyes. He could feel the hot coffee simmering through his veins, jarring his system into a state of nervous wakefulness.

''We can't ignore the possibility,'' he said. ''Hudson had a motive—you. He had the opportunity and the means. It would've been easy enough for a man his size to smother an invalid with a pillow. But suppose you're right. What are the chances John would have died of natural causes?''

''The doctor had examined John a few days earlier. His

heart was strong, his lungs clear, his appetite as good as could be expected.'' Rose sank back onto the edge of her chair, too shaky to stand.

''Tell me about the ransacked office.'' Latigo forced himself to pull back emotionally and step into the familiar role of investigator.

''Someone had gone through the drawers and files and just dumped everything back, something John would never have done. When I told Bayard he was anxious to help me—''

''You told Hudson about this?'' Latigo regretted the snapped question at once, but it was too late to bite it back.

''The office was open,'' Rose said quietly. ''He saw that I had been going through John's papers.''

''Did he seem nervous? Agitated?''

Her eyes glinted like shards of ice. ''I'm quite aware that Bayard could have been the one who went through John's things,'' she said. ''Unfortunately, as with everything else, we haven't a shred of proof.''

''No proof except what may still be in that office.''

Her fingers raked her tumbled hair, pushing it back from her face as she spoke. ''I've gone through everything in the drawers and files. It was a waste of time. There's nothing there.''

''Then why was Hudson so all-fired anxious to help you?'' Latigo was too tired to hide his irritation.

''Maybe he just wanted a reason to get me alone.'' Her indigo eyes challenged him from across the table. Latigo groaned inside, thinking that for two bits, he would gladly chuck this whole line of questioning, seize her roughly in his arms and take up where they had left off outside on the porch.

But it would be no good, he realized. The ghosts had awakened. They were prowling the night, demanding jus tice, demanding truth; try as he might, he could never run far enough to escape them.

Rose Colby's quest had become his own. He was doomed to stay and fight at her side, not only because of what he felt for this gallant woman, but because neither of them had a choice. They had uncovered a glimpse of something so monstrous, so evil, that there could be no more turning away.

Chapter Twelve

"It's no use, there's nothing here." Rose snuffed out the lamp and slumped dejectedly into John's big leather chair. She and Latigo had just spent three hours going through the papers again. Her head ached, her nerves were raw, and the two cups of coffee she'd drunk had turned to pine tar in her stomach.

All for nothing.

"Maybe we just don't know where to look." Latigo leaned back on his boot heels, his buttocks braced against the edge of the desk. His black Apache eyes were sharp and alert in the morning shadows. "Or maybe we're looking for the wrong thing."

"Perhaps there's nothing to look for." Rose sighed wearily. "Maybe Bayard, or whoever it was, found what he needed. Or maybe we're chasing a phantom that never existed in the first place."

"Then, for now at least, that's all we have to go on." He eased his body away from the desk, stretched his spine and shook his shoulders lightly like a long, lean cat rearranging its fur after a nap. Outside, the first rays of sunlight were creeping across the yard.

"As long as I'm going to be here, I might as well mak

myself useful,'' Latigo said. ''While I take care of the chores, you get some rest. You look as if you could use it.''

She stared at him, too exhausted to mask her surprise with civility. ''Is this your way of telling me you plan to stay?'' she snapped.

''Do you want me to stay, Rose?'' Something flickered in the black depths of his eyes. The blend of caution and tenderness shattered her guard, leaving her vulnerable as a schoolgirl.

''That,'' she answered, weighing every word, ''depends on your reasons.''

''My reasons?'' He walked to the window, where he stood for a long moment listening to the crow of a rooster. When he turned back toward her, Rose saw that his expression had hardened like rawhide in the desert sun, and even before he spoke, she knew what he would say.

''Try justice.'' His voice was low and taut. ''Try the realization that what we're looking at is a hundred times bigger than the worth of my own miserable neck. The Ring has to be broken, and you may have put me on the trail of a means to do it.''

''Then you're through running?''

''I ran because I thought there was nothing else I could do. All that's changed now. Between what you know and what I know, the pieces of this monstrous puzzle are falling together, and I have no choice. I have to stay and fight this.''

''Then I'm with you.'' She pushed herself out of the chair, an electric shiver passing through her tired body as she spoke. ''This was John's fight. Now it's mine.''

An anguished groan stirred in his throat. ''No, Rose.''

''No?'' she flared.

''You can't be involved. It's too dangerous for you and the baby.''

"But I'm already involved! Blast it, Latigo, you need
me, we need each other! Why should you stay if you won'
let me help you?"

"Because I know what we're dealing with, and so
should you. Be sensible, Rose."

"It's not a question of sense! You have no right to keep
me out of this!"

She had flung down a challenge, and she braced herself
for a sharp retort, but Latigo's eyes were sad in the gray
morning light as he hesitated, then walked around the table
and gathered her gently into his arms. Her rigid body trembled, still resisting what he had told her.

"Hear me out," he said, his lips brushing the loose tendrils of hair at her temple. "I know we're in this together
but there's one thing you have to understand. For whatever
it's worth, I care for you, Rose. I'd give up my life before
I'd let anything happen to you or to that little one up
stairs."

"You think I'd risk Mason?"

"Not willingly. But what would become of him if you
were to risk yourself?"

Rose softened against Latigo with a low whimper,
knowing he was right. Whatever her own feelings might
be, she could not gamble her son's life or his future.

She buried her face against his hard chest, filling her
nostrils with the warm, leathery aroma of his skin, her ear
with the low, steady beat of his heart, as she pondered the
awful danger to this man whose arrival had shaken the
foundation of her whole world. *Run, Latigo!* she longed to
shout at him. *You were right the first time! Run and save
yourself before it's too late!*

But it was already too late. They had opened the door
on a world of darkness, and even if they wanted to, neither
of them could turn away from what had to be done.

Pride… Honor… Courage… Duty. The words engraved

on her husband's medal echoed in Rose's mind as her arms slid around Latigo's waist, binding him close. John's legacy to his son was, perhaps, a legacy to them all.

"Tell me what you want me to do," she whispered.

He sighed wearily, his arms tightening around her. "I'll stay here, Rose, but only under one condition—you don't know who I am, you don't know anything about me."

Rose pulled back far enough to stare up at him, her eyes shooting questions.

"You already know that if I'm caught, you could be charged with aiding a fugitive," he said. "You could go to jail, lose your son, and lose the ranch. I won't risk any odds of that happening. Are you with me so far?"

"Yes," she whispered, sagging back against his chest.

"I'm a drifter who came by on a spent horse, needing work. If the law catches up with me, that's all you know. You'll be properly shocked to learn I'm wanted for murder, then you'll smile and thank the deputies for hauling me off to a well-deserved hanging." He brushed a kiss across her temple. "Are you still with me?"

"And if I'm not?"

"Then I saddle up and leave right now. I can't involve you in this, Rose. Not openly, at least. Do you understand?"

Rose swallowed a protesting cry, knowing he was right. "I've no choice except to understand," she said, muffling the words against his chest.

He caught her jaw with his thumb, forcing her to look up into his stern face. "There'll be no scheming to set me free, no telling the judge I was framed. You won't know me, and you won't care. That's the way it has to be. Can you promise me you'll do it?"

Rose met the ferocity in his eyes, her heart pounding so hard that she feared it would explode in her chest. "Yes," she whispered. "For my son's sake, I promise you, Latigo."

He leaned down and kissed her, a chaste and tender kiss that lingered on her mouth long after he had let her go. When he stepped away Rose felt him withdrawing from her, as if he had already become a stranger.

Rather than stand and stare at him, she forced herself to move. Her skirt brushed his legs as she squeezed past him to stride out of the office and through the dining room. Latigo hesitated for an instant, then followed her into the kitchen.

Her hands shook as they cleared away the coffee cups, but she made an effort to smile at him. "So, stranger, what name should I call you?" she asked lightly, then frowned. "For that matter, what *is* your real name, Latigo? I've never thought to ask."

He hesitated, and for a heartbeat Rose ached with the hope that he would take her in his arms again. But this, she swiftly realized, was not Latigo's way. He would keep his distance now, making this desperate charade easier for them both.

"I have a number of names," he said, settling onto a chair, "none of any great use. My father's name was Augustin Baroja, and he called me Martin. My Apache name is Nao-tio-tish. When the reverend and his good wife took me in and tried to civilize me, I was baptized Martin Packer. Take your choice."

Rose shook her head, trying to appear amused. "Well, I don't suppose it would be smart to use your Apache name, and after what you told me about the Packers—" She shrugged. "Will you answer to Martin Baroja?"

"That'll do as well as anything." He stood once more, anxious, in his wild way, to be in the open, to be movin' instead of talking. Against all reason, she struggled to hold him there.

"The Spanish name will help explain your dark coloring to anyone who wonders," she said as she piled the cups, saucers and spoons in the dishpan. "You don't happen to speak Spanish, do you?"

"Only border Spanish, but that shouldn't matter. Basques have their own language, not that I know much of that, either." He made a move toward the door. "I'm going out to check the yard for any signs our visitor may have left behind last night. Then I'll move my gear into the bunkhouse and start on the chores. You'd better leave those dishes and get some rest while you can."

"As soon as I'm finished here." Rose averted her face to hide her emotions as she wrung out a cloth and began wiping off the table. She knew what Latigo had in mind. He was creating a safe distance between them, ending the intimacy that would make it unbearable, if and when the time came, to do as she had promised.

He was acting out of wisdom and consideration, she told herself. All the same, as he picked up the pistol, then paused in the doorway, she found herself yearning to call him back to her, to feel his strong arms holding her close and his mouth, sweet and strong on hers, for what might be the last time.

"Latigo." She did not realize she had spoken his name aloud until he turned around to look at her and she saw the naked hunger in his eyes. The cloth dropped unnoticed from her hand. She took a tentative step and would have flown to him then and there, but he stopped her with a warning shake of his dark head.

"Don't come near me, Rose," he said in a low, dangerous voice. "If you do, so help me, I can't be responsible for what happens next."

She froze where she was, but still, he did not go. For a long, poignant moment they gazed at each other through the rays of silver light that slanted onto the tiles. Rose struggled to hold back the words that would pull them both over the precipice. *"I love you, Latigo, don't you see? I want you now because now is all you and I can ever have."*

He groaned aloud as if he had read her thoughts. "Damn it all, Rose," he muttered. "Damn us both to eternal purgatory if I make one move."

The dawn air shimmered between them. Rose felt him hesitate, torn, just as she was, between longing and safety. She waited, forgetting to reason, forgetting, even, to breathe as he took a single step toward her.

At that instant, a plaintive little wail echoed down the stairway. Mason had awakened and was crying for his mother. Rose's face went hot as she felt an answering surge in her breasts. For better or worse, salvation had struck in the form of a tiny, demanding angel.

She saw Latigo turn away without a word, and she knew there was nothing she could say or do. Cold reason was already flooding her mind, drowning the madness of a moment that would never come again.

Mason's cry was growing more insistent by the second. After flinging Latigo a last desperate glance, she spun away and fled from the kitchen. As she mounted the stairs, she heard the click of the latch as he walked out, closing the door firmly behind him.

A rooster crowed from the coop as Latigo crossed the yard. The morning breeze cooled his hot face but not his simmering blood. A moment ago he had been ready for her, ready to toss all reason to the wind, seize her in his arms and carry her to the first blasted place he could get her under him. Even now, though the madness was fading from his mind, his body still raged with the fire of need, a fire that would have ultimately destroyed the tender, vibrant Rose Colby.

The crying baby had saved them both, he told himself as he scanned the still-damp earth for boot prints. The last thing he needed was more ties to bind him to this place. And the last thing Rose needed was the unforgivable stigma of having had an Apache lover.

A buzzard glided above the ranch, passing so low over the open yard that Latigo could see the pale ring around its eye. A momentary chill passed through his body as he watched the grim black wings flap upward again, rising on the morning air to spiral off above the mesa.

Only when he glanced down again did he notice the track, the round, unmistakable print of a bobcat. He dropped to a crouch, examining the impression in the soft, damp dirt. The animal had been a large one, big enough that Rose could have easily mistaken it for a human intruder in the darkness.

Cocking the pistol, Latigo followed the trail into the scrub, where it disappeared in a clump of brittlebush. It would be a waste of time to track the cat farther, he decided, releasing the hammer. In all likelihood, it had crept into the yard to steal a chicken or two, been scared off by Rose's shot and had long since hightailed it back to its den. With luck, it would be too frightened to return.

With a final glance around, he turned back toward the house, noticing as he did so that new salt grass was already sprouting amid last year's yellow stems. In a few days' time the desert would be ablaze with color and humming with new life.

In the old days, spring had been a time of renewal, hope and celebration for the Apaches. But no longer, Latigo noted darkly. On the bleak, dusty San Carlos, every day was the same: the women lining up outside the agency for their rations of flour and beef; the once-proud warriors, sick with frustration, drinking smuggled rotgut whiskey until they passed out; the children growing up in despair, their traditions dying, their futures uncertain.

As Latigo watched the sun's rays steal across the desert, his mother's people drifted softly through the shadows of his memory. He saw his cousins; he saw his mother and his baby sisters, long dead; he saw his grandmother with her precious herbs. And towering above them all, Cochise, the greatest Apache—no, the greatest *man*—he had ever known.

Latigo bowed under the bitter weight of regret. In his own pride, he had turned his back on these people—the old and the young ones, the wise and the foolish, the strong and the tender. He had walked away from them all, telling himself he was no longer one of them. Once he had dreamed of becoming their voice, the preserver of their history and traditions. Now it was too late, and in the final reckoning of things, he could blame no one but himself.

He entered the barn and found that the swelling on Sundown's leg was almost gone, the cut already knitting at the edges. If the leg continued to improve, he would allow the horse a little exercise tomorrow. He warmed with anticipation, thinking of how pleased Rose would be. He imagined her smile, the deepening of the tiny dimple in her cheek, the flash of sunshine in her eyes, blue and swift, like the flash of a jay's wing. He had seen far too little of that smile.

He milked the cows and fed the stock, including his own gray mustang, which had tired of wildness and wandered in sometime during the night. Then he gathered up his gear, including the saddle, and carried everything into the empty bunkhouse. As his fingers brushed a coil of the tightly braided whip, his arm muscles tightened sharply in response. His shoulder was still weak from the wound, but he could not afford to neglect the strengthening of it any longer. Tonight, when he could not be seen from beyond the ranch, he would begin working with the whip again.

Martin Baroja.

His lip twitched in ironic amusement as he remembered the name Rose had selected for him. He would need more than a name, Latigo swiftly realized. The hired help could return at any time, to say nothing of incidental visitors to the ranch. Any report that a tall, young Basque who looked suspiciously like an Apache was working at the Colby ranch would bring lawmen and bounty hunters swarming like flies to honey.

He would need to think of some way to change his appearance; meanwhile, it was time he went inside and told Rose about the bobcat tracks.

The sun had risen, flooding the landscape with its buttery warmth. Latigo heard the chatter of cactus wrens as he crossed the yard.

"Rose?" He entered the kitchen cautiously, not wanting to startle her, but she was nowhere in sight.

"Rose, can you hear me?" He strode through the dining room and called up the stairs. "Rose?"

The gloomy tick of the grandfather clock echoed in the silent hallway where the sun had yet to reach. A stray fly buzzed against the ceiling. There was no other sound to be heard.

Dread gripped Latigo's heart as he mounted the stairs, cocking the pistol as he climbed. He had been in the barn for a good fifteen or twenty minutes, ample time for someone to break into the house. If anything had happened to Rose and the baby—

He reached the landing, flattened his body against the wall and edged along the hallway toward the bedroom. Any unwelcome guests would have heard him come in. They would be waiting, most likely armed.

The tick of the clock droned up the stairwell, measuring

each heartbeat with cold, mechanical precision as Latigo approached the half-opened door. A bead of sweat formed on his temple, quivered for an instant, then trickled down the furrow between his cheek and his ear.

He could see inside the room now, almost as far as the bed. There was no movement, no sound. Tensing like a cat, he sprang at the door, swung it all the way open and burst into the room—only to find nothing but peace and stillness and heart-stopping beauty.

Rose lay curled on the coverlet, fast asleep. Her open bodice revealed, cradled in a nest of ecru lace, one bare ivory breast, like veined marble, with its exquisitely swollen mauve-brown nipple. Latigo's knees weakened as the tension drained from his body. His throat tightened as he struggled to avert his gaze.

The baby lay in the curve of her body, gurgling softly and playing with its fingers. Time froze as Latigo stood at the foot of the bed, staring through the barred gate of heaven. Rose's face was soft in the morning light. Her parted lips were moist satin petals, ripe for kissing, her tousled hair spun gold in the light of the new day.

Latigo ached to reach out and stroke the sweet, forbidden silk of her breast, to bend down and burn a trail of kisses along the delicate ridge of her collarbone, to touch, smell and taste her skin with such gentle ferocity that she would not even know whether she was awake or dreaming.

His fantasies broke rein as he imagined slipping her son back into the cradle, then stretching out beside her on the bed and pressing the full length of her lovely body against his own. He imagined teasing her to a drowsy wakefulness as he unbuttoned her gown, pausing to nip and nuzzle her throat and taste the moist richness of her mouth, all with such exquisite restraint that she would moan for more, her frenzied fingers raking his hair and clasping his shoulders.

Even then, he would take his time, stroking, licking and

grazing until both of them were hot and damp and quivering with desire. Only then would he invade the fragrant labyrinth of petticoats and drawers, sliding his hand up the warm, satiny length of her thigh until his fingertips nested in the crisp mat of curls that guarded the wet velvet heart of her womanhood. There the stroking, nipping and nuzzling would begin all over again, until...

Latigo's mouth had gone dry. His pulse was a ragged, racing torment. He swore under his breath as he wrenched his thoughts aside, forcing his mind to shatter the fantasy before it could carry him over the edge of madness. Making love to Rose would be the sweetest heaven he had ever known, he had no doubt of that. But the price, in guilt and remorse, was a hell they would carry for the rest of their lives.

He exhaled slowly, looking down at her where she lay curled protectively around her child. Even making love to Rose would not be enough, he mused in an agony of tenderness. He wanted to know every moment of this woman's life, waking and sleeping. He wanted to protect and cherish her, to fight for her, to provide for her, to surround her with the joy and devotion neither of them had ever known.

Heaven help him, he loved her.

He loved her beauty, her warmth and her courage. He loved her all-too-rare smile and the secret pain that flickered in the depths of her violet eyes. He loved her generous spirit, her passion for truth and justice.

He loved Rose Colby with all his being, as he had never loved before and would never love again.

And this moment, gazing down at her sleeping face with the bitter sweetness of knowing, was all of her he would ever have. It was a moment he would carry with him for the rest of his life.

Latigo allowed his eyes to linger for the space of a long

breath. Then he forced himself to turn away, walk quietly out of the bedroom and down the stairs.

As the clock struck eleven, Mason began to fuss. Startled by the noise, Rose jerked herself awake. What time was it? What day was it?

She sat up, blinking. The top of her dress was unbuttoned. Yes, she was beginning to remember now. Exhausted from the long night, she had stretched out on the bed to nurse the baby. That was the last thing she recalled. Until now.

The air in the room was hot and bright, and Mason was crying to be fed again. She had slept for several hours, she realized. The day was half gone.

Propping the pillows behind her, she gathered up the squalling Mason and snuggled him against her breast. He latched onto her nipple, making small, hungry, sucking noises as he drank. After last night's fever scare, the sound was heaven to Rose's ears.

She closed her eyes, trying to relax as she gathered her thoughts. Images and sensations swirled through her mind. Latigo, his fierce black eyes, his rough, tender mouth utterly possessing her, coaxing her to a frenzy of need. Hot color crept into her face as she remembered clinging to him, pressing her body against his hardness and begging him to make love to her.

Begging.

She stared down at her rumpled skirt on the coverlet, at her legs, her feet, still encased in their proper brown high-topped shoes. She gazed at her suntanned, work-worn hands where they cradled her son.

Who was this woman, Rose Colby? Merciful heaven, she was no longer sure.

In her marriage, she had submitted to John out of wifely duty and longing for a child. Their couplings had brought her, at best, a frustrating sense that real pleasure was just out of reach. She had never known, never even dreamed, that she could want a man the way she had wanted Latigo last night.

He had been the one to back off. He had been the one with the strength and wisdom to stop them short of disaster. She had been all too ready to give up her very soul for a deeper taste of the ecstasy that had rippled like hot honey through her body.

Latigo had been right, she told herself firmly. Now, with harsh late-morning sunlight streaming into the room, she could see the common sense of his actions. But last night in his arms, her reason had vaporized in the heat of desire. She had been all fire, all passion, a woman she scarcely knew.

Her thoughts scattered like quail at a sudden familiar sound from the yard below. It was the jingle of harness brass, the snort of a tired horse and the thin, rapid, oddly metallic patter of Mexican voices. Miguel and Esperanza had returned at last.

Rose's heart leaped, then somersaulted in sudden panic. Latigo. She had to warn him.

But he would have heard them by now, she realized. And even if he'd managed to get out of sight, he could not hide forever. He would either have to face them or slip away into the desert.

Mason was still ravenous. She shifted him to the other breast, helplessly waiting for whatever was to happen next. The seconds crawled by, marked by the ticking of the grim, old clock. Then Rose heard the door open and Esperanza's heavy tread on the stairs.

"¿Niña? ¿Dónde estás?" The shrill but motherly voice echoed up the stairwell. Esperanza had been John's housekeeper when Rose arrived at the ranch as a frightened young orphan. The pet name, *niña*, little girl, was an affectionate carryover from those painful early days. It was a name that Esperanza persisted in using even though Miguel and the vaqueros all addressed Rose as *Señora.*

"*¿Niña?*" She bustled into the bedroom like a bright-feathered bantam hen. Her sharp brown eyes rolled disapprovingly as she took in Rose's disheveled hair and red-laced eyes.

"*¡Santa madre!*" Her fingers stabbed the air, punctuating her words. "I go off for a few days and come back to find you looking like you slept in your clothes, if you slept at all! What in the name of the sweet Virgin have you been doing to yourself?"

"Mason had a fever. I had to sit up with him." Rose could not bring herself to explain more. Her thoughts were fixed on Latigo and his safety. Mexicans and Apaches had been bitter enemies for as long as anyone could remember. If Miguel and Esperanza knew that the law and the army were looking for a fugitive Apache scout, anything could happen.

"A fever? *¡Pobrecito!*" Esperanza kept up her chatter as she scurried about the room, straightening a cushion here, catching a flick of dust there. "But look at him now! Eating away like a little coyote, *gracias a Dios.* If anything had happened to him, *niña,* I would never forgive myself for not having been here! *Ay,* that devil rain! The floods washed out three bridges. We had to get back here by way of—"

She stopped speaking, her eyes suddenly fixed on the open doorway. Rose's heart jumped so violently she could almost feel it crash against her ribs, but when she turned, she saw only a plump, shy-looking Mexican girl, who looked to be about fifteen, standing hesitantly on the threshold.

"My grandniece, Juanita," Esperanza announced, beaming. "She's a strong worker and a good girl, not the sort you'd worry about sneaking into the hayloft with some no-good vaquero.'' Her tongue clicked like a castanet. ''I brought her from Fronteras to help you with the baby, *niña,* so you can rest and make yourself pretty again, maybe find yourself another husband, a young and handsome one this time, to make you laugh in bed, no?''

''But I don't—'' Rose bit back her protest as she saw the hurt flicker in the girl's large, chocolate eyes. She smiled and extended her free hand. ''*Bienvenidos,* Juanita. We're very glad you have come,'' she said gently.

The plump brown fingers crept timidly into Rose's clasp, then withdrew, still trembling, to hide in the folds of Juanita's faded calico skirt. Where was Latigo? Rose wondered frantically. Had he gone? Had anyone seen him?

''She doesn't speak a word of English,'' Esperanza added, chatting on as if nothing in the world were amiss. ''But then, neither does your little one. They can learn English together, *¿verdad?''*

Mason had finished nursing. Distracted by all the noise in the room, he pushed himself away from Rose's breast and began glancing curiously around. At the sight of his round blue eyes, Juanita's shy face burst into an ecstatic smile.

Softening, Rose eased her son into the girl's eager arms. Juanita gathered him close, rocking him in her arms and making little clucking noises that sent Mason into peals of baby laughter.

Esperanza nodded her approval. ''Juanita is the firstborn of my nephew's nine children. She is good with babies, no?''

''Yes, I can see that.'' Rose fumbled with her bodice, feeling strangely torn. She would need more help if she was to manage the ranch efficiently, she reminded herself. And Esperanza was getting too old and arthritic to be running after a growing child. But Mason was *hers,* and the sight of him, so happy in this young stranger's arms, sent an odd pang shooting through her heart.

Something quivered inside her chest as she remembered Mason lying snuggled against Latigo's bare, golden skin. Seeing him there, peaceful and contented, had seemed so natural, so right.

Rose struggled to calm her screaming nerves. Where was Latigo? What had happened to him in the hours since he had kissed her all too gently and walked out into the dawn?

"We should never have gone away and left you, even though you told us to, *niña,*" Esperanza was saying. "When the storm came and made us late, we were so worried about you, all alone, with so much work to do. How fortunate Señor Baroja happened along when he did!"

Rose's head jerked toward Esperanza. Questions flashed in her eyes, questions she dared not ask.

"Señor Baroja, the man you hired. He came out of the barn as we pulled into the yard and offered to help Miguel unhitch the horses." Esperanza's tongue clicked again. "A good hombre, I think. But what a pity you couldn't have found someone younger, with two good legs!"

Rose stared at her blankly.

"You look exhausted, *niña.* A nap and a warm bath will do wonders for you. Let me get Juanita's things into the little room off the kitchen, then as soon as she's fed, I'll put her to work heating some water and carrying it up-stairs."

She spoke in rapid-fire Spanish to Juanita, and the girl reluctantly passed the baby back to Rose. Then the two of them trooped out of the door, their chatter echoing along the corridor until they reached the first landing on the stairs.

Rose was off the bed as soon as their voices faded.

Clutching Mason in her arms, she flew across the room to the window, nudged aside the lace curtain and peered anxiously down into the yard.

She could see the wagon near the barn, with the two-horse team still standing between the traces. Two men were working to unbuckle the heavy harnesses and carry them inside. One was Miguel in his broad Mexican sombrero. The other—her breath caught in a little gasp as he came around the wagon, graying, stoop shouldered, and limping slightly on a stiffened left leg.

Rose's knees went weak as she watched him. The disguise was so perfect, so natural that if she hadn't known better, even she might have been fooled. Any visitor to the ranch, including the help, might mention the presence of a middle-aged Basque with a limp, but that should raise no alarm. Not when the law was looking for a young, virile half-breed Apache who, by now, had likely crossed over the Mexican border.

But danger was all around, she swiftly reminded herself, and anything could go wrong.

Chapter Thirteen

It was midafternoon when Rose glanced out of the upstairs window and saw someone approaching on the road from Tucson. Whipping John's old binoculars from their case, she lifted them to her eyes and focused, with effort, on the moving brown dot.

It appeared to be a lone rider, moving his mount at an easy trot. As he came into closer view, she saw that he was dark and slightly built. Mexican, she judged. Lashed to the back of the saddle was a bulky-looking package wrapped in brown paper.

Latigo had propped a ladder against the frame of the *ramada* and was working to restore its storm-damaged roof. Rose's gaze had secretly followed him for much of the afternoon, but he had not betrayed himself with so much as a glance in her direction.

The rider, sighting the ranch, had spurred his horse to a gallop. Rose weighed the wisdom of warning Latigo with a shout. As she hesitated, her hand on the window frame, she saw him freeze in midmotion. An instant later he had climbed down the ladder and limped swiftly into the barn.

Rose hurried downstairs, emerging half-breathless onto

the covered porch as the young rider galloped into the yard. He was everything she had guessed him to be.

"Señora." He pulled up short of the porch and swung his wiry body out of the saddle. The tall bay horse's sides were flecked with foam, Rose noticed, and the animal appeared much too fine to belong to him.

"¡Señora!" He grinned, doffing his hat in a deep, mocking bow. "I have brought for you a letter from Tucson, and also a package. A present, I think."

"Who sent you?" Rose asked, although she knew, with a sinking heart, what the answer would be.

"One very fine *señor*. Very rich. 'Find the most beautiful lady in all of Arizona,' he told me. 'Give these things to her. Then come right back to me with her answer!'" He reached into his leather vest and, with a flourish, whipped out a square, sweat-stained envelope.

Rose accepted it with a sigh. "There's feed and water for your horse in the corral. When you've taken care of him, go around to the kitchen and ask the cook for some eggs and beans. After that, you can go back to Tucson and tell your very fine *señor* to take his—"

"Wait!" The young Mexican halted her would-be tirade with a staying motion of his palm. "First you must see what he has sent you. I confess I took a small look myself. It is *magnifico!*"

He unlaced the package, swept it off the horse in a single motion and thrust it into Rose's reluctant hands. "The *señor* told me I was not to leave until you had opened this gift, and the letter also," he said, flashing his impudent grin.

"Then I shall open everything at once, just to be rid of you!" Rose wheeled and swept into the house, muttering under her breath as she closed the door firmly behind her. Bayard had his gall, sending her a present after the way he had behaved. She would send it back, she vowed, with a reply so scathing that it would end his courtship once and for all!

She carried the envelope and package into the dining room, hesitated, then walked into John's office and closed the door. Esperanza would be all too eager to see what the messenger had brought, and Rose wanted no meddling, motherly advice.

The envelope was sealed in wax, emblazoned with Bayard's own stamp, the gaudily entwined initials, *B* and *H*. Irritated by the mere sight of them, she broke the seal and ripped open the envelope.

The paper that tumbled out onto the desk was not a letter but a stiff, printed card. When Rose picked it up, she saw that it was an engraved invitation to the Governor's Ball and Reception at the Carillo Gardens in Tucson.

She stared at the elegantly raised letters, her annoyance mounting with each breath. She had told Bayard in no uncertain terms that she would not go to the ball with him. Why did he persist in this useless, maddening pursuit of a woman who could scarcely abide his company?

Flinging the invitation onto the desk, she slashed away the net of strings that bound the thick brown package. The invitation was presumptuous enough, but the idea that he would send her a gift was beyond all—

Her thoughts froze as the paper parted to reveal gleaming folds of ebony satin, lavishly embroidered with tiny jet beads. For all her dismay, Rose gasped as she lifted the gown from its wrapper and held up its full length. From the low, beaded bodice to the narrow waist, elaborately flounced bustle and elegantly flared skirt, the sight of it shook the very roots of her conservative Quaker soul.

Bayard's offering was the most scandalously beautiful piece of clothing Rose had ever seen.

The idea that it had come from him, that he expected her to wear it for *him*, filled Rose with cold fury. Her hand groped for the scissors on the desk as, for one blinding moment, she contemplated slashing the gown and sending it back to Bayard in tatters.

But then another image flickered in her mind—weary eyes straining to see black against black by the light of a guttering candle; hands, thin and work worn, stitching every inch of seam, every tiny bead, fashioning an object of heartbreaking beauty to be worn, admired and treasured. Some poor seamstress had put the hours and days of her life into this gown. It was no fault of hers that Bayard Hudson had been the one to buy it.

With reverence for its hard-won beauty, Rose quietly refolded the soft, black satin. The fabric glided like water beneath her fingertips as she laid it onto the paper and smoothed out the wrinkles. She would send it back with the messenger and give no other reply, she resolved. Words, even angry words, would only challenge Bayard to try again.

The string that had bound the package was too hastily cut to reuse. But hadn't she noticed a spool of twine in John's top drawer? Impatient to finish the task and send the insolent young Mexican on his way, Rose jerked open the drawer and began rummaging inside. Only as her fingers touched the twine did another notion strike her with such lightning force that she forgot the gown, forgot the messenger, forgot the Governor's Ball.

She and Latigo had spent hours going through John's files in an effort to find some link to the Ring. Wasted hours, because they had found nothing. But then, why should they? Why would John keep damaging evidence with his ordinary papers?

If there was anything to be found, it would have to be someplace else, someplace hidden where no one else would think to look.

Heart pounding, she pulled out the drawer where she

had found the twine. She tested the sides and bottom for thickness. She reached into the empty recess of the desk and explored the backing with anxious fingers. Nothing. But there were other drawers. Nine more of them to be exact.

Moving like a whirlwind now, Rose tugged out each drawer one by one. She tested each panel—bottom, ends and sides. She groped the space where each drawer was removed in the desk and cabinet. When her search yielded nothing, she dragged each heavy piece of furniture away from the wall and checked behind it.

She found no more than a few dusty cobwebs and one small, scurrying spider.

She sank into the big leather chair, wanting to cry with frustration. Someone else had searched, too, she knew. Someone with a compelling and fearful reason had invaded John's office and pawed frantically through his records. There had to be an explanation. There had to be something to find.

She remembered Bayard's anxiety, his insistence on helping her sort the papers. Every suspicion pointed in his direction. He had been here in the house countless times since John's accident. He'd certainly had no lack of opportunity.

But what about motive—a motive so black that it would drive a man to murder?

Rose stared at the half-crumpled invitation to the Governor's Ball as she struggled with the elements of a giant mental jigsaw puzzle, each piece so monstrous that her mind refused to grasp the entire picture. The Ring. The massacre of the Rooney family. The death of Major Scott, so close in time to John's accident and so chillingly similar. John's death and the ransacked drawers. And then, there was Latigo and his own tragedy. Latigo, moving the pieces of the puzzle, drawing them together, forcing her to examine what she was afraid to see.

Had Bayard Hudson ordered the murder of innocent people? Had he killed John in cold blood, with his own hand?

There was no proof. But if proof existed, she owed it to John, to Mason, to Latigo, and to herself to find it.

A shiver passed through her body. Finding proof, she knew, would demand a bolder course of action than searching John's safe, quiet office. It would demand all the courage she possessed.

Rose's hand shook as she picked up the invitation to the Governor's Ball and stared at the elegantly engraved script. Forcing herself to rise, she laid the invitation on the desk, lifted the black satin gown from its wrapping, shook it out to its full length and held it up to her shoulders. As her hand brushed the hollow of her throat, she felt the erratic throb of her pulse. She felt fear coiled like an ice-blooded living creature in the pit of her stomach, and for an instant, she all but lost heart.

She closed her eyes, marshaling her strength. This act would be her gift to a tormented man on the run, she vowed. It would be her gift to a little boy who would never know his father.

Opening her eyes again, she laid the gown over the back of the chair, turned and walked resolutely out of the office to find Bayard's messenger.

The moon that shone through the blackness was as round and yellow as the eye of a giant cat. Its cold light gleamed on Latigo's bare chest where he stood in a desert clearing, the long, braided whip coiled in his hands.

Taking his time, he worked his sore shoulder to loosen the muscles. Only when he felt ready did he uncoil the whip, bring it up behind him, then plunge it forward to send its full, sinuous length singing through the dark night air.

At the sound of the snap, a flock of roosting doves exploded from a nearby paloverde. Startled, Latigo froze as they scattered into the night.

He had put more than two hundred paces between himself and the ranch buildings. All the same, he could not shake the feeling that he was being watched.

Glancing around again, he brought his arm back and felt the ripple along the whip as it caught the air. He gave it an instant to straighten, then brought it forward with a forceful snap that triggered a jab of pain in his shoulder. He was still weak, he lectured himself. Slow and easy, that was the way of wisdom tonight.

A third time, then a fourth and a fifth, he sent the braided lash whistling through space. Only as he paused to catch his breath did he realize the darkness had fallen abruptly silent. Latigo dropped to a crouch, nerves quivering as he listened. His ears caught a sound as subtle as a heartbeat in the darkness—the faint crunch of a pebble, forced into the sand by the pressure of a single footstep.

His fist tightened around the whip, the only weapon he had brought with him. "Who is it?" he rasped. "Come on out!"

In the dead quiet that followed, the night wind rustled the small, new leaves of a mesquite bush. Then Latigo's breath caught as Rose stepped into the clearing clutching her skirt to avoid the treacherous clumps of cholla. His heart contracted at the sight of her.

The night wind lifted her pale hair as she hurried toward him, stunningly beautiful in the moonlight. Latigo steeled himself against the urge to catch her in his arms, crush her close and burn her alive with his kisses.

"What are you doing here, Rose?" He kept his voice

cool, his manner distant. "Why didn't you let me know you were out there?"

She stopped an arm's length away from him, slightly out of breath. Vulnerability flickered in her soft violet eyes, and he realized that his aloofness had hurt her.

"I was watching you, that was all," she said. "And I needed to talk to you. I've been waiting all evening. I—" Her raised hand crumpled into a small, indignant fist. "Oh, blast it, don't look at me like that, Latigo! I've done nothing at all to deserve that scowl of yours!"

Latigo sighed, disarmed once more. "How did you know where to find me?" he asked more gently.

"I didn't. I tried the bunkhouse, and you weren't there. Then I heard the sound of your whip and followed it."

"You shouldn't be out here, Rose. It could be dangerous for you."

"You're out here."

"That's different." He battled the wild sensations that her nearness evoked in him. She smelled of fresh lavender soap. He yearned to bury his nose between her soft, white breasts and fill his senses until he was staggering drunk on the scent of her. He wanted to touch her, to taste her. He forced himself to glance past her into the darkness.

"I see you're busy," she said guardedly, backing off a step. "Go on, then. Don't let me interrupt your practice."

"My arm's had enough for tonight." Latigo exhaled slowly, taking time to coil the whip into a tight circle and fasten it into the loop on his belt. "Come on, I'll walk you back to the house."

"As Martin Baroja, or as Latigo?" The lightly phrased question carried an edge.

"Take your pick." He placed a hand at the small of her back and steered her firmly in the direction of the yard. He could feel the resistance in the rigid posture of her spine. It was just as well she didn't know what he really felt like doing to her, Latigo mused darkly. But he could not afford to dwell on that now. He needed to get her back to the house before his willpower crumpled.

"I said I wanted to talk to you." She fought the impelling pressure of his touch. "The least you can do is stop and listen!"

Latigo exhaled slowly. They had come within fifty yards of the house and were passing beneath the crown of a large paloverde. Its limbs hung low, sheltering them from view. This was as good a spot as any. "All right," he said, a bit too curtly. "I'm listening, Rose."

She glared up at him, bristling with frustration. Once more, he ached to gather her into his arms and hold her until her sweet body melted into his, until the whole world drifted away from them, leaving them alone in the dark intimacy of night.

"Have your servants said anything?" he ventured in an effort to break the tense silence between them. "Do you think any of them suspect me?"

She shook her head, her hair moving softly in the wind. "They're trusting people. Good people. They'll take you at your word."

"Not if they find out I'm part Apache."

"They won't find out. But that's not what I came to tell you."

Latigo allowed the raising of an eyebrow to serve as a question. She stared down at her hands, then abruptly met his gaze again.

"I'm going to the Governor's Ball this Saturday," she said. "With Bayard Hudson."

Latigo felt his heart lurch. "So, are you asking for my blessing?" His voice was flat and cold.

She glared at him as if he'd slapped her. "Blast you, Latigo! Don't you even want to know why?"

"I'd say it's none of my business."

Her nostrils flared slightly. She took a half turn away from him, as if she were about to wheel off and stalk back to the house. So much the better for her, he lashed himself, even as he fought the urge to catch her wrist, spin her back against his chest and hold her hard.

He knew, of course, that Rose wanted to get information from Hudson. But that didn't make it all right. She would be putting herself in terrible danger, and he was largely to blame. He should never have told her a thing about himself or her husband. He should never have involved her in this unholy mess. He wanted her safe.

But even as he willed her to run away, she spun back to face him. "Don't you see? There's no other way to find the answers we need. We've exhausted everything we know. We've searched John's office and come up empty. I *have* to go to Bayard!"

"No, you don't, Rose." His voice came out rough and angry. "If the man is what we suspect he is, you'll be gambling with your own life. And even if you survive, what makes you think he'll reveal anything at all?"

Her hands came together at her waist, clasping so tightly that the knuckles whitened in the moonlight. "I know I'm taking a risk," she said. "And I know I may not learn much. But I've thought this out. It's an opportunity, an opening."

"Rose—"

"No, listen to me. The ball will be outdoors, at the Carillo Gardens. There'll be plenty of important people there, so Bayard will have to be on his best behavior. He'll have no chance to get me alone."

"What about getting you there and back?"

"I'll be staying at Esther Carmichael's boardinghouse on Main Street. It's only a few blocks away. More than likely we'll be walking to the Gardens. And even if we don't, Bayard's buggy is open, and the street will be crowded, and…'' Her fingers twisted in agitation.

''Don't do this, Rose,'' Latigo said softly.

''I have to.''

''Not for me, you don't.''

She looked up at him, moonlight glinting like Mexican silver in the purple depths of her eyes. ''Not for you,'' she whispered. ''For my son.''

''Even for him, don't do it,'' he said more forcefully. ''Find another way, Rose, or let it go. Nothing is worth your life!''

''And my life is worth nothing, not if John was murdered and I let his killers go free!''

''Don't be a reckless fool!'' he snapped.

''Have you got a better idea?'' she retorted hotly.

''I'll find one. Give me a chance to deal with the Ring in my own way, without dragging you into it!''

''We're running out of time,'' she flung. ''And as for dragging me into it, this is as much my battle as yours, and I'll fight it the only way I can!''

The stubborn jut of Rose's jaw emphasized her words, and suddenly Latigo was sick with fear for this headstrong, beautiful bundle of courage who, whether he willed it or not, had become the center of his whole world.

''I won't let you do it,'' he said, his free hand seizing her upper arm. ''I'll stop you any way I can.''

''You won't stop me,'' she said, her eyes suddenly cold. ''You can't stop me. I thought we were in this together, Latigo, and I came to you tonight for advice and support. If your male pride won't allow you to give me that, then there's nothing more to say.''

She made a motion to pull away from him, but he gripped her arm firmly, his emotions churning, his hard gaze drilling into her eyes. ''Damn it, Rose, do you think you can just walk away and do what you please?''

"Are you jealous? Is that it?" Her words raked him like talons. "Are you so possessive and narrow-minded that you can't stand the thought of my spending time with another man, even a man I despise?"

Something exploded inside Latigo as he jerked her hard against his chest. His rough and angry mouth caught hers, its searing pressure arching her neck, crushing her breasts against him as his kisses punished and devoured her. For the space of a breath she resisted him. Then he felt her body go molten in his arms. She clutched his neck, his hair, returning his kisses with a savagery that sent lightning bolts forking downward to the hard shaft of his desire. Latigo's head spun with the sudden rush of blood. He fought for self-control.

"Jealous?" he rasped, thrusting her away from him. "Listen to me, Rose Colby, I'm jealous of the air you breathe! I'm jealous of the ground you walk on and the bed you sleep in. I'm jealous of every blessed thing that touches you!"

He forced her to look directly into his face. "But, damn it, lady, jealousy has nothing to do with the reason why I won't stand for your going to that dance with Bayard Hudson."

"So you won't help me." He saw the cold anger slide back into her luminous eyes and the steel of determination settle over her moist, deliciously swollen mouth.

At that moment he knew he had lost her. Not that Rose had ever been his to lose, Latigo told himself bitterly. She was as distant and perfect as the moon, a dream he could never possess.

She was the only woman he had ever loved.

"You think you can keep things under control," he said, desperate to appeal to her reason. "But you can't, Rose. The man is powerful and ruthless. If what we suspect is true, he wouldn't hesitate to have you murdered, not if he saw you as a threat. And even if he's as innocent as a newborn lamb, you'd be crazy to be alone with him!''

"I know the dangers," she said curtly.

"And you'd be strictly on your own. There'd be no one around you could trust. Even the sheriff is more than likely in the Ring's pocket."

"I know."

"Then use the good mind God gave you. Leave Bayard Hudson to me."

"Why?" she asked. "Because you're a man and I'm not? How can you deal with Bayard or anybody else when you can't even show your face in Tucson without getting arrested? I have to do this, Latigo. I have to do it because you can't, and I can!"

"Can you?" Latigo seethed with frustration. His grip on her arm tightened as he bit back the urge to shake some sense into her. "I know I can't stop you, Rose. But by all that's holy—"

"You sound like a preacher."

"I was raised by one, or have you forgotten?"

She tore herself out of his clasp with an angry twist of her shoulders. "I came out here hoping you might tell me more about Bayard and the Ring, so I'd have a better idea what to say to him. But I'm not about to fall down on my knees and beg. I don't need you to help me fight my battles. I'm going back to the house, and you can go to—to blazes!"

She spun away and strode out of the lacy shadows into the gleam of full moonlight. Despair tore at Latigo's insides as she walked away. He knew what had to come next, and he knew what he had to say. This moment had been in the cards from that first night, when he had opened his eyes to the heavenly sight of her face.

"Rose," he said softly.

She paused and turned toward him, her hand at her throat, her soft lips parted.

"I'll have my things out of the bunkhouse and be gone before sunrise," he said.

For the space of a heartbeat, she stared at him. Then, without a word, she turned once more and fled, skirts flying, toward the safety of the house.

Latigo kept his word.

When he did not appear for morning chores, Miguel checked the bunkhouse and found his gear missing. By then, Rose had already noticed that his gray mustang was gone from the corral. In spite of what he had told her, the discovery came as a shock. Too anguished to sleep, she had spent most of the night staring down at the yard from the darkness of her bedroom window; even so, she had failed to see him leave.

A passing ghost, gone with the first light of sunrise. His words haunted her now as she sat on the front step, cradling Mason in her lap and watching an eagle drift on silent wings above the mesa. Those words had warned her that Latigo would not stay. But she had been ill prepared for the suddenness of his going or the aching void his absence would leave in her life and heart.

"A strange man, that Señor Baroja, no?" Esperanza sat in the rocker under the shade of the eave, picking bits of rock and chaff from the dry red beans in the hollow of her apron.

"Strange?" Rose was barely aware that she had spoken.

"You know the kind, *niña*. Too quiet. Quick nerves, like a cat's. I suspected from the first moment that he was not what he appeared to be."

"What do you mean?" A growing dread tightened the cords on either side of Rose's throat.

Esperanza's tongue clicked sharply. "What a child you

are! That man, he had the look of a desperado if I ever saw one! Did he steal anything from us?"

"He took nothing that wasn't his own," Rose answered quietly. "I really think you must be wrong about him, Esperanza. Mr. Baroja couldn't have been more kind and helpful, especially after the storm."

"*Quizás, niña.* Perhaps. Your horse, he is walking well today. Miguel had him out of his stall before breakfast for some exercise. Your Señor Baroja knows animals. But that in itself means nothing—and the way the man left, in the night, without a word..." She tossed a handful of tiny rocks off the porch, startling a half-grown rooster that was foraging in the dirt. "Perhaps when you go into town for the fiesta, you should speak to the sheriff about him."

"I'll do no such thing!" Rose masked her fear with an outraged glare. "The man did no harm to anyone while he was here. In fact, I don't know how I could have managed without him after that storm. Whoever he is, I owe him a great debt, and I'll not repay it by—"

Her words broke off as she noticed the shrewd expression in Esperanza's chocolate eyes. "What is it? Why are you looking at me that way?"

The older woman chuckled. "I have known you a long time, *niña,* and I have never heard you speak so passionately about any man. Are you quite sure you did not fall in love with him?"

Rose felt the heat surge upward in her cheeks. "Don't be silly!" she sniffed, toying with the spit curl she had shaped on top of Mason's head. "He was old, almost as old as—"

"Almost as old as your husband, rest his soul?"

"That's not what I was going to say."

The beans rustled sleekly as Esperanza stirred them with her blunt, brown fingers. "Your heart is awakening again. That is good. But you must take care that it awakens to the right man. That Señor Hudson, for one. Oh, I can't truly say I like his way. But he's rich, *niña,* and he desires you. With such a man, you would live like a queen! You would never want for anything!''

"Anything except tenderness and understanding," Rose added wistfully. "Anything except love."

"But love can grow in time! My Miguel and I, our families arranged our marriage. We barely knew each other at first, but as the years passed—"

A fussy little wail from Mason interrupted the story Rose had heard countless times before. She gathered him to her shoulder, grateful for the reprieve.

"Juanita can take him, *niña.* You look tired. You should rest." Esperanza rose heavily from the rocker, holding out her apron to cradle the beans. "She is in the kitchen. I'll call her."

"No, no, leave her be. He's hungry. I'll take him upstairs and feed him. Then it will be time for his nap. And for the tenth time, Esperanza, you're the one who needs Juanita. I can manage the baby just fine, but your arthritis—"

"*Ay, que cosa! Niña,* you are much too young to be telling an old woman like me what to do!" Esperanza's dark eyes sparked as she flounced into the house, making a visible effort to put a spring in her labored step.

Rose followed her inside and trudged upstairs with her son, who, by now, was whimpering to be fed. The massive clock marked the measure of her footsteps with its monotonous, droning tick, a portent of the empty times ahead. Awaiting her were days of watching the horizon for the sight of a lone rider, nights of listening in the darkness for the sound of hoofbeats and the snort of a horse, knowing, as time passed, that she would never see Latigo again.

She nursed Mason, feeling drained and exhausted. When he finally fell asleep at her breast, she was grateful. Tip-

toeing to the cradle, she eased him gently onto his back
and nestled the blue blanket around him. For a long moment she stood looking down at the rosebud perfection of
his tiny, sleeping face. Her quest would be for Mason, she
vowed. Whatever the danger to her, this child would know
the truth about how his father had lived and how he had
died.

The gown hung on the door of the wardrobe, jet beads
glittering in a ray of late-morning sunlight. Bayard had
chosen well, Rose mused bitterly. Black for her widowhood. Gleaming, low-cut elegance for a woman whose
price had been met and paid. The so-called ladies at the
ball would be properly scandalized. So be it. She knew
who her friends were, and she had never held much with
social climbing. As for Bayard, the scandal would touch
him, as well. But the men, who tended to wink at such
foibles or even admire them, would be swift to forgive.
Bayard Hudson had his eye on the governorship, and he
was a man who knew how to get what he wanted.

Unless she found a way to stop him.

Rose shuddered with apprehension, then turned her back
on the gown and walked swiftly out of the room. The
Governor's Ball was two days off. Brooding over it now
would only wear away her courage, just as pining for a
lost love would shrivel her spirit. She had a son to care
for and a ranch to manage. This was no time to huddle in
a corner whining like a spoiled child.

Head high, Rose marched down the stairs. The ledger
in John's office had been neglected since his accident last
summer. She would take the jumble of invoices, statements
and receipts that had piled up in the interim and enter each
one in its proper place. That dreary but needful task should
serve to occupy her for the rest of the afternoon.

And she would lay claim, at last, to John's office, she
vowed. She had searched the small room from floor to

ceiling. She knew every inch of space and every scrap of paper. It was high time she made the place her own.

After pouring a cup of coffee for herself in the kitchen, she crossed the dining room and flung open the office door. The stuffy air enfolded her in its stifling clasp as she stepped inside. John had always insisted on keeping the door closed, she remembered, even when he was working. But she would make a point of always leaving it open.

She set the cup of coffee on the desk. Then, striding to the file cabinet, she picked up the silver-framed tintype of John's first wife and son, folded the stand and slipped it gently but firmly into the back of a drawer. The photograph of John's militia swiftly followed it, then, after a moment's thought, the picture of John with the governor.

The last portrait, showing John on his favorite horse, she left in its place. This was the man she wanted to remember, strong as a weathered mountain cedar, fiercely proud, kind in his own gruff, distant way. He had given her a home, a life and a son. For that she owed him…everything.

Over the past months, Rose had let the ranch paperwork accumulate in a large Pima basket that she kept under the sideboard. Notes, receipts and bills made an untidy pile as she upended the basket on the desk, leaving the older items on top. She would sort everything first, then make the entries in the ledger.

Forcing her hands, eyes and mind to the task, she settled into the big leather chair and began sorting the papers— one pile for credits, one pile for debits, everything ordered by date. Yes, she had let this go much too long, she lectured herself, taking a sip of the still-bitter coffee. But never, never again.

Never again.

Rose quivered as the memories rushed out to drown her. Latigo…the gleam of sunlight on his golden skin, the black spark of flint in his eyes, his restless mind and body, the suppressed animal power in every motion. Latigo holding her in his arms, his mouth awakening womanly desires she had never known she possessed, his hard, hungry body igniting fires in the well of her being; his hands, so strong, so gentle...

She slumped over the desk, reeling with despair. They had parted so angrily, so senselessly. She should have turned back, run to his arms, begged him to stay.

But it was too late. He was gone, driven away by her own angry pride, never to return.

Rose's fist slammed the desktop in an explosion of anguish. The impact of the blow, or perhaps the motion itself, upset her coffee cup, sending a scalding, brown stream spilling over the desk, across the papers and into her lap.

With a yelp, she jumped to her feet and bolted for the kitchen. By the time she returned with a rag, the coffee had spread over the desk. The papers were so soaked and stained she would be lucky to salvage them at all.

Muttering at her own incompetence, Rose sponged the dark liquid from the surface of the desk, blotting the papers and leaving them flat to dry. Only then did she drop to her knees to clean the floor.

Her skirt and petticoats had absorbed much of the coffee that had spilled over the edge of the desktop. Only a few dribbles spattered the earth-colored Mexican tiles. It would take no more than a moment to wipe them.

Rose's heart lurched as she noticed the single tile far back beneath the desk, framed on all four edges with fragments of broken, clinging grout. Hunching lower, she reached out with a trembling hand. The tile was loose. A sharp tap with her fingertip evoked a slightly hollow sound.

Rose's breath came in taut little gasps as she clawed the

tile's elusive edge, struggling to catch it with her fingertips. But even for her nails its fit was too snug.

She had noticed a penknife in John's drawer. Scrambling to her knees again, she swung the office door closed, hard enough to click the latch. Then she swiftly found the tiny knife in the drawer, flung herself to the floor again and jammed the blade into the crack between the tiles.

Her pulse jumped as the tile lifted with a dry, scraping sound. Yes, there was a hollowed-out space beneath. Her groping fingers touched a leather notebook.

A few heartbeats later she had drawn it out and was kneeling on the tiles, clasping it in her hands, staring at the plain, brown cover.

John's portrait seemed to mock her from the wall, challenging her to learn the secrets of who he had been and what he had done. Time itself seemed to stop as Rose opened the book, turned to the first page, the second and the third.

Her shaking hands blurred John's immaculate script before her eyes as the chilling truth slid into place. The intrigues, the brutal schemes, the arranged murders. And the names were names she knew, names whose place in John's narrative shocked her to the roots of her trusting, innocent soul.

And through it all, one awful regret lay like cold stone on her heart. Latigo had departed too soon to see this; he would never learn the full truth. The burden of what she knew, and the responsibility to act on it, was hers alone.

Chapter Fourteen

Latigo crouched like a brooding eagle on the crest of a high sandstone bluff. The setting sun played its thin-fingered heat over his skin as he waited for the vision to come.

For the past thirty-six hours he had not eaten, drunk or slept. He had stripped away every vestige of the white man's world—his clothes, his boots, his weapons. Then he had climbed the rocks to this sacred pinnacle, fixed his gaze on the far horizon and waited for the power that would give him peace.

But now, as the dying sun turned the clouds to flame, Latigo knew that he had failed. It was one thing to strip all tokens of the white world from his body. Removing them from his spirit was another matter.

He had fled to these mountains seeking wisdom. But his heart had not been prepared to receive it. He had spent the length of the day brooding over the murders, the Ring, his days at the Colby ranch, and Rose. Rose, most of all.

He had left her, knowing she would be better off without him. He had left hoping that in his absence, she would abandon her foolhardy course, and hoping that with him out of the way, his enemies would leave her alone.

But now Latigo knew his choice had been wrong. Whatever the cost, he should have stayed and protected her. Even though she could never be his, Rose Colby had a child to raise, a ranch to perpetuate and a lifetime of love to give. She was a woman well worth dying for.

His quest all but abandoned, he remained to watch the colors change in the rocky arroyos below. His eyes followed the play of shadows on wind-weathered rock, the shifting nuances of shape and form.

Mingled with the breeze, he heard the murmur of remembered spirits, some mournful, some accusing and angry, filling him with a sadness so profound that he could have wept.

Forgive me, his mind whispered. *I should have known I was not worthy. I have forsaken the life way. I have wronged my people. Forgive me.*

The wind's harsh tone gentled, and the voice he heard now was that of the old *di-yin,* who had schooled the young boys of his mother's clan.

The question is not one of worthiness, my son. It is only that to begin a new path, you must walk the old path to its end. Only then, as the two paths become one, will you see your way clearly…

An eagle screamed in the dying light of the sun. Latigo flinched, blinked his eyes, and realized he had been dozing. The air had cooled. Blue-black shadows spilled like liquid velvet through the canyons below.

He stretched his cramped limbs and stood up, feeling, still, the sun's lingering heat where his bare soles pressed the sandstone. It was time to leave this sacred place to the spirits who dwelt here. Time to go his own way.

Twilight closed around him as he groped for the precipitous footholds chiseled into the cliffside countless generations ago. As he descended, the words of the old *di-yin,* or perhaps the words of his own heart, echoed in his mind.

To begin a new path, you must walk the old path to its end.

To its end.

He had not received his vision. But the answer had come, all the same. He would walk his old path to its end, the resolution of all that had brought him here.

Perhaps to the end of his life.

From the camp below he heard the mustang snort as its nostrils caught his scent on the wind. Latigo hurried his pace, intent now on what lay ahead and what he must do, and knowing, even now, that time was running out.

Tucson drowsed in the warm spring sunlight. Powdery brown dust rose in lazy swirls beneath the wagon wheels. Brown-skinned children played tag in the open plaza off Congress Street. Carmine-lipped saloon girls lounged in iron-grilled windows along Maiden Lane, their cheap lace fans stirring the indolent air.

A train of burros, their packsaddles loaded with Mexican pottery, plodded along the edge of Main Street. Rose turned her own buckboard aside to pass them. The morning on the road had been long, hot and dusty. For all her dread of the evening to come, she was looking forward to the coolness of Esther Carmichael's boardinghouse, a cup of fresh mint tea and Esther's easy flow of chatter.

Juanita perched beside her on the wagon seat, cradling Mason in the pool of skirt between her knees. The girl was pleasant, eager to please, and very capable with the baby. Rose was grateful to have her along.

The Carmichael boardinghouse, a low structure of sun-baked adobe, was set back from the street in the shelter of two giant cottonwoods. Esther Carmichael, a large-boned, handsome woman of fifty, was waiting on the shaded porch when Rose pulled the buckboard in through the gate.

"Well, it's about time!" She strode down the steps,

beaming. "I've been waiting for you since that smart-mouthed Mexican rode by with the message that you were coming. Your room's all ready, with a pallet for the girl and my old cradle for your little one. My goodness, look how he's growing!"

Rose climbed stiffly down from the wagon, feeling the cold weight of John's Peacemaker in the pocket of her skirt. Dropping to the ground, she hurried to meet her friend's embrace.

Esther and Levi Carmichael had settled in Tucson a decade ago and started a prosperous retail emporium. A few years later, after a series of calamities, Levi, a kind and generous man, had lost it all to Bayard Hudson, who had held a lien on the property. The night Levi signed the transfer papers, he had walked out into the desert and shot himself.

"Come in! Come in!" Esther swept the baby out of Juanita's clasp. "I've got some tea brewing, and fresh apple pie on the table. Leave the wagon. Jacinto can take the horses to the livery stable. I can't wait to find out what you're up to!"

"You'll know soon enough." Rose tottered into the parlor and sank onto a horsehair settee, fanning herself with the broad-brimmed sombrero she'd worn to protect herself from the sun. What would Esther say, she wondered, when she learned that her friend was going to a dance with Bayard Hudson?

"Let me bring you some tea and a slice of pie!" Esther bustled toward the kitchen, still balancing Mason in the crook of her ample arm.

"Not so fast!" Rose hoped her chuckle did not sound too forced. "I need a few minutes to unwind first. But Juanita's probably hungry now."

"I'll put this little mite in his cradle and get the girl a plate in the dining room. Then you and I can do some

catching up!'' Esther shouldered the baby and bustled off
to the kitchen with Juanita in tow.

Rose tried to relax while she waited. But the feeling did
not last. By the time her friend returned to the parlor, she
was staring agitatedly at the far wall, her eyes fixed va-
cantly on a gilt-framed floral arrangement fashioned of fine
wire that had been wound with lengths of human hair. The
locks, in rich tones of brown, red and gold, had been
snipped in youth from Esther's seven children. Esther herself had wrapped and looped the wires to make the exquisite little bouquet.

''Do you want to tell me about it, Rose?'' Esther settled
her stately frame on the opposite end of the settee, crossing
her legs beneath her brown nankeen work skirt. Her sharp
eyes were green, flecked with saffron, a fine foil for her
gray-laced auburn hair.

''I don't know where to begin,'' Rose said with simple
honesty. ''So much has happened, more than I dare tell
even you.''

Esther's eyes narrowed but her low, almost masculine,
voice was gentle. ''Suppose you start by telling me why
you're here and what's in that trunk Jacinto just brought
in from your wagon.''

''Not yet.'' Rose had recovered her steel. ''First I need
to ask you a favor.''

''My dear girl, you don't even need to ask.''

''No, I must ask you this, Esther. And you mustn't answer until you've heard me out. Promise me now, all
right?''

''All right. But I must say, you're looking far too serious
for such a lovely spring day.''

''You'll soon know why.'' Rose fidgeted with her skirt,
then forced her hands to lie still in her lap. ''I've written
up a will. It's in my valise. I plan to have it witnessed and
filed with John's lawyer this afternoon.'' She swallowed

the tightness in her throat, hoping her friend would understand. "Esther, in case anything happens to me, I want to name you as Mason's legal guardian."

"But what can you be thinking?" Esther's eyes widened. "Rose, you're young and healthy!"

"It's a precaution, that's all. John had no close living relatives, and neither do I. It would be foolish to leave such matters to chance."

"Of course, I would take him!" Esther burst out. "I would love him as if he were my own little boy! But Rose, dear, are you sure I'm the one you would want raising your child?"

"Why not?" Rose gazed at her, puzzled and more than a little hurt. "You're my most trusted friend, the person I would want to take my place if something were to happen—that is, if you're willing."

"With all my heart! But, Rose, nothing is going to happen. You're going to live to see your great-grandchildren!"

"I would want Mason to be raised on his land," Rose continued, her words coming in nervous spurts. "The ranch would be your home, just as it is mine. You could live there on the income for the rest of your life. And, of course, if you found a good man and wanted to remarry, he would be welcome, too, and even..." Her voice trailed off as she realized her friend was staring at her in horror.

"Rose Colby, what on earth is going on?" Esther demanded in a tone so vehement that it caused Mason to flinch. "You're talking as if you're planning to leave this life any minute, and frankly, it scares the living daylights out of me!"

"I was about to tell you." Rose tried to speak calmly but her shaking voice betrayed her. "I can't tell you everything because it's too dangerous, but—"

"Dangerous!" Esther's large, expressive hands spread

in exasperation. "What is it you're up to, Rose? Have yo
decided to take on the whole Apache nation by yourself?"

Rose's cheeks flushed as if they had been seared. Sh
knew her friend had meant the question as nothing mor
than a grim joke, but the humor had struck too close t
her heart. No, she swiftly resolved, she could not tell Es
ther about Latigo. She could not afford to tell *anyone* abou
Latigo.

"Rose?"

"It's Bayard Hudson and the Indian Ring," she said
blurting out the words. "I have a weapon to bring then
down, and I'm going to use it. For what they did to Levi
for what they did to John and to so many others, so hel
me, Esther, I'm going to destroy them."

The sun had set, slashing the western sky with bloodre
streaks. As the shops closed their doors, the lights went o
in the saloons. Behind one set of swinging doors, an out
of-tune piano began to tinkle. The evening air swam wit
the aromas of tobacco smoke and simmering chilies.

In the Carillo Gardens, the carefully hung lantern
winked on, one by one like emerging stars, their reflection
shimmering on the black surface of the water. Hired wait
ers and Mexican serving girls scurried back and forth fron
the wagons to the linen-covered plank tables, loaded dow
with trays of tamales, sliced beef and pork, relishes
breads, pies and cakes, chilled beer from the local Pionee
Brewery, and fruit punch sloshing in cut-glass bowls. Th
musicians drifted in and began tuning their instruments o
the small dais reserved for the orchestra. The whine o
discordant strings floated on the darkening air.

In an upstairs chamber of the Carmichael boarding
house, Rose, in her camisole and petticoats, was seated o
a low dressing stool while Esther brushed her hair. Wit

each stroke, tiny explosions of static crackled like summer lightning, underscoring the tension in the small room.

"I still wish you would tell me everything," Esther said. "Who knows, I might be able to help you."

Rose shook her head, pulling against the brush. "I want you safe. The less you know, the better."

"I know more than you might think." Esther twisted the hair experimentally, one way, then another. "In fact, I've been aware of the Ring for years. Men talk around the supper table, you know, and they don't pay much heed to the woman who's ladling out the mashed potatoes."

"I wish you'd told me sooner."

"So do I. But I thought it would only upset you. You were such an innocent, frightened little thing." Esther paused in her brushing. One callused fingertip lifted Rose's chin. The warm, green eyes scrutinized her face. "You've changed," she said. "I can't explain how or why, but you seem more sure of yourself, more purposeful, more... whole."

"Do I?" Rose felt the sharp rise of color in her cheeks, and she knew that Esther had seen it, too.

"Only one thing makes a woman look like that," Esther said gently. "Love. You've met someone, haven't you?"

Rose could not help it. Her eyes flickered away.

"Love gone wrong? Is that it?" Esther guessed. "So wrong that you would take this terrible chance alone?"

Rose swallowed hard, struggling against the anguish that surged like floodwater against a dam of twigs. "Oh, Esther," she whispered.

Esther dropped to her knees, bringing her eyes level with her friend's. "By all that's holy, child, you're not...?"

"No. No, nothing like that." Heat surged below the surface of Rose's skin. "You know what the doctor told me after Mason was born."

"My dear, you can't be certain. Doctors can be wrong."

"No." Rose shook her head vigorously. "It's not what you think. Let me tell you something, something so sad it's almost funny. I wanted him to make love to me, Esther. I wanted it so much that nothing else mattered. Heaven help me, I even begged him. He wouldn't do it. He said he didn't want me to be sorry later."

"He must be a very rare man." Esther stood and resumed her slow brushing. "If you want to talk about him, I'm ready to listen."

"It doesn't matter anymore." Rose could feel the shriveling of her spirit as she spoke the words, making them real at last. "He's gone, gone for good. And it's all for the best. At least that's what I keep telling myself."

"All for the best?" Esther paused in her brushing. "Since when is losing someone you love all for the best? Oh, Rose, he isn't married, is he?"

"No. It's not quite as simple as that. But he's an outsider, a man who believes he'll never belong anywhere."

"That can't be the whole story."

"There's more. He's in trouble, terrible trouble, because of the Ring. What I'm setting out to do tonight is as much for him as for—" Rose stared down at her hands for a long moment, struggling against emotions she could not allow herself to feel. Then, with a toss of her head, she forced a brittle laugh. "This is getting maudlin, isn't it? Help me into the gown, please, Esther. Bayard will be here soon, and I certainly don't intend to keep the gentleman waiting!"

"Your bravado isn't fooling me, Rose Colby." Esther retrieved the ball gown from its hanger on the door of the wardrobe. "But it's not too late to back out. In fact, I'd take great pleasure in meeting Bayard Hudson at the door and telling him you'd changed your mind. Anything to cause that man pain."

"No." Satin enveloped Rose's head, muffling her answer as the gown was pulled on. The fabric slid like cold, black water over her skin, settling onto the curves of her body as if it had been formed there.

"It's not pain I'm looking for," she said quietly. "It's justice."

Rose willed herself to stand still while Esther's patient fingers worked their way up the back of the gown, pulling each tiny button through its satin loop. Again she bit back the temptation to unburden herself and tell her friend everything: the damning evidence in the journal, the terrible scope of the Ring's influence, her strong suspicion that Bayard had arranged John's "accident," then murdered him with his own hands when he showed signs of recovering. And Latigo—all that he was, all that he meant to her, and all that had happened at the ranch.

But full knowledge would only plunge Esther into needless danger, Rose reminded herself as, once more, she resolved to leave the good woman in relative ignorance, and safety.

That afternoon the two of them had gone to John's lawyer. They had drawn up and signed the papers naming Esther as Mason's legal guardian in the event of his mother's death or disappearance. Mason's future was as secure as she could make it.

Not that she had the slightest intention of dying, Rose reminded herself as Esther worked the last button through its loop. She was going to survive and triumph. She had to keep believing that.

"Now for the hair," Esther announced, steering Rose back to the dressing stool. "No, don't turn toward the mirror. Not a peek until I'm finished." The steady, skillful hands twisted, pinned and pulled. "I wish I were dressing you for your wedding," she said wistfully. "To someone young and strong and gentle, someone who loved you as much as you loved him.''

''Don't,'' Rose whispered. ''There'll be no wedding for me, Esther. Not ever.''

''Then I pray to heaven I won't be dressing you for your funeral! Listen to me, Rose, be careful tonight.''

''Don't worry, I know what I'm doing.'' Rose's voice rang hollow, expressing a conviction she did not feel.

''Do you?'' Esther stepped back to survey her handiwork. ''There's something missing,'' she murmured, ''and I know exactly what it is.''

She opened a dresser drawer and drew out a small, carved wooden box. When Rose saw what lay on its crimson velvet lining, she gasped out loud.

''Cut smoky quartz.'' Esther's fingers caressed the necklace of brilliantly faceted gray-black stones set in a finely worked filigree of silver. ''Levi gave these to me for our tenth anniversary. Oh, they're hardly worth a fortune, but I've loved them all the same. Here, let me try this on you, first the necklace, then the earrings.''

Before Rose could protest, the cool rich weight had settled around her throat. One glance at her friend's face told her how it must look. Her hand flew up to touch it. It lay sensuously hard against the softness of her skin, the sharply faceted stones as large as quail eggs, the silver filigree as delicate as lace.

''Oh, Esther, I could never wear this!'' she whispered.

''And why not?''

''It's yours. You treasure it.''

''Then wear it for me. Wear it for Levi, and for the good years we had together. If you're going to do battle with Bayard Hudson, I want a part of us to be there. Please.''

Without waiting for an answer, Esther fastened the dangling earrings, made to be worn without piercing, onto

Rose's earlobes. "Now, stand up and turn around," she said in a voice as tender as a mother's. "Look at yourself, dear. See how truly exquisite you are."

Rose forced her trembling knees to straighten. She had no desire to see herself, not when she had dressed to please Bayard Hudson. Still, when Esther clasped her shoulders and gently turned her around to face the large dressing mirror, her heart seemed to stop for an instant.

The woman who stared back at her from the glass was a glittering, dazzling stranger. The ebony satin gown clung to her body, accentuating her swollen breasts and slender waist. From there it fell into a graceful skirt, its back caught up into a bustle that served to anchor an elaborate cascade of satin ruffles. The smoky, transparent stones accentuated the fairness of her ivory skin, the intensity of her large violet eyes and the rich, moon-spun gold of her hair, which Esther had pinned into silky coils and coaxed into soft, face-framing tendrils.

"John Colby was a blind fool," Esther murmured from behind her. "If he'd known what he had, he would have covered you in diamonds."

"No," Rose answered softly. "You're wrong, Esther. All John ever wanted from me was sons, and for what I gave him in his lifetime, he wouldn't have thought me worth a string of cheap clay beads."

"Don't be so unkind to yourself. You're a fine and lovely woman, Rose, and you deserve far more happiness than life has given you."

Rose turned and gave her a quick, hard hug. "Thank you, dear friend," she said, glancing at the pretty little porcelain clock on the dresser, "but this is a conversation for another time. I'll look in on Mason for a moment. Then I'll get my shawl and wait for Bayard on the porch."

"The porch?"

"I know what Bayard did to you and how you must feel

about the man. I won't dishonor your house by inviting him in.''

Esther returned the embrace swiftly, then broke away, leaving Rose with a spot of cool wetness on her cheek. "Be careful," she said.

Minutes later, Rose stood alone in the shadows of the porch. The plain gray merino shawl she clutched about her shoulders was a poor match for the elegance of the gown, but Rose did not care. In fact, as the minutes crawled past, she began to wish passionately for a woman-size tent that would cover her from head to toe. She had never felt more exposed.

The gown had no pockets, so that afternoon, on the way back from the lawyer's, Rose had slipped into a pawnshop. There she had purchased a sleek, evil-looking little derringer in a holster that strapped to the leg. Even now, she could feel its reptilian weight against the outside of her calf, hopelessly out of reach beneath the ruffled layers of her petticoats. Rose could only pray there would be no occasion to use it.

To brace her faltering courage, she forced her mind to rehearse the steps of her plan, one that was, of necessity, loose and open to change. She planned to play on Bayard's desire, coaxing him to talk until she had what she needed. Only then would she seek out one of the few men she could trust—the governor, Agent Clum, or even the president of the railroad. She would present him with the facts and offer, as evidence, John's journal, which was still safe in its hiding place at the ranch.

That journal was her most powerful weapon, Rose reminded herself. No one else, including Esther, knew of its whereabouts. But even for the journal, she had made careful provisions. Tucked into her valise, where her friend would look only if something went wrong, was a sealed envelope on which she had carefully written:

To be hand-carried to Governor Anson Safford in the event of my disappearance or death.

Disappearance or death.

The words shimmered darkly in Rose's mind as she looked down the moonlit street and saw Bayard Hudson's buggy rounding the corner.

Chapter Fifteen

"Take off that shawl and give me a look at you." Bayard cast Rose a lustful, sidelong glance. "I'd like to see how the rest of my present fits."

"It fits just fine." Rose sat rigidly on the buggy seat, struggling to relax. "Don't worry, you'll see it soon enough. It'll spoil the impression if I give you a peek now."

"Dash it, Rose, I'd like a lot more than a peek." His free hand snaked across the seat to rest on her knee. "Don't you know what you do to me? For two cents, I'd turn this buggy around and—"

"Oh, no, you don't! No free samples!" She slapped the hand lightly and removed it with a playful little laugh. "We're going to cause enough of a scandal at the ball without making a spectacle of ourselves in the middle of Main Street! Now, for heaven's sake, watch where you're going! The poor horse can't read your mind!"

The traffic grew heavier as they drove south, with more buggies, horses and wagons funneling into Main Street. The territorial legislature was currently in session, and nearly all of its members would be attending the ball.

Rose knew the women who attended would likely be

shocked by her behavior. Less than five months in mourning, and here she would be, wearing a gown that was a mockery to her widowhood, dancing, laughing and flirting. All of this Rose had rehearsed in her mind, and she had told herself it didn't matter what people thought of her. Still, as Bayard's buggy neared the brightly lit Carillo Gardens, dread tightened its cold knot in the pit of her stomach, and she struggled against the wild urge to leap out of the seat and flee into the dusk.

At the gardens' entrance, Bayard halted the buggy next to a tall cypress and turned the reins over to an attendant. Rose could hear the throb and blare of the music as he came around to lift her down from the seat. She stiffened as his hands closed around her waist, then spun away as he set her on the ground. This man was half-mad with lust for her, Rose knew. A shrewd woman would use that lust to her advantage.

She slipped off her shawl, tossing it carelessly into the wagon bed. Bayard grunted softly as his eyes raked her flesh, taking in the way the black satin clung to her curves and set off her creamy, bare shoulders. "Heavens above, but you're beautiful," he muttered, reaching for her again.

"People will see." Rose pivoted away with a toss of her head that loosened Esther's carefully placed hairpins. "Let's go into the dance," she said. "I've never met a president before."

Bayard's thumb fondled the sensitive inner flesh of her arm as he led her inside. A few couples were already dancing in the center of the broad plank floor, laid on fresh timbers for the occasion.

The reception line had formed in front of the speakers' platform, along one side of a large open square that was bound on the left by the richly laden buffet tables and on the right side by the darkly glittering reservoir. At the far end, red and white bunting had been draped across a row of cypresses, older by far than the park itself. Beyond these massive, shadowy trees lay darkness and desert.

Rose's gaze darted among the guests, singling out her enemies and her possible allies. Governor Anson Safford was easy to pick out. A small, neat man with a bristling mustache, he had no known connection to the Ring. But could she really count on his support? Even if she could get his ear, would he believe her claims or dismiss them as the rantings of a grief-stricken female?

Picking out the president of the Southern Pacific Railroad was also easy because he was surrounded by a large, anxious knot of people, all clamoring to be heard. They would besiege him for the rest of the evening, Rose swiftly surmised. And even if she could speak to the man, he had not known John, and he would have little interest in her.

Rose could see several army officers from nearby Fort Lowell, none of whom she knew. John had mentioned that the Ring had worked its way into the military, and that some high-ranking soldiers were taking bribes. She could not afford to trust any of them.

But there was another, a man even Latigo had said she could count on. If she could locate John Clum, the Indian agent—

"What are you up to, Rose?" Bayard's hand tightened on her arm. "Tonight you should have eyes for me alone. Instead your attention is wandering all over the place."

Rose forced herself to laugh. "Don't you know anything about women, Bayard? I was appraising the gowns and hairstyles and jewelry and making comparisons. See, all the other women are doing the same."

"And envying you." His hand moved higher on her arm, the knuckles deliberately skimming the curve of her breast. "And every man here is envying me. I knew you wouldn't be able to resist my invitation, Rose, especially after I threw in those fancy widow's weeds you're wearing."

"You have very elegant taste," Rose said coolly. "But the truth is, I came because I wanted to discuss some business with you."

"Business?" A shadow crossed his florid, handsome face.

"Wait until we've gone through the reception line. Then we can talk as we dance." Rose edged him toward the spot where the line was queuing up to meet the dignitaries and their wives. "By the way, I heard an amusing story about the agent on the San Carlos—Mr. Clum, isn't that his name? Would he be here tonight?"

"Clum?" Bayard's snorting laugh underscored his contempt. "Why, that cocky little Indian-loving fool wouldn't dare show his face around Tucson! He'd be strung up on sight!"

"They say he even wants to start a school for those Apache vermin!" A sedate, graying matron just ahead of them in line had turned around to speak. Rose recognized her as the wife of a prosperous merchant. "Can you imagine Apaches learning to read and write? Oh, they're clever enough, I suppose, in the same way monkeys are clever. But there's certainly no real intelligence there. Not, at least, as we understand it."

Rose's jaw tightened behind the mask of her frozen smile. Wisdom dictated that she nod politely and agree with what she'd heard, but the woman was attacking Latigo, his people and his heritage. Foolish or not, Rose knew she could not let such bland ignorance go unchallenged.

"Oh?" she retorted, in a conversational tone. "And how *do* we understand intelligence, Mrs. Pennington? I'd be very interested in hearing your opinion."

The woman squirmed under Rose's icy gaze. "Really,

my dear, certainly you know what I mean."

"No, I'm afraid I don't."

"Intelligence is the ability to be, well, *civilized!* I mean, good heavens, the Apaches don't even use cutlery when they eat! And their language! The soldiers say it's nothing but gibberish, like the chattering of so many wild baboons!"

A bitter smile teased at the corner of Rose's mouth. "Oh, but think about this, Mrs. Pennington. What if you and I, civilized creatures that we are, had to survive in their world? Could we track game over bare rock? Could we walk out into the desert and find herbs that would heal wounds and cure fevers? Could we raise our children with no doctors, no churches, no schools, and still teach them to be survivors and leaders?"

The woman glared at Rose over her ecru silk fan. "Really, Mrs. Colby!" she huffed. "You almost sound as if you admire them! You, of all people, should have nothing good to say about Apaches! They did murder your parents, after all!"

"And my father, good Quaker that he was, would have long since forgiven them." Rose ignored Bayard's insistent tugging at her arm. "If you ask me, there's been enough bloodshed on both sides! The whole territory needs to forget about avenging the past and get on with the future!"

"Well!" The woman's glare had become venomous. Other people in the line were turning around to watch. "You're certainly entitled to your opinion, but I know for a fact your late husband didn't feel that way, fine man that he was! If he could see the way you look tonight, Rose Colby, and hear what you just said, poor John would turn right over in his grave!"

Bayard was clearly embarrassed. His tugging at her arm had become an insistent pinch. "Come and dance with me,

Rose,'' he muttered, close to her ear. ''You can meet the president later!''

Still quivering, Rose allowed him to lead her onto the dance floor. The evening was off to a stampeding start in the wrong direction.

''For Pete's sake, why can't you just smile and look pretty?'' Bayard growled. ''A beautiful woman doesn't need to have opinions on matters that don't concern her.'' As they began to waltz, his fingers dug into the small of her back, as much in anger as in desire. ''And what you said, Rose! You of all people should know better! Have you ever seen an Apache up close? Have you ever touched one? Smelled one?''

Smelled one. Touched one. Loved one.

''They're human maggots!'' Bayard raged on. ''Gut-eaters! The world will be a better place when they're all dead!''

Rose swallowed her fear, forcing herself to smile as she struck Bayard with her only weapon, the truth.

''Don't be ridiculous, Bayard,'' she said lightly. ''Think what would happen if there were no more Apaches. My ranch would lose those lovely, fat government contracts it gets for providing beef to the fort and the reservation. With the danger gone, the army would move out, and the railroad would finally move in.

''Once that happened, your shipping business would be all but worthless, and so would the stockpiles of expensive goods you've brought in overland and sold to the local merchants. The wealthiest men in town could lose their fortunes, including the husband of Mrs. Pennington, over there.'' Rose forced a bitter chuckle. ''Why, if that poor woman knew what the Apaches had done for her, she'd probably drive out to the San Carlos in person, with a wagonload of home-baked cinnamon rolls and cof—''

She broke off as she glanced up at him. Bayard's ginger-colored eyes had narrowed to hostile slits. In the depths of his stone-black pupils, something hard and frightening glinted.

"You're talking about profiteering," he drawled, "and that's an ugly word, even in these parts. Now where would a pretty little lady like you get such wild notions? Don't tell me you thought them up all by yourself."

"It wasn't that difficult, even for me."

"Well, it's balderdash all the same. Apache raids on my wagon trains have cost me thousands of dollars and a score of drivers over the years."

"And by scaring off the railroad builders, they've earned you and other businessmen a hundred times that amount. It makes perfect sense, Bayard."

"I wouldn't be saying that too loud around here, Rose. There are folks who wouldn't take too kindly to such talk."

"The railroad president might be interested. So would the governor."

"Not when you can't prove a blasted word of what you're saying." He scowled down at her, all traces of good humor gone. "Is this the business you said you wanted to talk to me about?"

"Not exactly." Rose flashed her boldest smile. "I just wanted you to know that I'm not as naive as you seem to think I am."

"Maybe we'd better talk outside." He had stopped dancing. His hand gripped her elbow tightly, steering her toward the edge of the dance floor.

"No." She pivoted into his path, her heart slamming. "It's only business. We can talk while we dance. Please, Bayard." Her free arm slipped to his shoulder as she drew him back into the motion of the waltz. "I didn't mean to upset you, but I thought I could speak to you openly."

"What is it you want, Rose?" His voice was guarded,

his eyes still wary, and Rose knew she would have to weigh every word. She would be a fool to underestimate Bayard now.

"Your advice will do for the time being," she said. "The rest can come later, and only if you're willing, of course."

A muscle twitched in his full-fleshed, ruddy cheek. "I'm waiting, Rose. What is it you need advice about?"

Rose closed her eyes for an instant and pictured Latigo, hiding, dodging, hunted like an animal for the rest of his life. This was for him, she told herself as she took a deep breath.

"I'm concerned about the future of the ranch," she said, gazing up at Bayard with what she hoped was a look of womanly trust. "What I said about the railroad coming—the changes will affect me, too. I'll be competing with half the country for the sale of my cattle, and I'll have to cut my prices to the bone. The ranch is barely making expenses now. If things get so bad that I have to borrow money, I could lose my son's inheritance. I could lose everything."

His manner softened at once. "Rose," he declared in a patronizing tone, "if it's money you need, I can certainly arrange a loan to—"

"No." She shook her head in swift denial. "No, it's far too soon for that. But I am getting worried. John told me nothing about his business affairs. What little I know, I learned from his papers."

"I did offer to help you."

"No, you offered to take over the running of the ranch, and I can't allow that. I need to do this job myself, the way John would have wanted it done. But since you seem willing, there is something I need."

His hand tightened against the small of her back, drawing her closer. "When you look at me like that, you know there's nothing you can't ask for," he murmured huskily.

Rose checked the urge to shrink away from him. "It's really quite simple," she said with an engaging little smile. "As I mentioned, John told me next to nothing about his business involvements. But I was aware that he did have...friends, you among them. A group of friends who supported each other in times of need, who worked together for their common good. Now that I'm alone I could use that support."

"You have my support, Rose. Isn't that enough?"

"Not entirely." She forced herself to look straight into his eyes. "You see, I want to give as much as I receive. I want to be part of the things you're working for, just as John was."

Rose waited for her answer, her heart thudding so violently that she could scarcely breathe. She didn't really expect Bayard to say yes, but she did need more answers. If Bayard saw through her masquerade now, she was lost.

But even as her knees threatened to buckle beneath her, he smiled, the lamplight glinting faintly on one gold bicuspid. "There's a very simple solution to all that," he said, squeezing her close. "Marry me, Rose. I can give you everything John did, and more."

"I told you I have no plans to remarry," she said, chilled beyond playacting by his ardor.

"And I told you that one day you'd fall on your knees and beg me to be your husband. Has that day arrived?"

"I said I wanted to discuss business, not marriage."

"As a woman, my dear, marriage is the only business you are fit to discuss."

His words silenced her as abruptly as if he had struck her across the face. Fighting, again, the impulse to tear herself out of his arms and stalk off the dance floor, Rose forced herself to drift with the music while she regrouped her thoughts and took another tack.

"How is your hunt for that fugitive coming along, that half-breed scout from the San Carlos?" she asked, her pulse quivering. "What was his name?"

"Latigo!" Bayard snorted contemptuously. "The bastard's vanished without a trace, probably over the border by now. But yesterday we doubled the reward to two thousand dollars. That'll be enough to put every bounty hunter in the territory on his trail."

"We?" Rose asked, pouncing like a cat on a vanishing thread.

"What?"

"You said *we* doubled the reward. What do you mean by that?"

Had he paled slightly about the lips, or had she only imagined it? "Why, the citizens of Tucson, of course!" he blustered. "I contributed half the amount myself."

"But why?" She drove her advantage deeper, harder. "I could understand the townspeople putting up a reward if one of their own had been killed. But two federal agents on an Indian reservation? That's the government's business."

"The government's business and none of your own. Let's get some punch." He was all but dragging her off the dance floor. Rose resisted with all her strength, knowing her only hope of safety lay in keeping visible to the entire crowd. "You're hurting my arm!" she muttered. "Do you want me to start screaming, or do you want to talk about this?"

"Have you lost your mind?" His florid face blazed with heat as he began to dance with her again. "You don't know what you're talking about!"

"Don't I?" Rose retorted. "I've wondered all along why an army scout with an excellent record would murder two strangers he was assigned to protect. Now I know the answer—he didn't do it. It was someone from Tucson someone you and your friends are protecting.''

''You're babbling, woman.'' His eyes had gone hard ''But if you'd like to entertain me with your twisted line of reasoning, I'm ready to listen. Why would anyone from Tucson want to kill our two nosy government friends?''

''Two reasons.'' Rose's artificial smile glittered like cu crystal as she willed her feet to keep the rhythm of the dance. ''The two agents may have discovered some illega activity—say, the smuggling of guns or whiskey. That sor of thing does go on, you know. It's no secret to anyone.'

''If that's the case, maybe your half-breed was the smuggler. That would certainly give him a motive for kill ing the two federal men.''

''No, he was guiding them. If he'd been hiding some illegal activity, it would have been a simple matter to steer them away from it. Why would he kill them, especially when he knew he'd be blamed?''

Bayard scowled at her. ''You said there were two rea sons.''

''So I did.'' Rose felt as if she were balanced at the edge of a precipice, swaying dizzily. ''Whoever did the killing, they could have planned to kill Lat—this Latigo too, then blame it on the Apaches and use it as an excuse to stir up more trouble. Only it didn't work. He got away so there was no choice except to blame him instead. That way nobody would believe his version of what happened.'

She felt his shoulders tighten beneath her hand. ''That' a mighty interesting set of ideas, little lady,'' he said in a cold voice. ''But there's a small matter of proof, and you don't have a shred of it.''

''I never claimed to have proof of anything.''

''Then, who's to say this Latigo you're defending with

so much passion isn't a cold-blooded killer who ought to be strung up on sight?''

"How could even a cold-blooded killer shoot himself in the shoulder—from behind?"

Rose's heart seemed to stop as his whole body went rigid. "What gave you the idea he was wounded?" he rasped, his arm tightening around her waist.

"You did." She groped for a way out of her own trap. "You told me that day you came to the ranch with the posse."

"No." His hand gripped hers, crushing the knuckle-bones so tightly that the pain shot up her arm. "I told you no such thing, Rose."

"Then I must have read it, or heard it."

"No, the papers didn't mention it. Nobody knew."

"Then how did *you* know?" She twisted away with all her strength and stood facing him, her hair tumbling loose from its pins, her breath bursting out of her chest. The other couples had stopped dancing. Rose felt every eye in the room on her as she confronted her enemy.

"How did you know about the wound, Bayard? Were you there to see it happen, or did your hired gunmen tell you about it? You can't hide anymore, not from me or from the truth!"

Bayard's face had gone crimson. Rose spun away from him, risking everything now as her frantically searching eyes found the governor standing next to the railroad president in the reception line. He looked thunderstruck, as did everyone else who could see and hear what was happening.

"I have proof." What she had intended as a shout emerged from her fear-constricted throat as a gasp. "I have written proof—of a conspiracy—"

For the space of a breath Rose almost believed she had won. Then the whole world seemed to crash down around her. Bayard's powerful arm encircled her ribs, jerking her

off her feet. His huge, fleshy hand covered her mouth
blocking her scream and holding her immobile against the
great bulk of his chest.

"My apologies," he said in a calm voice that was none
theless audible to everyone present. "I'm afraid Mrs
Colby hasn't been herself since her husband's death. She
insisted that I bring her here tonight, but I see now tha
she's not yet up to meeting people. If you'll be kin
enough to excuse me, I'll take her back to her room an
send for a doctor. The poor woman is clearly sufferin
from a nervous disorder."

Rose struggled like a wildcat, clawing at Bayard's hand
as he carried her off the dance floor, but she was no matc
for his bulk and strength. Her frantic gaze darted from on
face to another, her eyes pleading for help, but no on
came to her aid. They had all believed Bayard's lyin
words.

Merciful heaven, they really believed she'd gone mad

Wild with terror, Rose sank her teeth into the fleshy bas
of his thumb. She tasted the salty wetness of blood an
heard him mutter, "You bitch!" But he did not let her go
His brutal arms crushed her ribs as he swept her out of th
circle of light and safety into the darkness of night.

His boots crunched gravel as he strode into the ope
area where the horses and wagons had been staked. For
moment Rose thought he might be planning to put her i
the buggy. Her muscles relaxed in an effort to lull hir
while she gathered her strength for a leap or a scream.

But Bayard passed the buggy without a pause, and now
as the darkness closed around them she felt the full impac
of her desperation. Wherever he was taking her now, h
did not intend that she return.

As she began to struggle again, the slight, cold weigh
of the derringer pressed against her thigh. There was n

way to reach it now, but its presence represented her only hope, if she could get Bayard to lower his guard.

They were in the open desert now, surrounded by moonlit darkness. Here and there, lights from outlying shacks flickered like earthbound stars, none of them close enough to be of help to a desperate woman.

Bayard glanced around cautiously before he spoke. "I don't know how far you were planning to take this, but the game's over, Rose. You might as well tell me where it is."

She stared straight ahead in determined silence, knowing that once he had what he wanted, she would be of no further use to him.

"Don't play innocent with me." His arm jerked tighter around her ribs. "You said you had evidence. Where is it, Rose?"

"Safe and secure," she gasped. "And I've made sure that if anything happens to me, the first person to see it will be the governor." She squirmed in his arms, fighting for breath. "It was you who ransacked John's files, wasn't it?"

"I don't have to answer that question, or any others."

"No, you don't need to!" Rose muttered through pain-clenched teeth. "I already know the answers, and all those people who saw us leave the party together are going to be suspicious if I don't turn up in one piece later on!"

His arms softened but did not release their grip. "Lord, do you really think I could hurt you, Rose?" he murmured against her hair. "There's a solution to all this. Marry me, girl. Marry me now, tonight, and you can have it all. Money, status, power, whatever you want."

"What about justice?"

"The world doesn't work that way, honey. I discovered that a long time ago. You take what you can, any way you can get it. And I want you, Rose, now."

She gasped as he spun her around and she saw his fu
face in the moonlight. It was a monstrous mask of lust an
greed. This was a man who had cheated, lied and murdere
his way to wealth and power. He would do as he wishe
with her, Rose knew, and whatever story he devised t
cover himself, people would believe it. Even the letter sh
had left with Esther would be dismissed as the raving c
a demented female.

No one would believe the truth, just as no one had be
lieved Latigo. No one except the woman who loved him

"You arranged John's so-called accident, didn't you?"
she said, struggling vainly to pull away. "You arrange
the killing of Major Scott, too, and the massacre of th
Rooney family."

Bayard's body had gone rigid. He twisted her arm be
hind her back, hurting her. "And I suppose I shot Abrahar
Lincoln, too," he growled. "Why don't you throw that i
while you're at it?" He forced her close to him once more
"Quit stalling, Rose. You're not calling the shots here.
am. And I'm telling you, it doesn't have to be this wa}
With me, you'd have everything a woman could eve
want."

"All I want is the life I have," Rose retorted coldly
and even as she spoke, she realized that life was gon
forever. "Let me go, Bayard" she whispered, giving in t
her fear. "No one will ever believe the things I said bac
there. You've seen to that yourself."

"I can't do that," he said, still clasping her close. "Yo
said you had evidence. I want that evidence, Rose. Now."

"Suppose I give it to you?" The desperate seeds of
plan had sprouted in Rose's mind. "What will you do wit
me then?"

His mouth nuzzled her bare shoulder. "That, my dea
girl, is up to you."

Rose willed herself to relax in his arms. "I have a son to raise," she said. "I want to live."

"Then you will, but on my terms, Rose, and I think you know what they are." He licked his lips nervously. "You said you had the evidence."

"Yes." Her shaking voice betrayed her fear. "I have it with me—someplace, uh, private. Let go of me, and I'll get it."

"No tricks, Rose, or you'll be sorry." His arms released her. She staggered backward, righted herself and began fumbling with her skirts.

"Turn around," she said. "Please."

He laughed roughly in the darkness. "No more turning around, Rose. I'm not going to take my eyes off you."

Rose's heart sank as she lifted her petticoats, keeping them bunched in her left hand to hide the sight of the derringer. Bayard was not going to make this easy for her.

"I'm waiting." His voice was clotted with lust, his breath a low rasp in the darkness. Rose's fingers closed on the teaspoon-sized handle of the tiny weapon. Thumbing back the hammer, she jerked it from its holster. A wave of hot rage swept through her as she pointed the muzzle upward at his chest.

"I should kill you right now," she said in a flat voice. "Go on, give me an excuse. Make me do it."

He stared down at her, eyes bulging in momentary shock. Then, slowly, he began to laugh.

"Why, Rose, honey, you wouldn't really shoot me. Don't you know what they'd do to a lady who put a hole through the next governor of Arizona? Even if you only wounded me, you'd never see that pretty little baby of yours again, I can promise you that."

Rose's eyes narrowed as she lowered her aim. "If I could put you out of business as a man, it might be worth it," she said, bluffing for all she was worth. "I'm a good shot, Bayard, and you're no puny target. There are plenty of places I could damage you. Now turn around and start walking back toward the reception.''

''Anything you say, little lady.'' He turned as if to follow her order. Then, with a move so uncharacteristically swift that it caught her off guard, he wheeled backward and struck her with the hammer of his swinging arm. The pistol discharged with a harmless pop as it flew out of Rose's fist to vanish into the darkness. In the same motion he lunged at her, the momentum of his heavy body carrying them both to the sand.

''Now, this is more like it,'' he muttered as she struggled under his panting weight. ''I'm going to have you here and now, Rose. Maybe that'll tame your spirit and show you who's boss!''

Chapter Sixteen

Rose writhed against Bayard, biting and clawing as his hand found its way beneath the tangle of her petticoats. "This is no way for a woman to behave!" he gasped as he raised up to unbuckle his belt. "You can't fight me anymore, Rose, so you may as well relax and enjoy—"

His words ended in a choked gurgle as something long and thin hissed out of the darkness to snap and coil around his neck. Some invisible force wrenched him backward onto the sand. He lay there gasping and clawing at his throat as Latigo, whip in hand, stepped into the open.

"Did he hurt you?" he glanced swiftly at Rose.

"Not as much as he meant to." She scrambled to her feet. Joy, confusion, relief and worry pinwheeled inside her as her eyes took him in, straight and lean and hard as a living blade in the darkness.

"We've got to get away from this place," she said.

"What do we do with your friend?" He glared contemptuously down at Bayard, who lay sprawled in the sand. Latigo's long, brown fingers balanced the uncoiled whip, ready to strike again at the first treacherous move.

Bayard's eyes bulged with fear and recognition. He had known Latigo during the Apache wars and had no trouble remembering him now. "So that's how it is!" Bayard's gaze swiveled angrily toward Rose. "You're too damned highfalutin prissy for a future governor, but you'll spread your legs in the dirt for a filthy, murdering, half-breed...*Apache!*" He spat out the word as if a scorpion had invaded his mouth.

"Mrs. Colby is a lady," Latigo said coldly, "and she deserves far better than either of us. But I'm not here to dispute a woman's honor, Hudson. I want you to tell me about the hired guns who murdered those two federal agents and nearly got me, too. Who were they working for?" His fist shot out, clamped onto the front of Bayard's shirt and jerked him half-upright.

"I don't know what you're talking about," Bayard muttered, his weight sagging against Latigo's grip.

"He knows," Rose said quietly. "He as much as told me so."

"Do you want to live, Hudson?" Latigo growled. "Then tell me the truth. We've got a reliable witness right here."

"Reliable?" Bayard's lips tightened in a grimace. "Why, half the territory thinks she's crazy by now. And if they find out she's thrown in with you, they'll string the two of you up side by side without so much as a nod from the judge."

"He's right," Rose said, her spirits plummeting. "He made sure of that himself."

"You're as good as hanged right now, you dirty Apache bastard," Bayard said. "And nothing you can make me say is going to amount to a dime's worth of difference."

Even as he spoke, Rose caught the sound of men's voices on the night wind and saw the distant flare of lanterns from the direction of the party. "Someone's coming," she whispered frantically. "They must've heard the gun go off. We've got to get out of here." She glanced down at Bayard. "He's bound to talk. We could take him with us."

"No, he'd only slow us down. We'd never get away." Latigo scowled at Bayard as he weighed the dangers against his choices.

A look of sick fear passed like a shadow across Bayard's face. "Don't kill me," he pleaded. "For the love of heaven, man, I won't say a word."

Latigo raised the thick, braided handle of the whip. "You of all people should know I'm not a murderer," he said gruffly. Then the handle came down sharply across Bayard's temple. Bayard grunted once and collapsed unconscious in a pool of moonlit sand.

"Come on! My horse is this way!" Latigo grabbed Rose's wrist and began to run. She stumbled after him over the rough ground, prickly pear and cholla spines clawing at the fabric of her gown. Soon Bayard's friends would find him. Soon he would regain consciousness and tell them everything. They had minutes, perhaps, to get away.

A lightning jab of pain shot up her leg as she stubbed her toe on a sharp rock. He caught her against him as she staggered and nearly fell. "You can move faster without me," she gasped. "Save yourself, Latigo. Leave me here."

"Leave you to what?" His eyes blazed in the moonlight. "If Hudson and his friends get their hands on you, you'll never live to talk about it."

"No. I've got something to bargain with. John's journal. I found it under the floor at the ranch. It's still there, and if anything happens to me—"

"Damn it, stop arguing and come on!" he snapped, sweeping her up in his arms. "Say I'm kidnapping you, if you like, but any way you want to put it, I'm getting you out of here!"

Rose clung to him in silence as he strode through the thickening scrub. She could see his horse now, tied in the shadow of a mesquite clump. "Latigo!" she whispered, seized with sudden panic. "My baby! He's at my friend's boardinghouse! We've got to get him!"

"Your boy may be safer where he is." He gripped her waist and, with no time for tenderness, hoisted her onto the front of the saddle.

"No! Bayard knows he's there! They could take him."

Latigo understood at once. He jerked the reins loose from the bush, flung them to Rose and vaulted up behind her.

Unaccustomed to the added weight, the skittish horse snorted, bucked and bolted into a headlong gallop. "Hang on!" Latigo muttered as they tore through the scrub, headed back toward town.

By the time they reached Main Street, Latigo had brought the mustang under control again. Avoiding the crowded thoroughfare, he slipped down an unlit side alley, skirting the backs of the low adobe buildings. The nighttime sounds of Main Street—music, laughter, curses— were muffled here.

Rose held her breath, afraid to break the silence with so much as a word. Seconds, every one of them precious, crawled by as they wound their way through the darkness. When Bayard regained his senses, the boardinghouse was the first place he would send his cohorts to look for her. If she did not arrive in time, they would take her son. Bayard would use the child to draw her back and bend both her and Latigo to his will.

Only when Rose saw the two big cottonwoods, blotting out the stars where their branches spread against the sky, did she realize they had reached the rear of the boardinghouse. She could see a lamp glowing through Esther's kitchen curtains and two others in the bedrooms upstairs. Aside from those signs of life, the place appeared quiet.

"Wait in there." Rose motioned Latigo toward the shed. "They mustn't see you. I'll get Mason."

"Be careful." His strong hands clasped her waist as he lifted her off the saddle and slid her gently to the ground. "If you need me—"

"It's all right." Rose avoided his eyes, knowing that if she so much as looked at him, all the longing she had ever felt for this man would come bursting out of her. And there was no time for such emotions. Not now.

"If I'm not back in the next few minutes, or if you see any danger," she whispered, "leave. Ride out of here fast and don't look back."

It was the closest she dared come to telling him she loved him.

Without another word, Rose spun away, sprinted across the moon-dappled yard and disappeared into the darkness of the side of the house. Even now, she knew that time was running out.

What had he done to this woman? Latigo lashed himself as he watched her go. Rose's life had been safe before the horse dragged him, wounded and bleeding, into her yard. Because of him, there was a powerful chance she would never feel safe again.

He would protect her with his very life, he vowed. But as he slipped into the darkness of the shed to wait, Latigo knew it would not be enough. Maybe he could spend his days on the run, but there was only one place where Rose and her baby belonged. Whatever the cost, he would find a way to return them to their ranch to live out their days in peace and safety.

Latigo prowled the darkness as he waited, so wary that his nerves jumped at every mouse rustle. Each passing rider in the street snapped him to quivering alertness.

He went limp with relief as the back door opened and

she slipped outside, wrapped in a shawl and carrying her son and a sack of supplies. "We've got to get out of here," he growled, masking tenderness with irritation. "What took you so long?"

"I'm sorry," she whispered. "I had to gather some things for the baby. Esther insisted on sending some food with us. Here, you take this. It's loaded." She slipped the Peacemaker into his hand. Savoring its cold weight, Latigo slipped it into his empty holster.

"How much does your friend know?" He swung into the saddle, intending to pull her up behind him.

"No more than she needs to. Esther's a good friend and she hates the Ring. We can trust her."

"We'll have to." He lifted the baby and the sack from her arms, then offered his free hand to help her scramble up behind him, a more comfortable position than over the saddle horn. Young Mason's eyes were luminous in the moonlight, and for the space of a heartbeat, Latigo was crushed by the weight of his responsibility for these two precious lives. No sacrifice he could make would be too great for their safety.

Rose had settled into place behind him, astride the horse's rump. Ruched above her knees, her petticoats flashed white in the moonlight. "Give Mason to me," she said. "I can hold him between us."

Latigo passed her the infant, then nudged the horse to an easy walk. Rose gripped his shoulder with one hand as she cradled the baby with the other. There was no question of going faster. A gallop, or even a trot, would throw them both to the ground.

"Why did you come back?" she whispered as they slipped between the adobe walls of a narrow alley.

"Because I had nothing to lose." Latigo did not trust himself to say more. He concentrated on guiding the horse through the treacherous shadows, steeling himself from the warm pressure of her thighs against the backs of his legs. The tense silence lasted until they reached the outskirts of town.

"But how did you find me?" she asked at last. "How did you know I was in danger?"

"You'd told me about the dance. I stayed beyond the trees and watched, hoping that you'd come to your senses and wouldn't be there. When I saw you come in—" Latigo swallowed as the rush of emotion swept over him again. The sight of Rose in that elegant gown, on the arm of a rich and powerful man, had brought home with the force of a gut kick how far out of reach she was for a wretch like him.

"I watched you as closely as I could," he said, "but it was crowded and hard to see. When I realized you'd gone—" Again the memory of his panic and despair tightened his throat.

"But you found me," she said when he did not continue. "You found me in time."

"After tearing around the desert like a crazy man—yes, I heard voices and then the shot—" He broke off again, racked by the thought of how close she had come to rape and death in the darkness. "What the devil did you think you were doing?" he exploded. "You told me you'd found your husband's journal. Couldn't you have taken it straight to the governor in broad daylight? Damn it, Rose."

The baby stirred and whimpered, unsettled by the vehemence in Latigo's voice. He heard Rose soothing her child, making motherly little cooing sounds.

"I realize I could have gone straight to the governor," she said at last. "But I didn't know enough. John's journal entries ended the day before his accident. I was hoping Bayard would tell me more."

"More?"

"Oh, I knew he would never confess to killing John.

But I had hoped, if I tried to be charming and pretende
to trust him, he might tell me about the two federal agent
on the San Carlos, and about you. But I should hav
known better. Bayard was much too clever for—''

''Wait.'' Latigo stopped her, his heart slamming
''You're saying you pulled this whole damn fool stunt fo
me?''

''You saved my son's life.'' Her voice faltered. ''I fe
I owed you that much. If there was a chance, any chance
I could clear you of those terrible charges.''

''Damn it all to hell, Rose, I'm not worth it!'' Latig
swore to hide the emotions that were ripping him apar
That this beautiful woman would risk her future, her honor
her very life, for a homeless fugitive was beyond imag
ining.

''You're worth it,'' she said softly. ''You're worth mor
than you could ever know. I love you, Latigo.''

He moaned as if she had jabbed a steel blade betwee
his ribs. ''Don't, Rose,'' he whispered.

''Don't what? Don't tell the truth?'' Her hand grippe
his shoulder, the pressure of her thin, cool fingers swee
torture through his shirt. ''When you left the ranch, I fe
as if my life had ended,'' she said. ''It began again tonigh
when you stepped into the clearing. Whatever happens
you need to know that. I don't want either of us to di
with those words unsaid.''

Latigo knew Rose was waiting for a reply. He struggle
to speak past the aching lump in his throat. All his life h
had been treated as an outcast, hated and reviled whereve
he went. That any woman would say those words to hir
was a miracle in itself. That it could be Rose was beyon
belief.

''Don't you know why I left?'' he said, his voice roug
with emotion. ''And don't you know why I came back?''

Her hand tightened on his shoulder. ''I think I do,'' sh

answered gently, "but tell me anyway. There are some things a woman needs to hear."

Latigo could feel the baby breathing softly in the space between his body and Rose's. The tiny boy drowsed contentedly, lulled by the warmth and the easy motion of the horse. The town lay behind them now, its lights all but indistinguishable from the stars in the sky. What could he do with this woman and her precious son? How was he going to take care of them? The questions tore at him even as he groped for the words Rose wanted and so deeply deserved.

"So why did you leave?" Her whispered question probed emotions he scarcely understood himself.

"I left because I thought it was the only way to protect you," he said, clutching at a way to begin. "But that wasn't the only reason. Maybe I hoped that my going would undo the harm I had done you, that you'd forget me in time and go on as if the past week had never happened."

"You were wrong." Her fingertips brushed the back of his neck, lingering to caress his hair where it curled thickly down over his shirt collar. "You were so very wrong, Latigo," she said. "I would never have forgotten you. And as for my going on—"

"I tried to forget you, too," he said, spilling the words out before they could block up like a jam of logs. "I went high in the mountains and tried to put everything behind me. But it was no use, Rose. Even up there in the spirit place, where no white person had ever been, you were with me. Even then I knew I had to come back, if only to finish what you and I had begun."

"And what have we begun?" Rose's question trembled with anxiety and wonder. "Where do we go from here, Latigo?"

"You know I have to leave," he said gently. "And you know I can't take you and Mason with me."

"Yes, I know," she whispered, "just as you know that I can't face the rest of my life without you."

"You're a beautiful woman, Rose." The words shattered his heart, but he had to say them. "Things are changing in the territory, new people are coming in. You'll find someone else, a good man, and you'll marry again."

"No." Her hand lay quietly on his collar. "No, not that. Not ever."

Silent once more, Latigo nudged the horse through the thick scrub that bordered the foothills. He knew Rose wanted to hear finely wrought phrases and romantic vows he had no hope of fulfilling. But he would not make promises he could not keep. He loved her too much for that.

There was only one vow he could keep, the one he had made to himself. That vow had brought him back to Rose. In the end it would separate them forever.

When they reached the foothills, Latigo paused in the shadow of a tall mesquite clump. "We need to rest the horse," he said. "My camp's farther up, a good two hours of climbing at our pace, but it's well hidden. You should be safe there."

He slipped one arm around the baby, then offered his free hand to help Rose slide off the back of the horse. Her legs were numb from the long ride. They buckled under her as she dropped to the rough ground.

"Are you all right?" He swung out of the saddle with Mason cradled against his shoulder.

"I'm fine." Rose scrambled to her feet, but her strained knees would not support her full weight. Latigo caught her as she sagged against him. She felt him hesitate, struggling against her nearness. Then his breath caught as he drew her close. Her arms locked around his waist, and they held each other, binding the length of their bodies with the fierce desperation of two people who know their time is running out.

"Damn it, Rose." His lips, cool velvet to the touch, devoured her hair, her forehead with nibbling, urgent kisses. "Why did you let me drag you into this mess? You could have had a good life, you could have stayed safe."

"Shh." Her fluttering fingertips touched the clean, sharp planes of his face as if memorizing the feel of him. "Right now I'm as safe as I need to be. And I'm with you. That's all that counts."

She strained upward and would have kissed him then, but Mason chose that instant to cry. His lusty little wail filled the darkness as he squirmed and kicked between them, suddenly wide-awake and hungry.

Rose sighed as she reached for the small, protesting bundle and drew her son close. "He has to be fed. Can we spare that much time?"

Latigo's fiercely gentle gaze met hers as he nodded then turned away to tend the horse. Rose sank into the deep shadow of the mesquite, fumbled with her bodice and nestled her son against her bare breast. She was too exhausted even to cover herself, but she swiftly realized it no longer mattered. Nursing her child with Latigo standing guard seemed as natural and right as anything she had ever done.

Latigo busied himself with rearranging the gear and letting the horse lip canteen water from his cupped hand. Rose watched him from the shadows, her eyes following the easy grace of his movements. Latigo had never told her he loved her. Not even her own heartfelt confession had stirred the words in him. But maybe words weren't all that important. He was here. He had risked his life to come back for her. For now, that would have to be enough.

They had talked impersonally in the past hour, mostly about the Ring. Rose had told him everything she'd

learned from John's journal—the names, the plans, the in
trigues and murders. Latigo had listened quietly. "Why
didn't you bring the journal with you?" he had asked her

"I was afraid something might happen to it," she'd an
swered, clutching Mason tightly as the horse lurched down
the steep side of a wash. "I put it back under John's desk
to keep it safe."

The soft crunch of a boot heel snapped Rose's attention
back to the present. Latigo had turned away from the horse
and was walking slowly toward her. A few feet away, he
sank to an easy crouch, his gaze resting on her with a
tenderness that transcended the need for words.

"I've been thinking about the journal," he said after a
long, pensive pause.

"So have I," Rose said. "We have to get it, Latigo.
We have to use it to break the Ring. It's the only way you
and I will ever be safe."

He shook his head, his narrowed eyes gazing at her
through the darkness. "It's not enough, Rose. The Ring is
too big, and its members are too powerful. Even with
what's in the journal, you'll never bring them all down.
There'll always be someone out there who can hurt you."

"What are you saying?" She stared at him, half
incredulous. "Are you suggesting that I give up?"

He shook his head. "I'm suggesting that you use the
journal to protect yourself and Mason. Hudson knows you
have it, but he doesn't know how much damage it can do
to him. Right now, nobody knows." He toyed with a stick,
tracing circles on the moonlit sand. "The real power of
the journal lies not so much in what it *does* contain as in
what it *might* contain. Do you understand what I'm say
ing?"

"I understand, but I don't agree with you," Rose re
torted passionately. "You want me to strike a bargain with

he Ring, to tell them I'll keep the journal locked away as
ong as they leave me alone.''

"I want you alive and safe, Rose, at any cost."

"Even the cost of your life?" she flung. "The only way
o clear you is to break the Ring and force its members to
confess everything."

Latigo gazed into the darkness, strangely silent. An om-
nous chill crept over Rose as she waited for his answer.
When he did not speak she began again, the words flowing
out of her in a torrent of agitation.

"I have my own plan," she said. "We get the journal.
We take it to John Clum on the San Carlos. He'll have
outside contacts who can be trusted—someone in the army
or the federal government, or even some newspaper outside the territory. We'll break the Ring, force them to clear
you."

"It won't be enough." He stood with a weary sigh.
"Believe me, Rose. You'll be doing well to save yourself
and Mason. Take my advice and leave the territory. I could
get you to Prescott in a few days. Your bank in Tucson
could wire you enough cash to get you to Santa Fe or Salt
Lake City."

"No, I can't do it." Mason had finished nursing. Rose
pulled her bodice together and struggled to rise on legs
that were already beginning to stiffen. Latigo moved to her
side and lifted her gently by the elbows. She stepped back
from him, knowing she would be lost if he took her in his
arms again.

"John had loans on the ranch, notes for stock and feed.
If I leave, the bank or the Ring could contrive a way to
foreclose. I have to go back." *And I have to find a way to
save you,* she almost said, but she knew it was not what
he would want to hear. "Don't worry," she added, "Mason and I will be safe there."

"Safe?" He swung away from her and bent with a liq
uid motion to pick up the loose reins.

"I'll send for my vaqueros. With enough guns, we coul
hold off an army in that house."

The small sound he made could have been either a groa
or a darkly bitter chuckle. "Let's get moving," he sai
"The sooner we make it to my camp, the sooner we ca
get some rest."

"Then you'll take us back to the ranch? You'll help m
get the journal to Clum?"

He glanced over his shoulder, his black eyes hard a
chiseled flints. "All right, Rose," he said quietly. "We'
do it your way. I'll take you back to the ranch."

A hollow undertone in his voice touched Rose with
dark chill. At that moment it was all she could do to kee
from flinging herself into his arms and pleading with him

*Take me away, take me to Mexico, to California, an
place where we can be together. We can start over a
different people, build a new life. All I want is to be wit
you.*

But those were words she could never speak. Her firs
duty was to Mason and the ranch that was his heritage
Whatever the cost to her own happiness, she could no
sacrifice John's legacy to his son.

She flashed Latigo a swift, searching glance, filled wit
questions she dared not ask. "Let's go," she said.

Only when he had boosted her onto the saddle and lifte
Mason into her waiting arms did Rose realize that Latig
meant to lead the horse the rest of the distance. She soo
understood why. The mountain trail climbed dangerously
snaking along steep ledges and over falls of sharp rock
The weight of two people would have been too much fo
the tired horse. Worse, even one misstep could have le
to a deadly fall.

She kept her eyes on the pale outline of Latigo's bac

as they wound their way through the darkness. Rose had never liked heights, and even a sidelong glance off the trail was enough to jerk a noose of fear around her heart. Latigo was taking her where no white men could follow.

When the trail leveled out along the top of the high mesa, Rose felt herself begin to breathe again. Little by little the soft beauty of the desert night stole in upon her senses: a clump of evening primrose in full bloom, white against bloodred earth at the side of the trail; the silver gleam of moonlight on a lone cholla; the swish of unseen wings in the darkness; a sky as vast as forever, hung with the blaze of a million stars.

Latigo had said little on the way up the mountain. Thus, Rose had no warning when he suddenly turned the horse off the trail and entered a narrow cleft that, only an instant before, had appeared to be no more than a shadow on solid rock. The horse splashed through a trickling stream in the darkness. Then, before Rose had time to do little more than gasp, the rock had opened up again into a small, secluded glade overhung by desert willow and tamarisk.

Latigo halted the horse and reached up to take Mason while Rose swung wearily out of the saddle. "It's beautiful here," she whispered, trying not to wake her sleeping son.

"But not very comfortable, I'm afraid. I wasn't expecting visitors." Latigo busied himself with the saddle. "Have you ever slept under the stars on a horse blanket? It's the best I can offer you."

"It's a warm night, and there's a first time for everything," Rose answered with a determined little smile. "Are you hungry? Esther sent along some fresh bread and sliced corned beef."

"It'll taste even better in the morning." He bent swiftly to unbuckle the cinch. "But if you're hungry—"

"It can wait." She stepped back to watch him, filling her eyes with the feral grace of his body, the ripple of his

shoulders as he lifted the heavy saddle off the horse and
laid it over a rock. She found herself wanting to burn every
inch of him into her memory so that she would have his
image to keep like a treasured photograph in her mind.

Mason stirred in her arms, whimpered once and drifted
back to sleep. Rose found a soft, dry tuffet of grass close
by and, after checking carefully for scorpions, made a nest
of her woolen shawl and settled him gently into it. He
slept, lulled by the whisper of the night wind.

Rose raised her arms high, reaching toward the stars as
she stretched the kinks from her tired body. Now that she
could rest, the terror and uncertainty of the past hours began to spill over the edges of her courage.

Need was like a cry in her, and as she watched Latigo
move through the shadows, her whole soul ached to feel
the strength of his arms holding her close. She loved this
man, and she wanted him here, now, under the glory of
the open sky. Tomorrow might be filled with danger and
despair, but tonight they were safe. They were together,
perhaps for the last time.

Latigo had slipped the bridle off the horse and tethered
the animal to graze. He paused in the shadows, watching
the play of light on Rose's moon-bright hair. Watching
and aching.

With the breeze lifting the tatters of her black satin skirt,
she looked like a spirit of the night, as wild as the wind
itself and so beautiful she almost stopped his heart. Her
pale arms were streaked with crimson scratches from riding through the thorny scrub. Not once had she com-
plained, he remembered now. She was a miracle of beauty,
toughness and courage, his Rose.

His Rose.

But she was not his at all, Latigo reminded himself.
They belonged to two different worlds, and she could no
more follow him than a dove could follow a hawk. He

oved Rose Colby with all his soul, and he knew there
vere words she was waiting to hear. Even now, those
vords were inside him, struggling to break free. But he
vould be wise to hold them back. The less he told Rose
1ow, the less she would be hurt when he was gone.

Forcing himself to stir, Latigo carried the horse blanket
o a level, sandy spot on the ground, shook it flat, then
:rouched to cover it with his bedroll. "It's the best I can
)ffer you," he said gruffly, smoothing out the wrinkles.
'Get some rest. I'll keep watch. We'll move out at first
ight, all right?"

There was no answer.

"Rose?" He glanced up at her. She was standing where
1e had last seen her, but now she had turned toward him,
1olding out her arms. Moonlight glistened on her tear-wet
:heeks.

At the sight of her, something cold and resistant shat-
ered inside Latigo, like the last vestige of winter ice in a
nountain stream. Almost without his willing it, he felt
1imself stumbling to his feet and striding toward her,
lrawn by a need that had burned too long and too deep to
)e denied any longer.

She gave a little cry as he caught her in his arms, and
hen they were kissing, their mouths and tongues blending
n frantic abandon, tasting, touching, licking. Her hands
·aked his hair, pulling his head lower, to her throat, her
:ollarbone.

Latigo felt his whole body ignite as his lips grazed the
ull, silky softness of her breasts. He buried his face in
heir sweat-dampened cleft as he had ached to do for so
long, drowning his senses in the feel and taste and musky
woman scent of her.

Rose moaned as his hands slid up her ribs to cup her
sensitive, swollen breasts. Her own hands ranged franti-
:ally over the barrier of his clothes, seeking the buttons,

the buckles that separated his body from her touch. She wanted more of him, all of him.

His pulse leaped as her eager fingers crept downward to discover the iron-hard ridge of his desire. Rose gasped as he jerked her against him once more, bringing their hips in full contact through her skirt. She moved with him as they stood clasped in the moonlight, pressing close, transfixed by the sensations that rippled like molten fire from the place where their bodies touched.

Latigo's breath rasped as he struggled to speak. "Rose, if you want me to stop, for the love of heaven, tell me now," he whispered, his voice rough velvet in her ear.

"No." Her eyes were closed, her whole being throbbing and alive. She burned to feel the coolness of his coppery skin against hers, to know his hardness thrusting into the hot, liquid center of her womanhood. She pressed closer, needing him as she needed air and water and nourishment. "Don't stop, Latigo," she murmured wildly. "Please don't stop."

Their own momentum carried them to the blanket. For the space of a breath, he paused above her, his eyes seeking hers in the darkness. His finger traced the path of a tear down her cheek. Then he bent and kissed her with a gentleness that triggered new swells of desire, rising and falling with the power of great ocean waves. "Yes," she whispered, trembling as he caressed her breasts, her hips, her willing thighs. "Yes."

Latigo was not an expert lover. The wonder with which he touched her body was evidence enough of that, but his very innocence moved Rose to a depth of tenderness she had never known. When he fumbled with the busk of her corset, she helped him with the stubborn fastenings, eager to give him every part of her.

Her breath caught as he slipped out of his clothes and leaned above her in the moonlight. So magnificent was his body that for the first moment Rose was acutely conscious of her own shortcomings—the motherly sag of her breasts, the marks of childbearing that streaked her belly. But then he bent to kiss her, his mouth moving over her breasts, her ribs, then downward to caress the very scars that she had thought so ugly, and she knew that to Latigo every inch of her was beautiful.

She whimpered softly as his fingers grazed her thigh, then slipped upward, brushing the wetly swollen center of her need. She was ready for him, so ready that her whole being throbbed with desire.

He paused for a heartbeat, then a single stroke brought him home. Rose arched upward to meet him, her low cry of joy blending with the night. Stars swirled in her vision as they began to move, slowly at first, with a sense of discovery and delicate wonder, then with more urgency, in perfect union, as if they had been lovers from the beginning of time. Rose felt every sense singing inside her, every part of her tingling with an exquisite, unfolding pleasure like the opening of a hundred pink buds. She heard Latigo gasp, felt him shudder as his love burst inside her. Then came the ecstatic spiraling, down and down until, at last, they lay quivering in each other's arms, rich with contentment.

The moon had climbed the crest of the sky to hang low, now, above the western peaks. Rose lay curled beneath the blanket with her son in her arms, both of them sleeping soundly.

Latigo crouched beside them, listening to the night and thinking as he kept watch.

If all went well, the winding mountain trail would take them to the Colby ranch by tomorrow night. But even if they managed to get their hands on the journal, the days ahead would be rife with uncertainty and danger. Come what may, he resolved, Rose's safety, and that of her child, would be his first concern. He would be there to protect her, to care for her, to fight at her side.

Rose had given him the most precious of gifts—not only her love but her trust. Whatever happened, he would not betray that trust.

Not even at the cost of his own life.

Chapter Seventeen

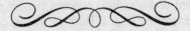

The setting sun washed the flats and mesas with violet as Rose and Latigo came over the last rise. A light evening breeze had sprung up, carrying the aroma of wood smoke, chilies and fresh corn tortillas. The horse, scenting its own kind, snorted and pricked up its tired ears.

Latigo turned the animal so that Rose, behind him on the cantle, could share his view. She twisted against him, straining to see through the gathering twilight. Below them, the ranch lay silent in the fading shadows. Horses milled quietly in the corral. A wisp of smoke curled from the kitchen chimney.

"It looks peaceful enough," she said softly. "No strange mounts or wagons. No visitors in the yard."

"I don't like it," he said. "It's too quiet. You're not going down there alone."

Her arms tightened around his waist. "Last night you promised me you'd stay here and wait," she said.

"I'd have promised you damn near anything last night," he muttered huskily. "That doesn't mean the promise was a good idea."

Rose paused to check on Mason, who lay cradled in a sling that Latigo had fashioned from Rose's petticoat.

Slung over her shoulder and under her arm, the device had freed her hands and given her son comfortable, safe support.

"Trust me, you mustn't be seen, not even by Esperanza and Miguel." She slid off the horse, to stand looking up into his worried face. "Sooner or later the sheriff will question them. The less they can be forced to tell him, the better."

He scowled down at her, concern masking tenderness. "We'll have to move fast. If Hudson and his cronies figure out where we're headed, it's all over."

She reached up to clasp his lean, leathery hand. "I won't be twenty minutes. All I have to do is change my clothes, get the journal and some provisions and saddle a horse. Then I'll meet you back here." Rose gripped his fingers hard. "If you don't see me come out in half an hour, or if you see any sign of trouble, head for the border and leave it to me. Don't even stop to think."

She saw his throat move as he pressed the Peacemaker into her hand. "Just hurry," he said.

Rose felt his gaze on her as she zigzagged her way down the hill with Mason slung under one arm and her satchel under the other. Even then, she knew that if she looked back at him she would be lost once more in the memory of last night, and this was no time to be sentimental. She needed to think clearly and act swiftly.

It was deep twilight by the time she reached the yard. In the east, a platinum sliver of moon had risen above the horizon, casting the barn and windmill into pools of shadow. The windows of the house were dark. With no dinner to serve, Esperanza would have long since gone home to the small hacienda she shared with Miguel. So much the better, Rose reminded herself.

Mason's whimper broke into her thoughts as she mounted the porch. "Ssh, love," she whispered, cradling him close. "Be patient a little longer. We'll get both of us changed and out of here fast. Then you can have dinner in the saddle."

The door was locked, but there was a key in her satchel. Rose heard the familiar click of the tumblers. Then the door swung open into the hallway. There was no sound except the steady, familiar tick of the grandfather clock—the stern taskmaster that had marked the minutes and hours of her life for the past nine years. Only now did Rose realize how much she hated the gloomy sound of it.

The stairwell was dark, but Rose knew her way by heart. Holding the pistol loosely, she mounted the steps without hesitation and hurried down the hall toward her room. She would change first, then pick up the provisions and the journal on her way out. If she could manage the whole thing without lighting a lamp, there would be that much less chance of being seen.

She stepped into her bedroom, her mind checking off the things she would take. Her riding skirt, boots and a simple blouse would last her to the San Carlos and back. But the baby would need diapers and nightgowns and—

Rose's thoughts shattered into terror-stricken fragments as a powerful hand exploded out of the darkness, grabbed the pistol and wrenched her off her feet. Another hand clamped over her mouth, cutting off her scream. She recognized the hot, smooth palm and the smell of sweat and pomade even before she heard the voice.

"I knew you'd come back here sooner or later, you little Apache-loving bitch!" Bayard muttered. "Now I've got you, and you're never getting away from me again!"

As Rose clawed his hand away from her mouth, she heard the sound of other men's voices in the room, one harsh and guttural, one a nasal, whiny tang. Fear and rage burst inside her as she heard Mason shriek and felt him being jerked out of the sling, away from her side. "No!"

she gasped, fighting like a madwoman. "Give me my baby! *Give me my baby!*"

"Light the lamp. I've got her." Bayard's voice snapped the order. An instant later, at the touch of a match, the dresser lamp flickered on. Rose stared at the room in mute horror. The place had been completely ransacked. Drawers and chests lay overturned, their contents spilled across the floor. The carpet had been thrown back, the covers ripped from the bed. Even the mattress had been slashed open, wisps of its cottony stuffing floating in the air like snowflakes.

Mason was screaming in the awkward clasp of a burly, unkempt stranger who was wearing what appeared to be a grime-encrusted preacher's frock. "Please," Rose gasped, struggling like a wild animal to reach him. "For the love of heaven, don't hurt my baby!"

The other stranger, a wiry weasel of a man with a straw between his yellowed teeth, laughed. "Oh, we ain't gonna hurt him, lady. Leastwise, not as long as you do what the boss here says." He drew a huge knife from the greasy-looking leather scabbard at his belt and used its tip to scrape the dirt out from under his left thumbnail. The effect of the knife was not lost on Rose.

"Please!" She twisted in Bayard's crude embrace. "Bayard, if you've any spark of decency left in you—"

Bayard laughed low in his throat, an ugly sound. "Just pay my price, Rose. Nate and Preacher, here, can be pretty inventive if I turn them loose. They'll start with one little pink toe, then maybe a finger or an ear."

"No!" Rose sagged in Bayard's arms, sick with dread. Mason's screams had faded to heartrending little sobs. He hung over the big man's arm. "Tell me what you want," she said. "I'll do anything. Just don't let them hurt my baby."

"That's better." Bayard emitted a raw chuckle. "Now,

Rose, honey, there are three things I want from you if you want to keep that little nipper in one piece, all right?''

"Just give me my baby," Rose muttered, stalling for time any way she could. "And tell me what you've done with Miguel and Esperanza."

"Your hired help?" Again Bayard laughed. "You don't really think Preacher and Nate could leave those two old Mexicans alive, to talk, do you? Are you interested in the details?"

"No." Rose felt as if the life had been kicked out of her, but she knew her only hope—and Mason's—was to keep fighting any way she could.

"I'm going to let go of you," Bayard said. "One false move, and Nate skewers your boy like a brisket of beef. Understand?"

When Rose did not reply, he flung her onto the bed. She landed hard, sprawling across the ripped mattress. Mason shrieked, startled by the sudden movement. Preacher clamped a hand over his tiny mouth, a hand so huge that Rose feared her son would be smothered. "Just give me my baby," she pleaded. "You can have anything else you want."

"All in good time." A smug grin crawled across Bayard's face. "First things first, Rose. You mentioned you had some evidence against me and my friends."

Rose stared at her child imprisoned in Preacher's arms. Her gaze darted to Nate's knife, and she sensed the small, evil man would not hesitate to use it. "Downstairs in John's office," she said, her desperate eyes still fixed on Mason. "Under the desk, next to the wall, there's a loose floor tile."

At a nod from Bayard, Nate slipped out of the room, leaving Rose with the two men.

"You did it after all, didn't you?" She flung the words

at Bayard. "You arranged John's so-called accident, and Major Scott's, as well."

"You can't prove a damned thing," Bayard snapped, and Rose knew that the words made no difference because he did not intend to let her live. "I have a dozen friends who'll vouch for the fact that I was in Tucson the whole time."

"Of course you were!" Rose said, knowing she had nothing to lose. "You always paid others to do your killing for you, except for the time when you murdered your own best friend."

The shock that whitened Bayard's face told her all she needed to know.

"You killed John with your own hands, didn't you?" she said. "He was getting better, and you were afraid he'd talk. How did you do it? Did you smother him? Strangle him? I want to hear you say it, Bayard!"

"I did it for you, you little fool," Bayard snarled. "I set you free from a sick old man who was going to die anyway! You ought to thank me and—"

His words broke off as Nate slipped back into the room, carrying a lantern from downstairs and the journal. Bayard leafed through the slim leather volume, nodded and slipped it into his hip pocket.

"You've got what you came for," Rose said, knowing the fight was lost. "Now, give me my baby."

"Oh, but we're not finished," Bayard growled. "I said I wanted three things from you. Now I want you to tell me where that filthy Apache lover of yours is hiding out."

"He's gone—on his way to Mexico."

"You're lying!" Bayard's flattened hand cracked across Rose's face, knocking her back into the bedclothes. "You didn't come here alone. He's out there waiting for you, and I want you to go out and get him in here!"

Rose blinked the spots out of her vision. She could feel

the flesh beginning to puff over one cheekbone. "Give me my son," she whispered.

"So you and your lover can hightail it into the scrub? I'm not the fool you take me for, Rose. The baby stays, and if you want to see him again in one piece, you'll come back with the half-breed."

Knowing she had no choice, Rose forced herself to stand up and walk to the door. Behind her, Mason began to cry.

"Shut the brat up, damn it, or I'll shut him up for good," Nate snarled. "Babies make me nervous."

"You shut 'im up, then," whined Preacher. "I never was cut out to be no nursemaid!"

"Both of you shut up!" Bayard growled. "Rose, you've got ten minutes. Get moving."

Sick with fear, Rose flung herself out the door and raced down the hallway.

As she burst onto the front porch, she paused for an instant, catching her balance against a post. Her eyes searched the moonlit hillside. Perhaps he had already given up and gone, vanishing in his shadowy way without so much as a goodbye. But no, Latigo would be there, she knew. And she would have no choice except to betray him.

As she stepped off the porch, she heard his whispered voice in the shadows. "Rose, I was getting worried and came down. What is it?"

Rose turned to see him beckoning from the corner of the house. She ran toward him, stifling the little cry in her throat. Her anguish exploded as he caught her in his arms. Her fists pounded his chest in an irrational fury of despair. Why was he here? Why hadn't he run away and saved her from this heartbreaking act?

He held her fiercely as the storm subsided. His hands stroked her hair. "I'm here," he said, and no more words were needed.

"Bayard and two men—horrible men—" she whis-

pered, quivering against him. "They've killed Miguel and
Esperanza, and they've got Mason. They'll hurt him if I
don't bring you back."

"Guns?"

"They've all got guns, and they took the Peacemaker.
Bayard's got the journal, too. I think they mean to kill us
all. Latigo, it's all my fault. I'm sorry."

"Don't be." He gave her a swift, hard kiss. "Let's go,"
he said. Then he took her arm and escorted her back inside
and up the stairs like a grand lady.

As he mounted the steps with the woman he loved, a
dozen plans flashed through Latigo's mind. One by one,
he rejected them all. Saving himself would be easy. Saving
Rose would be possible, but not without sacrificing her
tiny, helpless son, and that was out of the question for them
both.

He had only one bargaining chip left, and he would use
it without hesitation. But even that might not be enough.

"Stay back," he whispered as they approached the door.
"Let me go in ahead of you."

Rose did not answer. He could sense the fear that
choked off her throat as she moved behind him. Inside the
room, a lamp flickered on the whitewashed walls. Bayard
Hudson's shadow loomed grotesquely, bent by the angle
of wall and ceiling.

As he entered, Latigo recognized the gunmen at once
from their ambush of the two federal agents on the San
Carlos. He had only glimpsed them at the time, but their
faces and the difference in their sizes had made an indel-
ible impression. He let his narrowed eyes flick over them,
lingering long enough to make them both uncomfortable
before he turned, at last, toward Bayard Hudson. "I've
come to bargain," he said.

Bayard Hudson snorted. "You're in no position to bargain, half-breed. I've got you and your white whore roped and hog-tied. I'll do what I please with the both of you, and there's not a blamed thing you can do about it.''

"Maybe not." Latigo was aware of Rose's presence behind him. "Unless I can convince you I'm worth more alive than dead.''

"Hell, man, you're not worth the saddle under your butt!" Bayard spat on Latigo's boots. Latigo, aware of Rose pressing close behind him, did not move.

"I may be worth more than you think," he said quietly. "I was with army intelligence before this debacle broke out. They're on to you, Hudson. They've got evidence that you planned the murder of Major Scott, and as soon as they have a solid case, they'll be coming to arrest you.''

Latigo paused to gauge the effect of his words. What he had just told Bayard Hudson was a bald-faced lie, but it was the only weapon he had. He saw the flesh whiten at the corners of Hudson's mouth.

"So what's this bargain you're proposing?" he asked in a tense voice.

"Let Rose and her baby go," Latigo said. "Give her a horse and time to get safely to Tucson. Do that, and when you turn me over to the law, I promise I'll confess to the murder of Henry Scott.''

Rose stifled a little cry. Bayard hesitated, clearly shaken by what he had heard.

"Think about it," Latigo said. "You'll be cleared of all suspicion, and even if Rose talks, nobody's going to believe her. You told me yourself that everyone from the governor on down thinks she's deranged. As for me—'' He shrugged, feigning a bitter smile. "After all, how many times can you hang a man?''

In the silence that followed, Mason began to whimper. Latigo could feel Rose's agitation as she pushed past him, straining to reach her son.

"What do you want, Bayard?" she pleaded. "You've
got three innocent people at your mercy! Let Latigo go
free, and give me my baby. I'll do anything."

Bayard Hudson had been scowling in pensive silence.
Suddenly he laughed, a clotted, evil sound. "By thunder,
this is even more fun than I expected! Latigo, I accept your
offer, but not on your terms, on mine. She will live, but
I've got my own plans for her. Nate—tie the half-breed
bastard to the bed. I want him to watch."

Latigo submitted grimly, knowing he had no other
choice. He was outgunned and outnumbered, and a struggle would only risk harm to Rose's tiny, fragile son. His
only hope lay in biding his time, waiting for the right moment, if it ever came. He cursed silently as the man named
Nate used the sash from Rose's discarded dressing gown
to lash his wrists to the bedpost—tightly, despite Latigo's
effort to expand his wrists by tensing his muscles. Even
when he relaxed, the thickly woven flannel did not loosen
enough to give his hands the play they needed.

Mason had begun to cry again, a full-throated wail this
time. Seeing, suddenly, that Nate was occupied, Rose flew
at the big man who held her son. Latigo's heart stopped.
The sash cut into his flesh as Bayard, in a lightning move,
caught her wrist and spun her hard around to face him.

"Your lover may have just bought *your* life," he
snarled, "but if you want that noisy little brat to survive
in one piece, you'd better start behaving yourself."

Rose glared up at him through the web of tangled hair
that had fallen into her face. "All I want is my son!" she
retorted. "For the love of heaven, just tell me what I have
to do."

"Why, Rose, honey, I was just getting to that." Bayard
laughed harshly. "Believe it or not, Preacher, here, is a
lawfully ordained minister, and I've even taken the liberty
of having the documents drawn up. It's well-known that a

wife can't testify against her husband. Besides, I've always had a fancy for you, my dear, to say nothing of this fine ranch. That's why you and I are getting married here and now.''

Rose stared at him in horror. When she spoke, her trembling voice made a mockery of her bravado. "First of all, the ranch isn't mine to give you, even in marriage," she said. "It's Mason's, and there's no legal way you can take it from him. Second, it so happens I can't stand you, Bayard. If you think I would ever agree to marry you—''

Something flickered in Bayard's eyes, something so darkly evil that it ended her words in a gasp. Taking his time, he turned away from her and nodded toward the wiry man with the knife. "A toe, I think, to start with, Nate. That should be sufficient to convince the lady.''

Nate probed the folds of Mason's blanket and came up with one tiny, exquisite pink foot. With his free hand he drew his knife from its scabbard. Latigo struggled like a wild man, but the stubborn sash held.

"No!'' Rose's cry clawed at Latigo's heart. "Bayard, I'll do anything you ask—anything! Just don't hurt my baby!''

"On your knees.'' Bayard grinned, relishing the moment as Rose dropped to a kneeling position. "I said you'd beg to marry me one day, remember? Now, do it. Kiss my boots and beg, Rose. For your son!''

Latigo groaned under his breath as Rose crouched to the floor and pressed her soft, pink lips to the muddy toe of Bayard's boot. Bound fast, he forced his rage inward as his groping fingers explored the range of what they could touch—the oiled smoothness of lathe-turned pine; the joint where the footboard fastened to the rail of the bed, secured by a single iron bolt. The bolt had been hastily forged, leaving a slight burr around its top edge, which pricked Latigo's fingertip when he touched it.

"I'm waiting, Rose," Bayard was saying. "Come on, girl. Let's hear you beg."

"Please…" Rose's body quivered like a bowstring. In the yellow lamplight, her violet eyes glittered with loathing as she forced out the words. "Please marry me, Bayard."

"Now, that's more like it." Bayard interlaced his fingers, flexing them and cracking the knuckles. "We'll sign the marriage document and have a simple ceremony, my dear. Then you and I will enjoy a private honeymoon in the guest room."

His smile mocked chivalry as he pulled Rose to her feet and, with a flourish, drew a folded paper out of his yellow serge vest. A pen and inkwell seemed to appear from nowhere. Bayard signed first, smiling as he did so. Rose, white-faced and drained of emotion, glanced at the document and scrawled her name. Sweat slimed Latigo's wrists as he worked the flannel sash hard against the bolt's fine, sharp edge.

Nate signed last as witness. Bayard refolded the paper, slipped it back into his vest and turned to the other gunman. Then he gripped Rose's arm, forcing her to stand beside him.

"Preacher, if you'll do the honors—"

Preacher stepped forward, still clutching Mason, whose cries had diminished to a pathetic sniffle. "I ain't never performed no marriage holdin' no baby," he announced in his nasal whine, "and I'll be damned if I'm doin' it now! Here, Nate, you hold 'im for a while!" Without waiting for Nate's consent, he shoved Mason into the smaller man's reluctant arms.

Nate recoiled as if someone had passed him a rattlesnake. Mason, sensing the tension, began to cry at the top of his lungs. "I'm not holdin' no damn baby!" Nate growled. "I told you before, the stinky little brats make me nervous!" With a speed that bordered on panic, he thrust Mason into his cradle, where he lay on his back, still crying.

"Go on!" Bayard snapped at Preacher, who was distracted by the sound of the screaming infant. "Just get it done, you fool!"

Preacher took a deep breath. Piety slipped like a glazed mask over his fat, greasy face. "Dearly beloved—"

"Get down to business," Bayard interrupted sharply.

Preacher cleared his throat. "Do you, Bayard Hudson, take this woman to be your lawful wedded wife?"

"I do," Bayard growled, his grip whitening the flesh of Rose's upper arm. Latigo felt the flannel fabric begin to fray and weaken where it rubbed against the bolt, but it still held him fast.

"And do you, Rose Colby, take this man to be your lawful wedded husband?"

Rose's face was ashen. She stood rigidly in Bayard's grip, looking as if her legs were about to buckle beneath her. The baby's forlorn wail quivered on the lamplit air. Rose strained toward the sound, then sagged in despair as she realized her efforts would be hopeless. "I do," she whispered dejectedly.

"The ring?"

Bayard wrenched a gaudily set garnet band off his little finger. Rose shut her eyes, looking ill as he slipped it onto her hand. The ring hung loosely, pulled askew by the weight of the stone.

"I now pronounce you husband and wife," Preacher intoned, and Latigo felt his heart plummet. The seamed edge of the flannel strip cut into his flesh, drawing blood as his hands writhed and twisted.

"One last thing before we retire, my dear." Bayard turned to his bride with a triumphant leer. "There is the matter of your late husband's journal. We wouldn't want it to fall into the wrong hands, would we, now?" He fished the small leather-bound volume out of his hip pocket, then glanced around the room. "Preacher, would you fetch Mrs. Hudson's necessity from under the bed? That should serve our needs."

The plump gunman, demoted to lackey again, ambled to the bed, reached underneath and pulled out Rose's empty porcelain chamber pot. Bayard placed the pot on the nightstand, picked up the lamp and removed the chimney. Opening the journal to the middle, he touched its pages to the flame.

The dry paper ignited like tinder, blistering Bayard's hand as he dropped the burning book into the chamber pot.

"No!" There was a sudden, desperate cry from Rose. She plunged toward him, frantic to save the precious journal.

"Damn you to hell, woman!" Bayard clutched his burned hand, cursing as she crunched into him. Then, in a scene that, to Latigo, seemed to take on the slow-motion quality of a nightmare, Bayard stumbled against the nightstand, sending both the lamp and the chamber pot crashing to the floor.

A curtain of flame leaped upward from the rug.

Rose dived for the cradle as Latigo struck. Hands still bound, he braced against the bedpost and lifted his feet in a swinging arc that clubbed Nate from behind, just below the shoulders. Nate went down, gasping for breath as he fell.

"Run, Rose!" Latigo shouted as the flannel sash parted against the bolt. "Get your baby out of here!"

The room was filling with smoke. Rose bundled her son in his blanket and started for the door. Bayard, all but ringed by flame, saw that his prisoner was free. Jerking his pistol from its holster, he aimed it squarely at Latigo and pulled the trigger.

Everything that happened next was jammed into the

same beat of time. Rose, passing Bayard on her way out of the room, flung herself against his upraised arm, throwing off his aim as he fired. Nate chose that instant to lurch to his feet. Bayard's bullet struck him in the neck. He reeled, then sagged to his knees, bleeding and cursing horribly.

Instinctively Nate's hand groped for his own holster. He yanked out his pistol and, with the last of his strength, squeezed off a single shot that struck Bayard in the chest.

Bayard grunted, sounding more surprised than hurt. Then, as if his bones were dissolving from the ground up, his knees began to buckle. By the time he collapsed on the smoldering rug, Nate was already dead.

"Get out of here, Rose! Now!" Latigo seized Nate's pistol and turned on Preacher, who had cowered in the corner, intent only on saving himself. "Move it, big man," Latigo barked. "Throw down your gun. Then grab your boss's feet and drag him out of here. I need live witnesses."

Rose had already vanished into the smoky hallway. Praying she would have the sense to go straight outside, he kept the pistol trained on Preacher, who was all but blubbering with fear. "That's it," Latigo instructed as if encouraging a backward child. "Get him onto his back. Now grab his ankles and pull him down the hall. I'll be right here."

The stifling, burning smoke was all around them now. Latigo could hear Preacher coughing as he dragged Bayard's limp body along the tiled hallway. The house would go up fast, he calculated. Its thick adobe walls were little more than mud and straw, and once they got hot enough—

A sharp moan from Bayard interrupted his thoughts, and Latigo realized they had reached the stairs. "Get around and support his shoulders," he ordered Preacher.

"Hell's bells, just let me out of here," the big man whined. "He's gonna die anyway, and I don't want to burn up in no fire!"

"Do as I say," Latigo growled, "or I'll shoot you here and now and drag Hudson out myself!"

Inch by inch, they somehow made it downstairs, through the open front door and onto the porch. Rose was waiting at the foot of the porch steps. She'd evidently put Mason down somewhere safe. Latigo blessed her when he saw that she'd had the presence of mind to fetch a rope.

Preacher dragged Bayard out onto the sand. Bayard lay still, his eyes closed and his breathing labored. His blood had left a long, thick smear across the porch and down the steps. It gleamed eerily like black tar in the moonlight. Flames danced in the upstairs windows of the house.

"I'll need you to hold the gun on our preacher friend while I tie him to the fence." Latigo's lungs and nostrils burned from the smoke. He felt so light-headed he could scarcely focus on the words he was saying to Rose. "When he's safely out of action, then we'll see what we can do for…your husband over there."

Something glimmered in her eyes. "I had to do it," she said. "You know I had to do it."

"Yes. I know you did." Latigo nudged Preacher with the muzzle of the gun, prodding him toward the corral. Singed and cowed, the big man made no effort to resist. Latigo's eyes flickered to Rose as she moved quietly beside him through the moonlit darkness. Her head was held high, her sweet, full mouth braced against any show of emotion. He had just watched her humiliate herself on her knees before a man she detested. Yet, even in the smoke-grimed tatters of the black satin gown, with her house burning behind her, she walked as proudly as a queen. She was magnificent, his Rose.

His Rose.

Lord in heaven, how he loved her!

Tying Preacher to the corral fence took less than a minute, but by the time Latigo finished, smoke was pouring through the roof of the house. Rose could hear the roar as the flames sucked air. She could hear the tiles clattering down as the supporting timbers burned and collapsed beneath them. There was no way to save the house John had built.

Latigo tightened the last knot. Preacher slumped in his bonds, all the spirit gone out of him. He would talk, Rose was certain, and there was every reason to hope his confession would clear Latigo of all charges.

And what then?

Bayard lay on his back where they had left him, his chest jerking painfully as he breathed. A lung shot, Rose calculated. Dangerous but not always fatal.

Latigo took the pistol from her hand and slipped it into his own empty holster. Rose hesitated beside him, half hoping he would take her in his arms, but she swiftly realized there was no time for that. Bayard was losing blood so fast that every second was critical.

"We have to save him," Rose said softly, trying not to think of how convenient and easy it would be to simply let Bayard Hudson bleed to death.

"Yes. Yes, of course we do," Latigo muttered as he strode back across the yard to where Bayard lay, his blood soaking into the thirsty sand. "First we've got to stop the bleeding. Bring some rags from the barn. Hurry!"

Rose raced to do as he asked as Latigo dropped to his knees beside his wounded enemy and began tearing open the blood-soaked shirt. She was halfway to the barn when some instinct—she would never know exactly what—made her glance back over her shoulder.

The upper floor of the house was a torch by now, but

that was not what caught her eye. No, it was Latigo, lean
ing over Bayard's chest, intent on stopping the wound
And it was Bayard's hand, holding something small and
black, raising it in one shaking hand, thumbing back the
hammer.

"*Latigo!*"

Her scream ripped through the air, all but drowning out
the pop of the tiny derringer. Then Rose's whole world
shattered as Latigo crumpled on top of Bayard and lay still
a crimson rivulet of blood trickling down his temple.

Latigo drifted in a bright liquid void, floating between
the worlds of life and death. He remembered, dimly, the
sound of a gunshot and the sensation of a lightning bol
creasing his skull, but that no longer seemed important. He
was warm and comfortable and so very tired.

From somewhere beyond the void came the sound of
voices. He heard and recognized his mother, his grand
mother, his uncle the great Cochise, but only one voice
spoke clearly, and that was the voice of the old *di-yin* who
had been his teacher.

Why are you here, my son? Your quest is not over.

Not over, Grandfather? Latigo's spirit asked. *But how
can I go on? I have lost the path.*

*The path is there. You have only to keep climbing, and
it will unfold before you, leading to things more wonderful
than you have ever dreamed. Go now, search for some
thing golden....*

The old man's words faded as Latigo began to climb
The trail was steep and treacherous, overgrown with thorns
and brambles that clawed his flesh. His body ached with
strain and fatigue. Once he slashed his leg on a sharp out
crop, and in his cry, he heard all the cries of his people
the injustices, the anger, the heartbreak. *Be our voice in*

e world, they called to him. *Be the keeper of our memories, the teller of our stories.*

Latigo was crawling now, fighting his way upward, inch y perilous inch. Then, just when he began to fear he could ot go on, he saw it, or rather felt it. The golden softness urrounded him with such an overpowering love that his eart seemed to burst with it. He reached out.

And his eyes opened.

He was lying in the shadows on a hard, narrow bed, overed by a flannel sheet and a thin, rough blanket. Only s his head began to clear did he recognize the bare rafters f the bunkhouse.

He shifted his gaze, and there, in a shaft of pale sunlight, at Rose, much as he had seen her that very first time. She vas looking down at him, her face thin and careworn, her yes bathed in weary violet shadows. To Latigo she had ever looked more beautiful.

"Rose," he murmured hoarsely.

She glanced up, her face transformed by joy as their yes met. "I thought I'd lost you," she whispered. "Oh, atigo."

"What happened?" He strained to sit up, then sank back nto the pillow. "How long have I been here?"

"Lie still," she said, her eyes glowing with love. "Baard shot you. The bullet grazed your skull. You've been nconscious for two days."

"Bayard shot me?" He blinked, struggling to remember ll that had happened—the mock wedding, the fire, the two unmen, Bayard's wound.

"What happened?" he muttered. "Rose, tell me everyhing!"

She reached out with her left arm, caught his hand and ressed it to her lips. Her eyes, he saw, were red laced om tears and fatigue. "When you're stronger," she said. Then I'll tell you the whole story. All you need to know

now is that the murder charges have been dropped. You'r
free.''

Free. Latigo clasped her hand, knowing he would neve
let her go again. "I love you, Rose," he whispered, ar
the words, spoken for the very first time, were as sweet o
his tongue as wild spring honey.

Epilogue

~~~~~~~~~~~~~~~~~~~~~~~~~~~~

May 1892

The years had flown—fifteen of them, each one as rich and full as the last. Only this morning Rose had glanced into her mirror and noticed the first strand of silver at her temple. She had frowned, then laughed and welcomed it, as she welcomed every day of her life here on this ranch with the family she loved.

Now, as she sat on the front porch watching the sunset streak its glory across the desert, her mind drifted back once more to the day when her life had stopped, then begun all over again.

In spite of her efforts to save him, Bayard Hudson had died a few minutes after shooting Latigo. Weeks later Rose learned, to her astonishment, that their marriage had indeed been legal, and she was the heir to his estate. Loath to touch a cent of Bayard's fortune, she had restored the mercantile to Esther and donated everything else to the Sisters of Saint Joseph, to be used for the benefit of the poor.

The sun was lower now, the gilded clouds deepening to hues of mauve and violet. Stretching her legs, Rose gazed beyond the paloverdes, watching the distant smoke from

Esperanza's cookstove curl against the sky. She had found Esperanza and Miguel in the barn after her ordeal, bound and gagged, but otherwise unharmed. The memory of her joy still brought a tightness to Rose's throat.

Miguel and Esperanza were elderly now, living in quiet retirement in their small home on the ranch. Juanita had taken over as cook and housekeeper, and the young vaquero she had married now did Miguel's work, a happy arrangement for everyone concerned.

Preacher's full cooperation with the authorities had saved him from the hangman's rope, and he was now serving a life sentence in the territorial prison at Yuma. His testimony had exposed the "accidents" that had brought down John and Major Scott and the murders of the two federal agents on the San Carlos. Latigo had been cleared of all blame.

The burning of John's journal had saved several other prominent Ring members from exposure, but then justice had found its own path. The coming of the railroad in 1880 had brought new prosperity to Tucson and broken the Ring's power once and for all.

The shadows had grown long across the yard. Beside the porch, the night-blooming cereus, flowering early this year, had begun to unfold its treasure of moon-white petals. The familiar scents of wood smoke and chilies lingered on the air. Rose felt the protecting peace of her home around her, the home Latigo had built for her with his own savings after the fire. It was low and rambling, with a shaded inner patio, harmonizing with the land, open to wind and sun and flowers.

One entire wing of the house was devoted to Latigo's library. There he had written his three-volume history of the Apache Nation, from the earliest legends to the last surrender of the fiery Geronimo. The books had brought him honors and recognition from all over the world, and part of the profits had gone to build a school and medical clinic on the San Carlos Reservation.

"Mama, what are you doing out here?" Rose felt a nudge as Miranda, the bolder of her dark-eyed twin daughters, snuggled against her right arm.

"Are you waiting for Papa and Mason?" Melinda, the more sensitive, soft-spoken sister, curled up on her left. The two girls were always together, and as beautiful as twin flames. They were Rose's own small miracles, proof, as Esther had once said, that doctors could be wrong.

"Juanita says supper's ready," Miranda said, running long, thin fingers, so like her father's, through her silky black hair.

"But I told her you would want to wait," Melinda added swiftly. "I know how you like having everyone together."

"We'll wait a few minutes longer." Rose snuggled her daughters close in the twilight.

"I see somebody!" Miranda cried, jumping to her feet. "It's Papa and Mason! They're racing, and Mason's ahead!"

Rose stood with Melinda to cheer the riders on. Mason was indeed leading through the gate. A fine, strong boy of fifteen, he was as close to Latigo as he might have been to his own father. Around his neck, always, he wore the tarnished medal Rose had salvaged from the ashes of the house.

Pride... Honor... Courage... Duty.

The words were John's legacy to them all.

Rose's heart skipped as Latigo rode in through the gate behind Mason and wheeled his mount to a halt. He was laughing good-naturedly, the sound warming the darkness around him.

Rose and the girls ran to him as he swung out of the saddle, her joy complete as he gathered them all into his arms.

* * * * * *

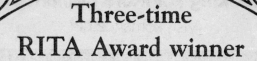

COMING NEXT MONTH FROM
HARLEQUIN HISTORICALS